FLYOVER FICTION

SERIES EDITOR
Ron Hansen

TWELFTH AND RACE

Eric Goodman

University of Nebraska Press | Lincoln and London

Library of Congress Cataloging-in-Publication Data

Goodman, Eric K.
Twelfth and race / Eric Goodman.
p. cm. — (Flyover fiction)
ISBN 978-0-8032-3980-7 (pbk. : alk. paper)
1. Interracial dating—Fiction. 2. Race riots—
Fiction. I. Title.
PS3557.O583T94 2012   813'.54—dc23
                2011041937

Set in Iowan Oldstyle by Bob Reitz.
Designed by A. Shahan.

For Susan

It demands great spiritual resilience
not to hate the hater whose foot
is on your neck, and an even greater
miracle of perception and charity
not to teach your child to hate.

JAMES BALDWIN

In order to get beyond racism,
we must first take account of race.
There is no other way.

JUSTICE HARRY A. BLACKMUN

ACKNOWLEDGMENTS

Although novel writing is the most solitary of activities, those of us who sit alone in a room and in our own mind understand that the necessary solitude and, indeed, the final form of the manuscript often require the assistance of many organizations and individuals. I'd like to thank the Ohio Arts Council, the MacDowell Colony, the Ragdale Foundation, the Headlands Center for the Arts, and the Department of English at Miami University for the time and space to write this book. Karen Mitchell, Justin White, Michael Sabbia, Dr. Constance West, and Lewis Diuguid helped with research. Stefanie Dunning, Lucy Ferriss, Ron Hansen, Jim Heynen, Richard Kolesnick, and Tim Melley made up a dispersed village of friends and helpful eyes. My agent and dear friend, Michael Carlisle, never gives up or allows me to. Susan Morgan is my first and final reader. And very special thanks to Brandon Black, who was instrumental to the writing of this book.

Finally, although *Twelfth and Race* is a work of fiction, set in the imaginary metropolis of Calhoun City, Missouri, the events that inspired some of this narrative occurred on the banks of the Ohio River. To honor the memory of that place and time, and, in some small way, to keep alive one who died too young, too soon, I have chosen to retain some of the actual Ohio names.

SPRING 1972

Brooklyn

PROLOGUE

Sliding to noonday sleep, crossing the gauzy border from dream to memory, Lorr stands again outside the Fillmore, waiting for the doors to open for the second show. It is 1968, and despite that evil war, everything feels possible. Lorr is as young, as innocent, and as wild as she will ever be. Sixteen, a Brooklyn girl, every hippie boy's fantasy. She wears her blue magic boots and a shimmery Indian dress. Dark hair tumbles almost to her ass. Her best friend, Jackie, who claims to have slept with half the boys in their homeroom as well as the Turtles' drummer and bass player the same frantic night after a show, began dragging Lorr, who didn't need dragging, just direction, to the Village the summer after their sophomore year. Three months later, on a warm and perfect October night, Jackie nudges Lorr's arm.

"See that kid? Don't look. He's looking at *you*."

At first glance, he isn't much: bone thin, her height or maybe a smidge more. Then she finds the melting eyes under all that hair, and he doffs his hat, releasing dark brown wave after wave and golden, foreign skin. The doors fly open, and her heart beats faster, it's the same every time. The lights, the smells, the feeling inside her that this could be the greatest concert ever, the very best night of her life. And now he's not just looking at her, he's smiling, she smiles, and for a moment it's just the two of them in that great and crazy crowd of kids.

When Lorr wakes after only a few hours of troubled sleep, her twentieth birthday is almost over. She lolls in bed, the curtains in Pammie's bedroom pulsing with late afternoon light. With consciousness comes anxiety; the last time she came home, she had a really bad fight with Mom. She doesn't want Mom or,

3

even worse, Daddy to return from work, find her still in bed, and start their ragging. *Find a job, go back to school. Do something with your life.* Lorr raises herself on an elbow. God, she's tired. Last night's Black Beauty really took it out of her. She tries not to notice Pammie's Monkees poster, which hangs over the dresser, focuses instead on her sister's alarm clock. *Five-thirty. Uh-oh.*

When she starts downstairs, Daddy is just coming through the door. For a moment she watches him unobserved, and she is struck by his attitude of joyous anticipation, which she doesn't believe is to see her. She feels for the first time in years what she felt at thirteen and fourteen: how strange to have such a gorgeous dad. Her girlfriends were always like, "Lorr, your father's really good-looking," or "Hank's *really* sexy," and she'd have to stick her finger down her throat and pretend to gag. He feels her watching him and turns: auburn, almost copper hair; blue eyes; prominent cheekbones. He smiles, and she remembers how happy she was when he called her "Lori-Lorr."

"Lorraine. I was hoping you'd be here."

"And here I am."

"Come give your old dad a kiss."

She runs barefoot down the stairs, quick and light, and throws herself in Daddy's arms. His cheek is stubbly, and there's his familiar smell: Pall Malls and the ghost of English Leather. He bends to kiss her, and Lorr's glad she remembered a bra because Daddy squeezes her tight, and he wouldn't like it, and she wouldn't either, if he could feel her through the blouse.

He murmurs, "I've really missed you."

"Missed you too, Daddy."

Then he flinches, at least that muscle in his cheek does. "You didn't bring anyone, did you?"

"Just me."

That should have made everything okay, but they stand an awkward arm's length apart, everything and everyone she might have brought home suddenly between them. Why did he have

4

to spoil it? For shit's sake, it's her birthday. Then little Richie and Pammie enter the dining room from the kitchen.

"Daddy!" Richie cries. "Daddy, Dad—*dy!*"

He breaks into a toddler's lurching trot, and Hank beams. He catches Richie in his arms and tosses him in the air, nuzzling him as he falls before catching and tossing him again. Each time little Richie squeals happily. And Lorr, poor Lorr, sad amid all this joy, is certain Daddy has forgotten her birthday.

But he hasn't. Everyone remembers: April fifteenth, tax day. Daddy's already made reservations at Senior's, where a full dinner includes appetizer, main course, two sides, and dessert. The portions are enormous, and the menu includes Jewish specialties like matzo ball soup and kishke, which you wouldn't expect in a restaurant that also features lobster and shrimp prepared every way under the sun. There's even a choice between water and seltzer, which Daddy calls two cents plain. As soon as they're seated, Lou, fifty-five and bald, his body shaped like a pear, sets down the complimentary dishes of half-sour pickles, green tomatoes, and pickled red cabbage Senior's is famous for.

"Evening, Mister Gordon. I see you brought the whole kit and caboodle."

Lou winks at Lorr, who smiles despite making him for the lech she knows him to be. Lou swabs his face with a cloth napkin fished from his back pocket. He wears dress pants shiny in the seat, a white shirt and bow tie, which on a fat man like Lou look foolish.

Daddy gifts her a birthday gin and tonic. He and Mom call for whiskey sours followed by a bottle of Mateus. Pammie's sentenced to soda for another six months, and they position her across the round table from Lorr, next to Richie's high chair, with Mom on the other side of the baby. They always seat her as far from little Richie as possible, which hurts her feelings. After last night's Black Beauty her nerves feel scraped; everything hurts her feelings. She gulps her gin and tonic, despite knowing what Mom will think, and smiles at Daddy.

"Can I have another?"

She watches Hank, who's forking pickled red cabbage, glance at Marilyn, whose eyes pull so close to her nose all that shows is black liner. Mom nods, and Lorr waves her glass at Lou, who's serving the next table.

"Another gin and tonic, barkeep!"

Lou grins.

Richie holds up his plastic cup. "Udder OJ, dar-beep."

Lorr and Pammie crack up. Daddy, too, and Richie, not knowing what's funny but realizing it's something he said, sings out, "Dar-beep! Dar-beep!"

Only Mom is unmoved. She places a roll in front of Richie and tells him to pipe down.

Lorr keeps her shit together through a shrimp cocktail, Long Island duckling à l'orange, baked potato, and onion rings. It's a consciousness-numbing feed, and everyone appears half-stunned, hence content. Mom is less effusive than Daddy, but that's not unusual. She's always been squirrely, given to silences that may mean nothing but that at other times blow up into bitter recrimination. So maybe Lorr should be careful, but it's her birthday, for shit's sake. She wants to be a kid again, fed and feted one last time.

Although all the other desserts are included with dinner, Daddy insists Lorr order Victory Layer Cake, despite the $2.50 surcharge. It's the closest Senior's serves to birthday cake, and it isn't every goddamn day his daughter turns twenty. Lorr, who's eaten enough for a small country, has been fantasizing about the ice cream cake with hot fudge, but Daddy will not be turned aside. In his insistence there's something that makes her feel she *ought* to want it, something in his eagerness to do something, *anything*, for her—two gin and tonics!—that she's scared.

So she accepts his gift of Victory Layer Cake, which, a few minutes later, floats out on Lou's tray. The devil's food slice slathered with whipped cream is six inches high. A single pink candle flickers. Lou sets down the slice and joins the Gordons in singing "Happy Birthday." Little Richie waves his fork, and he looks so happy, cheeks flushed with excitement, Lorr can't help herself; she starts to bawl.

The singing stops. She blows out the candle. And though she knows it's wicked, bad, bad Lorraine, she wishes, *Make little Richie mine again.* She is so instantly pummeled by guilt, she peers around, wiping tears from her cheeks. From Mom's expression— eyes narrowed to black-rimmed slits—Lorr believes she knows.

That night she lies in the dark beside her sister on her twin bed high-rise. It's not too late; little Richie's not even two. Pammie, still so innocent, whispered, "Happy birthday, Lorr," then boom, down the rabbit hole, while Lorr has lain awake haunted by all she has done and not done, by all she must somehow do. She feels so much older than Pammie, it's like they're not even sisters. Pammie isn't just a virgin; Lorr's pretty sure she's never let a boy feel her up. By Pammie's age she'd been doing it for two years, while the only penis her sister has handled is little Richie's, and she calls it "his thingy." Lying beside her, Lorr feels so dirty and used up she might as well be some forty-year-old selling blowjobs on Avenue D.

She climbs out of bed. Pammie's window faces the Hubbards, who have the only real yard in the neighborhood. Hank and Marilyn's row house shares a communal back driveway, and Lorr thinks, not for the first time, how nice it would have been to grow up with flowers and trees. *As if that would have made any difference.*

What kind of thought is that to have on your birthday? What kind of birthday is this anyway, twenty years old, listening to her sister sleep? If only Daddy hadn't made things so miserable Ricardo stopped loving her. If only she hadn't been such a coward and told Mom and Daddy right away he was Puerto

7

Rican. If only she hadn't been such an idiot and gotten pregnant. If only she'd had the abortion, but then there'd be no little Richie. If, if, fucking if. If she scoops up her son and gets on the Greyhound, she could be upstate before anyone finds out. She knows these kids, Sal, Jack, and Lisa, who used to hang around Tompkins Square before they moved to this commune outside Ithaca. Lisa was making it with both guys and said if Lorr ever wanted to come up and hang out, that'd be cool. The commune had cats, dogs, horses, goats for milk. Some of the older members had kids. They grew their own food and their own dope, lived in yurts. Winter, Lisa admitted, was a drag, but you got used to it. And on this warm April night, thirty minutes from twenty years and a day, winter doesn't worry Lorr.

She gathers her clothes, all her clothes, and slips from the room. Mom and Daddy's bedroom is down the hall. She should wait another hour to make sure they're asleep, but she's afraid she'll lose her nerve. She has two hundred dollars in her purse, ten crisp twenties. When they returned from Senior's, Daddy totally surprised her, said, "Don't tell your mother and don't use this to buy drugs," then pressed the bills in her palm. He was like that, Daddy. Lorr tiptoes to the room that used to be hers. The door is unlatched, an inch or two ajar; little Richie insists they leave it open when they tuck him in. When her eyes adjust, there he is in what the family calls his big boy bed: cheek down, the mass of curls he inherited from Ricardo half-obscuring his forehead. He lies so still she gets frightened. *Don't be an idiot, he's just asleep.* Still, she fingers his cheek. Plump and warm.

He wears Superman PJs, and Lorr decides to leave them on; she doesn't want to wake him. She stuffs his diaper bag with clothes and the Pampers he uses only for sleeping. She's about to lift him then thinks, *Omigod, where's his stroller?* She sneaks down the carpeted steps, avoiding the third from the top, which got her busted sneaking out in tenth grade. The red and blue stroller is folded up in the front hall. She sets the diaper bag

8

and her boots beside it. If she's leaving forever, or until Mom and Daddy get used to this, she ought to take her winter coat. Mom stores off-season clothes in the basement, and suddenly the enormity of what she's doing nearly knocks Lorr over.

When she returns to the main floor, she sets her blue down parka beside the pile of her other things and starts up the stairs to get little Richie then decides, no, she better open the front door and put her things on the porch before she has the baby in her arms. She opens the first of three locks, a keyed dead bolt, then the brass chain, finally the thumbscrew. Outside it's a warm spring night, no traffic, just the blinking yellow light at the corner. Lorr reenters the house, careful not to let the screen door slam, and takes the stairs two at a time. Wrapped in his blue blankie, little Richie weighs almost nothing. He doesn't speak or wake, just shifts slightly, resting his cheek on her shoulder. In a dash she's down and out the door. She descends the brick steps, steps into her boots, sets Richie in his stroller. His lids flutter, and he seems to see her. Then his chin settles, and he's gone.

Lorr is halfway to the station, crossing Ocean Avenue, the synagogue on one side, St. Mark's, where her Catholic friends went, on the other, when she realizes she can't do this. Mom and Daddy would absolutely kill her. And what does she know about babies? *How to make them.* But she also knows she really, really, really loves little Richie. *God,* she thinks and starts to cry, *you are so fucked.*

Instead of heading home, she detours down Ocean Avenue and follows it to Emmons and the Sheepshead Bay piers, where the party boats tie up. Daddy likes to fish, and when she was nine and ten, he used to take her out for the day, proud she wasn't all squeamish and girly. Happy days, just Lori-Lorr and Daddy. Now the boats' shadows and the sound and smells of the Bay, waves lapping against wooden pilings, saltwater and machine oil, bring that time back so powerfully—she was such a Daddy's girl, and everything she did pleased him—she's fighting tears. He'll be a good daddy to Richie, she knows he will, better than he was to her, the whole father-daughter-boyfriend tension won't fuck things up.

Lorr turns onto Bedford Avenue and heads away from the Bay. She's wearing her winter coat, carrying the diaper bag over her shoulder and pushing little Richie, who hasn't made a peep. She passes under the Belt Parkway overpass, where it always smells like piss. There are broken bottles everywhere; bums hide out here and drink. She hears something move in the shadows, and she's suddenly as frightened as she was at eight, when the underpass was known as the Scary Place and she was forbidden to walk here alone.

Whatever it was scurries into the deeper murk, and Lorr hurries on, reemerging into the relative brightness of Bedford Avenue. Richie still hasn't made a sound. It's like he doesn't even know she's there, or maybe in his baby-ness he totally gives it up to her, knowing she'll take good care of him. And she would have, if anyone had trusted her, if she'd trusted herself.

When she crosses Voorhies and starts down the row of attached brick houses, she senses something's wrong and in a moment sees what it is. Their house, fifth in line, is a blaze of light. *Oh shit, oh shit.* Mom must have woken up and checked on Richie. She cannot do this, she cannot fucking do this. She stops in front of the house and bends to the stroller. "I love you, little Richie. I love you."

She kisses him once, twice, three times. His eyes startle open.

"Or," he says and reaches toward her. "Or."

She kisses him one last time, says, "I gotta go. Be a good boy."

Then she's running away from the stroller, from the diaper bag, from the family manse, running toward the station, wondering how far, how very far, Daddy's two hundred dollars will take her.

BOOK 1. FALL 2000

Calhoun City

ONE

Imagine a boy, then a young man, then a man not so young, never quite at ease with himself. Smart but nebbishy. Not a nerd—in fact, a decent athlete—but assigned a permanent place on the geek side of the street. Not funny looking but not especially handsome either. No circle of freshman girls ever whispered behind open palms, "Ooh, Richie Gordon, he's so hot!"

Perhaps the adolescent zits put them off; he loved pizza, square and round, and its greasy, multitudinous toppings. There was the prominent forehead, which made him look like the brain he was. The sallow skin, a Jewish nose, more than a little hooked. *Aquiline*, Hank Gordon, originator of that nose, liked to say, but on Hank it looked good; on Hank everything looked good. Later, with his father dead, there was no way of catching up, not in the house of odd women in which he grew, his much older sister treating him like a houseplant and his mother, strange, abstracted, and celibate after Hank died, and who knew about before? It was a miracle, Richie sometimes told himself, he wasn't gay.

And now that same awkward, self-doubting boy was picking a shirt for a date with a woman he not only hadn't met but no one he knew had ever met. Who would have guessed that when the Calhoun City, Kansas, police called to say they had recovered his wallet, it would lead to this. The off-white? New blue pinstripe? He angled a red and blue club tie in front of his bedroom mirror and leaned in for a closer look.

Idiot. No one wears a tie to coffee. Maybe he should have invited her to brunch. Noon, Sunday? Of course, brunch. Call, say, *Don't eat, I'd like to take you out to brunch.* But he didn't want to imply she couldn't afford to feed herself. If he did call, she might conclude he was waffling, or overanalyzing. (Overanalyzing? Richie?) Or remember she had something better to do, and what a stupid idea it had been to say yes in the first place, some random white guy your baby's daddy's been scamming, some loser pissed off about a cable bill.

Richie dropped the tie and the off-white shirt still wrapped in its dry cleaner paper cuff and raised his arms, first the right then the left, burrowing nose-deep into springy black hair. Why was he so nervous? She was probably just some sistah who would hate him because he wasn't wearing a hoodie and baggy jeans that fell halfway off his ass.

You disgusting racist, he thought. *How could you even think that?*

For a moment Richie considered phoning to say he couldn't make it. Or better still, flushing both shirts down the crapper then taking a running jump off his balcony onto the train tracks eight stories below.

He inhaled his own distress. Maybe he *was* a bit ripe; maybe it wasn't just his own psyche declaring he was rotting meat. If he hurried, he had just enough time for his second shower of the morning. He started toward the bathroom, undressing. In a moment he was steaming under a warm cumulus of spray soaping his underarms, remarking on what a kick-ass job his colleagues, BMs of C&M's deodorant brands did day in, day out, how they were so good there ought to be a law against marketing deodorants to teenagers, just as there was a law against marketing cigarettes to them. Until that happened, however, what a fine, easy outrage it was to convince the newly mature and sexually inexperienced they smelled too funky to find love. Why, he wondered, not for the first time, why at thirty years old did he still fit that pliable demographic?

At five to twelve, with his carefully combed hair still wet, Richie settled into a small table just past the espresso bar, adjacent to

the floor-to-ceiling bookcase lining one wall of this most unusual of C. City, M.O.'s establishments: a combination used
bookstore and coffeehouse. Why invite her to Kaldi's? It was
unlikely LaTisha was a book hound like the assistant professors
Dave and Laura were always setting him up with. Richie understood his friends wanted him to be happy, but he also knew he
was the only straight bachelor of their acquaintance. Without
intending to, therefore, Richie had become part of the semi-
official welcome wagons in Dave and Laura's departments at
UMCC. In a little more than four years Richie had been out to
drinks or had dined at their home with an unmarried female expert in every century, British and American, from the sixteenth
to twentieth, as well as a clinical, cognitive, and social psychol-
ogist. He'd washed out with each and every one, not because
there had been no second or third dates, and even sex with two
of the women, a Jungian named Marie and Yvette, a postcolonial British scholar, who'd moved on to a more prestigious job
in Ann Arbor. He'd liked Marie quite a bit despite her fear of
the dark, which made after-dinner dates problematic, and her
theories about oppression, which she saw everywhere and in
all things, including their lovemaking.

He should have picked someplace else, he was certain of it.
The assistant professors had liked Kaldi's but had never liked
him, at least not for long. Or not in the way he wanted to be
liked. Or maybe he didn't like them. Richie blew into his palm
to test his breath. He had a sample size bottle of Score, C&M's
top-selling brand, in his pocket. Nope, he was good. He glanced
up at the front door, twenty feet away. He'd decided on the pinstripe, tucked into jeans. Hardly hipster, but at least with the
pinstripe he looked marginally handsome, the crisp blue and
white cotton setting off his olive skin.

There was no sign of LaTisha at noon or, for that matter, any
African American. The dark wood tables were mostly occupied
by white Gen-X'ers, students at the art school a few blocks

away. At five after Richie pulled a book down from the shelf above his table, *Fisherman*, by a Czech expatriate, Franz Herring. At ten after, tired of putting off the multi-pierced waitress (nose, chin, six or eight in each lobe, and suspicious bumps under her blouse) with the lame excuse—*Waiting for a friend*—he ordered a double cappuccino. He sipped half; then, fearful he'd been stood up, invoked powerful magic absorbed from his father on the party boats they took from the Sheepshead Bay piers all those years ago. If the fish weren't biting and he'd already checked his bait, let the weight kiss bottom then cranked up three turns; had even chummed with the tuna fish sandwiches Dad insisted they bring to piss off the fish. *Get them biting mad, Richie.* When all else had failed, one of them needed to propitiate the God of Fishing and Peeing. Everyone, Dad said, knew fish wouldn't bite unless someone was inside that smelly head.

So Richie headed to Kaldi's bathroom, two urinals and a single stall, every inch of dark paneling (except for the chalkboard above the urinals) covered with posters for readings and the jazz shows Kaldi's hosted on Wednesdays, featuring its house band, the Kevin Kane Trio, not because he needed to pee but because peeing might conjure LaTisha. Shaking himself dry, he tried to remember the last time a hand other than his own had touched this sad and lonely tip of his anatomy, realizing with a sort of anti-frisson it had been nearly eighteen months. He washed then hurried toward his empty table and found himself halfway past before perceiving it was no longer empty. As he turned, the honey mustard voice he'd been hearing in his head for days asked softly, "Richard Gordon, where you been?"

Did he want his first words to be *In the bathroom*? "LaTisha? Sorry to keep you waiting."

"I just got here, but looks like you been here awhile. Unless someone else been drinking your coffee."

Richie grinned at the medium-complexioned woman, whose short, processed, nearly black hair framed her face. LaTisha was big but not heavy. Broad shoulders, smallish breasts, brown eyes.

"You just gonna stand there?"

Her full mouth, lipsticked purple plum, a shade or two darker than her skin, parted; taken together, her lips and eyes softened the almost masculine lines of her face. Smiling, her face was not just intriguing and sexy, he thought, but full of whimsy. Behind it almost anything might be concealed.

"No, I'm not just going to stand here." He extended his hand, and when she joined hers to his, it felt warm and nearly as large as his own. He had this crazy idea to raise her creamy palm to his lips. But that was so obviously goofy, he simply sat down. "I'm glad you could make it."

"Me too." That killer smile again. "I almost couldn't find no one to mind Jada."

"You could have brought her."

"Nah," she said, "better this way."

"LaTisha—"

"Tisha."

"Don't worry. I'm not freaky."

On her cheeks just below and beside each ear a black curl glistened, upturned like a fish hook. "I'm not worried, I can take care of my daughter. Been doing it her whole life. Anyway, you kind of little." Her eyes laughed. "But cute."

This hot black woman thinks I'm cute? "You're kind of cute your-self."

"You slamming on me, Richard?"

He assumed *slamming* was a net positive and wobbled his head, a gesture that in his long-dead grandmother had meant *Maybe* but in the present circumstance meant *Absolutely*. He almost said, *My friends call me Richie.* Instead, he responded, "I nearly called you back to say, 'Maybe we could have brunch, not just coffee.' Are you hungry?"

She nodded.

17

"Well, then, let's eat."

He passed her one of the menus the waitress had left.

"Belgian waffles," Tisha said. "I love 'em."

"Eggs Benedict for me."

Waiting for their food, he kept thinking he ought to be pissed at her. He just knew she knew about the cable bill, the whole tawdry scam; she'd probably been in on it. But he was too intrigued by meeting her and perhaps getting to *know* her, oh you hopeful, horny white boy, to maintain an angry edge, so they talked about the weather, *cold*, and her coffee, *strong and really hot*. When their food arrived, rescuing them both from this pathetic awkwardness, Richie asked, "What do you think is Belgian about those waffles?"

Tisha raised a forkful of strawberries and cream that was mostly cream toward her lips. "They known for their dairies in Belgium."

He wondered if what they said about black women was true. What *was* it they said about black women? They couldn't get enough? *Not of you.*

Tisha swallowed, set her fork down, and patted her lips with a napkin. "I read somewhere Belgian waffles was introduced in this country at the World's Fair in New York."

"I'm from New York."

She smiled, and he smiled back at her.

"Why were you reading about the World's Fair?"

"I was reading about waffles. Used to major in food science."

She swallowed another forkful, tonguing errant cream from the conjoined heart of her lips. Richie answered the disruptive whisper of desire, *Stop it, she's just eating.* He glanced at his untouched plate and sliced into the hollandaise-topped poached egg. Yolk oozed from its white cave, mixing with the paler hollandaise below. He savored the contrasting textures: slightly rubbery Canadian bacon, yielding muffin, runny yolk, and hollandaise.

"Look like you enjoying that." She grinned. "You like to eat?"
Is she flirting? He nodded.

"Me too."

He was still trying to gauge her sub and subber subtext, when the skinny waitress leaned over them. "Everything all right?"

"Everything fiiiiine." When the waitress retreated, Tisha continued, "I suppose you want to hear all about Reece and your IDs."

He nodded.

"I met Reece my first month in C. City, M.O."

"Where'd you move from?"

"Not New York, I can tell you that."

"No, where?"

"That's right. Little town between nowhere and nothing much." She smiled, settled her fork, and with the thumb and second finger of each hand smoothed and shaped the glistening curl on each cheek. "About as dumb country as I could be, eighteen, and Reece, he pretty slick. Read everything, and boy, the—" She stopped. "He could talk."

For the first time jealousy flared in Richie, hot and red, at his Other, the ur-Richie who'd been using his IDs. Tisha raised her knife and fork. "Don't know how or where Reece got them cards, but by the time I'm here six months, I'm pregnant and he's in the County. Maybe he bought them inside. When he came out a few months before Jada born, we stayed to his Granny's in Ruskin Heights. Reece told me 'bout the IDs like they some joke, say he going be someone else, and I'd say, 'Nah, Reece, you always gonna be you.' I was real sweet on him back then."

She sipped her coffee. Richie reminded himself to take another bite of eggs.

"Anyway, Reece in some kinda trouble he wouldn't talk about, and when it came on Jada's birth, said we couldn't use his name. I say, we can't use mine, I promised my baby she gonna have her daddy's name. Reece say, 'Okay, use my other name,' which is how Jada came to be Jada Reece Gordon. Everyone know Reece her daddy, but she have this other name too."

"Jada Reece Gordon, that's pretty."

"I think so."

"When's her birthday?"

"May 19, 1996."

Richie thought a minute. He'd been in town about a year then. He could have lost the IDs, which included his social security card, that fall or winter, just like he thought. "So Reece never said where he got them?"

She shook her head.

"Do you know what he did with them? Did he get credit cards?"

"We didn't talk about things like that. You wanna know the truth?" She sipped her orange juice through a straw, and the color disappeared from the cubes in her glass. "We didn't talk much about anything, though Reece, he liked to read, and he liked to talk. But talking wasn't what he liked to do with me."

Some other Richie might have asked, *What did Reece like to do with you?* This Richie was pretty sure he knew and doubted he'd get the chance himself. "So if you were me," Richie began, thinking, *You are so wonderfully not me,* "would you get a new social security number?"

"Hell, yes." She laughed, and a sweet silvery sound slipped from her lips. "Reece good-looking, he funny. But even when I loved and stayed with him, and I haven't done neither since Jada was one year old, I didn't trust him. You think there something Reece mighta done? He probably did it."

"What about that cable bill on Pleasant Street? That was only last year."

"I can't tell you nothing about Pleasant Street."

Can't or won't?

"Once burned, twice shy." Again, that silvery laugh, her face softened by a grin. "Hell, burned five or six times, you get kinda scabby."

Richie took another bite of his egg stack. He'd been so enthralled by LaTisha? Tisha? (he wasn't sure what to call her, just as he wasn't sure if he should let her keep calling him Richard. Maybe he wouldn't be so shy as Richard), he kept forgetting to eat. "Do you have a picture of Jada?"

"'Course I do."

Her face assumed the hard expression, especially around the eyes, that she'd given the interrupting waitress.

"Before you start looking at me like that—"

"Like what?"

He hardened his own face, or tried to, narrowing his eyes and scowling down his nose. Whatever it looked like, he suspected it wasn't hard because Tisha laughed.

"Like someone stole your last piece of food."

"Oh, that face."

"Before you start, let me ask you something." Richie paused, hearing the pronunciation he hadn't used but which he thought she might. *Let me axe you something.* "Officially, Jada's father is Richard Alan Gordon?"

"That's right."

"Richard Alan Gordon would like to see a picture of Jada Reece Gordon."

He met her eyes, and this time he didn't find laughter or whimsy, more like shrewd consideration. He wondered what she thought of him, of white people in general. "I already told you." He longed to touch her hand, which lay upturned and bare beside her coffee cup, but he didn't because he was such a wimp. "You've got nothing to worry about."

And I already told you, Tisha did not say but must be thinking, he could hear it as clearly as he could hear the clacking heels of the approaching waitress, the hiss of the cappuccino maker across the room, *I can take care of my daughter, been doing it her whole life*. Tisha hefted her purse, paler yellow than her blouse, drawing from it a woman's red wallet. From the wallet she withdrew a school picture of a pretty little girl: narrow face, lemony walnut skin, hair arranged in cornrows ending in alternating pink and lavender beads. Jada's mouth, missing a front tooth, was open as if she were about to sing.

"That from this fall." Tisha met his eyes. "Jada always talking."

"She's pretty." Richie hesitated then said what he knew Dave Manning would. "Like her mother."

The compliment hung awkwardly.

"If you think complimenting Jada . . ." Tisha tapped the back of his hand with a shaped nail, and the shock of first contact burned through him. "Well."

Soon, too soon, they finished eating. "Something else?" he asked. "Dessert?"

"I should go."

"What's the hurry?"

"Don't laugh. I have to study."

"I think it's great, you're in school. What are you studying?"

"Nursing. What about you?"

He thought about claiming he was also in school: first semester, life science. Since they'd arranged to meet he'd been nervous about exchanging bios, fearful his might put her off as much as his white skin. But he was such a bad liar. "I work for Clay and Mason."

"Doing what?"

"I'm a brand manager."

"That pretty good?"

"It's all right."

The shrewd, appraising look she'd given him when he asked to see Jada's picture reshaped her features. "You're not boastful, are you?"

"I haven't done much to boast about."

"Brand manager, that some kind of executive?"

He nodded.

"Lotsa men woulda been talking about they job, they money, trying to impress me."

"Would it?"

"I'm impressed you didn't."

Soon they were out on the street, dressed in gray December light. Tisha turned right, and he fell in beside her, walking closer to the gutter. The bars, clubs, and galleries of the entertainment district were empty. Just a very few blocks had been gentrified, and it wasn't yet clear if the city's financial plan was going to work; the area drew nighttime crowds only. During the day and more than a block or two either side of Kaldi's, it was the same run-down neighborhood it had been for decades, since the end of Prohibition. Back then, Richie had read, there was real money being made, by whites and blacks both, in the bars, speakeasies, brothels, and jazz clubs that made C. City, M.O. famous and drew blacks from all over the South and Southwest, Arkansas, Texas, Louisiana, Mississippi, as far away as the Carolinas, so long as they could abide by Boss Prendergast's unwritten laws (not that they had much choice because Prendergast controlled the police, just as he controlled the flow of Prohibition hooch). Whites could come into the district to drink, whore, dance, and party, but blacks who provided many of those services weren't welcome in the white parts of the city, loosely defined as west of Troost Avenue. Things hadn't changed much since those days, at least in terms of where blacks were welcome. *They know their place*, he'd been told, when he first moved to town. It wasn't really that much different from New York. What had changed was that the jazz district had died and was slowly, tentatively, coming back, although glancing around now, he couldn't say for sure how far back it had come. Boarded storefronts, the Serve City Pantry, Second Chance Rehabilitation Center, and the Purity Clinic, just across the street, which Richie had heard referred to as the Not So Pure. A sign in the window promised twenty dollars for a pint of blood. Whenever Richie came to Kaldi's, or occasionally to hear jazz at the restored Blue Note on the corner, he parked as close as he could. It was asking for trouble not to; at the very least it was inviting panhandlers. Growing up in Brooklyn, riding the subway to high school, beggars would pick him out. A soft touch, a sap, an easy mark, though nothing really bad had ever happened. Still, he hated how they made him feel, like a coward or, worse yet, a racist.

He glanced at the daunting lines of Tisha's face in profile, a single shiny curl flat against her cheek, a black hook plangent on a field of brown. This was the first time he'd walked on Eighteenth Street or a street like it with someone from the race he felt threatened by, and not just someone, a sexy woman. Maybe passersby would think he was hip and they were together? *Never.* Wait, the first part wasn't true. In high school, walking to football practice at the fields adjacent to the East River and Sixth Street, the white players tried to buddy up with the blacks and Ricans. Back then the Alphabet (the bus dropped them at Eighth and D to begin their hike to the river fields carrying stuffed duffel bags of football manhood) hadn't yet yielded its current crop of boutiques and bistros. Collateral protection from black teammates had seemed prudent. It suddenly occurred to Richie that maybe they'd been scared too.

"Where are you parked?" he asked.

She turned, an uncomfortable look on her face above the raised collar of her red wool car coat. "I rode the bus."

He almost asked, *Why didn't you say something, I would have picked you up?*

"No biggie," she added, "one bus up Troost."

"Let me drive you home."

"If it's not too much trouble."

Too much trouble? Since the afternoon began, he'd fretted about it ending and having to return the baby picture of Jada the

C. City, Kansas, police had given him along with his IDs. He glanced at Tisha's eyes, realizing they were the same dark brown and the same height as his or maybe a little higher. "No trouble at all." He hesitated then took her black-gloved hand in his own gloved fingers. "When were you going to tell me we weren't walking to your car?"

He loved how a smile transformed her face.

"At the bus stop?"

When they crossed Troost, he spotted a panhandler in a ratty green parka halfway up the block. When they'd closed to fifteen feet and the panhandler stepped in their direction, grinning, Richie observed how dark he was, except for gray in the beard climbing his thin cheeks.

"My man, do a brother a solid?"

Which would look better? Give him money or not?

"I won't lie." He grinned, glanced from Richie to Tisha and back again. "This cold night's gointa be warmer wid a bottle."

Christ, I don't give him, I look cheap. If I do, I'm a racist? Richie dug in his jeans, no coins, then looked in the panhandler's moist, possibly crazed eyes. He could hear his father's warning, *Never take your wallet out on the street.* "Sorry."

"My man. Don't look like you gointa have trouble keeping warm wid that fine sistah."

Tisha grabbed Richie's hand. "Come on," she said, then fired over her shoulder, "You stupid, you rude! You woulda got that dollar you kept your big mouth shut." She turned to Richie. "Ain't that right?"

"That's right," he said, but only to Tisha, without looking back. They were almost to the corner. She was mashing his gloved hand in her gloved fingers, and it felt as if they were running away together or perhaps toward something he couldn't see.

TWO

Wednesday night, already past seven-thirty, in fact almost seven-forty-five, Richie turned off Brush Creek Boulevard. He was meeting Dave and Laura at a new bistro near the Plaza, and he hated to be late. It had already been a hairy she-bear of a week: foul breathed, mean eyed, and petty. There were water cooler rumors of forced retirements and buyouts (no one was fired at C&M, but ABMs and BMs were routinely coached out after bad evaluations), even whispers of whole divisions being sold, more fallout from last June's resignation, the über-coaching out of former CEO Brad Vanderwohl. No one had said anything directly to Richie, and with so many of Project Turf's start-up costs already spent, it remained unlikely, but he'd begun to fear his product launch would be pushed back or even canceled. Turf was the sort of innovative project Brad had been let go for supporting, too far, Richie now feared, from C&M's core product lines. Something had just felt off at the NBD managers' Monday morning meeting. He could see it in the other new business managers' faces as they hurried out of the conference room, no one making eye contact. Richie remained in the office until ten that night tearing down and rebuilding his model. He was back by seven Tuesday morning and seven-fifteen today. And not just Richie but the whole array of fluttery, gray-suited BMs, as if as a group they'd sensed some shadowy predator rising from the corporate deep. He'd been planning to work late tonight too, was settling in at his desk at seven-fifteen, twelve hours after he arrived, when he remembered, *Oh, my God. Dave and Laura.*

Last Wednesday he'd met Dave, as he did most weeks, at the Havana Martini Club a few blocks from his office.

"Richie," Dave had said, looking up from his second dirty Grey Goose martini. "What are you doing about your wallet?"

"Not much."

"For a smart guy you can be really dumb."

Dave grinned. Professionally, he was an expert on paranoia in postmodern fiction. He was also, and told anyone who would listen, more than a tad bit paranoid himself, which didn't mean people weren't after him, although mostly, Richie thought, it was Dave who was after everyone else. Dave ashed his cigar, and Anne, at whose table they sat most weeks, slipped in beside them, replacing the sooty glass ashtray with a clean one. "You guys okay?"

"Richie is dying of lonely."

Schmuck, Richie thought.

Anne, cute as a new penny—coppery curls fringing a heart-shaped face—produced a smile of questionable sympathy. "Would another martini help?"

"Absolutely. Richie wants one too."

They watched Anne's petite bum disappear behind the bar.

"You ought to ask her out."

"I'm finished with waitresses. It never works." He'd paused, thinking, as he suspected Dave was, *It doesn't work no matter who you're dating.* "What were you going to tell me about Laura's sister?"

"Oh, yeah, this friend of hers, Stan something, had his wallet stolen too."

"Mine wasn't stolen."

"Just listen." Dave drained his cocktail. "First, whoever had the wallet began running up huge balances on his credit cards. When Stan canceled them, the crook applied for new cards, using Stan's social security number. Then the same crook, or maybe it was someone else—they sell your identity, you know—got a loan for a new Harley in El Paso. Mind you, the wallet was stolen in Chicago. Of course, this was a top of the line, fifteen K hog—"

Dave paused to chew the last olive off his toothpick then poked Richie's forearm with it.

"Goddamnit, Dave."

"Pay attention. When whoever it was stopped making payments, the finance company went after Stan. For starters they torpedoed his credit then attached his tax return. Didn't matter that whoever had gotten the loan misspelled what was supposedly his own name, Stanley, on the application."

Richie chewed the garlic-stuffed olives off the toothpick in his own martini. "Why are you telling me this?"

"I'm trying to make sure nothing bad happens to my buddy."

"Nothing has."

"You don't know that."

Anne returned, martinis balanced on her little tray. She set them on the table beside a fresh dish of mixed nuts.

"Anything else?"

Under flaming hair her eyes looked gray as smoke. She was what, twenty-three? No wedding band. Richie slapped his Amex on the tray.

"Do you ever date customers?" Dave asked.

Anne smiled. "Once or twice."

Christ, Richie thought, blushing.

"You are such a jerk," he said when Anne left with his credit card. When he returned from the Havana's all-marble bathroom, which still had a uniformed attendant, an ancient black man, who'd called him "Suh" as he passed a white hand towel, Dave said, "There's a problem with your card."

Richie searched Dave's face for signs this was a joke.

"Apparently it's over the limit." Dave handed Richie his platinum Amex and a piece of paper. "You're supposed to call this number."

Goddamnit, Richie thought. I just paid that bill. Then he read what was written on the paper. "Anne. 279-6497."

Dave grinned. "Got you."

"You are such a schmuck."

"Point is, when your IDs are stolen by a lowlife, a crook . . ."

"We don't know that."

"Oh sure, that's why he's in jail, with your signature on fake IDs, because he's such a citizen. Point is, someone steals your identity, you don't sit around waiting for something bad to happen, for malevolent forces in the modern world—"

"All right, what should I do?"

"The only absolutely safe response is to get a new social security number."

"You think?"

"It was me," Dave said, "I wouldn't hesitate. I've been doing some research. It's easier than you think."

They attended to their martinis. Soon both were empty, and Richie stood, muzzle-headed, miserable, and ready for sleep. "Come on," he'd said. "I need to get home."

"Are you going to call Anne?"

Richie shook his head. Dave called him a pussy, and at the time he'd felt like one. Now, turning right on Middleton, with Yip's Bistro just ahead, as promised, but no place to park, he was glad he hadn't called Anne. *Tisha*, he thought. He circled the Plaza once, then again. There was never any fucking place to park. By the time he'd found a spot four and a half blocks away and ran back with his center-vented coattails opening behind him like black tail feathers, he was fifty minutes late. Dave and Laura were seated halfway back on the right side of the restaurant. As he hurried toward them rehearsing the tone and timbre for *I'm sorry, I'm sorry, I'm sorry*, he was struck, as he was each time he hadn't seen them in a while, by how much they resembled each other, if not sibling then kissing cousin–close: tall with dark blond hair, solid, all-American features, their eyes the same pellucid blue. Like fucking your sister, Dave would sometimes say and wink.

Dave stood to shake Richie's hand. "Mister On-Time arrives late."

"I'm sorry, I'm sorry, I'm sorry. I hope you didn't wait."

"Of course, we waited."

Laura rose and hugged him, her full body pressing against his. He kissed her high on both cheeks, inhaling a whiff of perfume or perhaps it was shampoo, a C&M brand, Pantene or was it Wella? He sat between them in the lemon candle-scented semidark. Dave was working on his second or by this time probably his third martini; Laura wasn't drinking. Dave insisted Richie order, in fact ordered for him. "Dirty Grey Goose martini, extra dry, extra olives."

When the drink arrived with appetizer portions of tuna tartare and fried calamari (Dave and Laura always included him in their orders, assuming all three would share, their *mange à trois* the gastronomic equivalent of Laura's hug), Dave raised his glass, dimples forming on his cheeks.

"We have news." He glanced at Laura.

"We're pregnant." She beamed. "Eight weeks."

A cloud of joy rose in him for his friends. "I'm so happy for you." He tapped his martini stem against Dave's and Laura's glass of Evian. *That's* why she wasn't drinking. "To the baby."

They weren't kids, Dave and Laura, either of them, close to forty. Richie set his glass on the table and clasped his friends' hands. Laura smiled and took Dave's, completing the circle. Richie leaned left and kissed her on the lips. *What the hell.* He leaned the other way and kissed Dave's stubbly cheek.

Eyes shining, Laura said, "We'd like you to be the baby's godfather."

And Richie, who felt almost every day how alone he was, turned from his friend's wife to his friend, tears starting down his cheeks.

When he reached home, Richie decided to call his sister. Since moving to Florida five years ago to sell real estate to the-soon-to-be retired, she'd been busy, busy, busy. If he didn't call her, they didn't speak. His whole life she'd been more like a young aunt than a sister; she ought to pick up the damn phone now and then. It wasn't like she had anyone else in her life, which was something else he didn't understand. Even in her midforties, Pammie was sexy, at least he'd thought so the last time he saw her, almost a year ago. Pale blue eyes like their dad. Sandy hair—white-blonde in baby pictures—and a very grown-up body: large breasts, wide hips, the same short legs Richie had inherited. Why Pam hadn't found someone and why she never had kids, well, those were mysteries.

Her machine picked up. Richie left a short message, doused the lights, and gazed out through his living room picture window high in the Western Auto Building. Western Auto, once proud corporate headquarters until converted to condos a few years back, was shaped like a pie wedge turned sideways; it straddled downtown train tracks in C. City, M.O. His living room window faced west, overlooking the train yards, which had provided C. City with its first source of wealth and reason for being. Location, location, location, as he'd heard his sister say about her business: in C. City's case the eastern terminus of the transcontinental railroad. He'd bought the condo a little over a year ago, when he was promoted from assistant brand manager (ABM) to brand manager (BM) and assigned to new business development (NBD). (Pammie had sent flowers and a card, congratulating him for being elevated from antiballistic missile to bowel movement).

He was pulling down one-twenty-two, and because BMs were Band Three, he could count on a sizable year-end bonus. All this, and Richie still had his hair, which his mother's father had lost in his twenties. Since the fall of eighth grade, when he mastered the basics of Mendelian genetics, Richie had assumed a similar fate awaited him. *Dome-head.* For years he'd fretted and did still, despite the mirror's thick assurances. Any moment it could all vanish, like his father and later his mother had. Luxuriant, was how his biz school lover Liz had described Richie's hair, and follicular health had turned out to be more than the sum of vanity or fear. Richie's brand, Folgrow, known in-house as Project Turf, was C&M's entry in the hot hair regrowth market, and a thick head of hair, well, he could sell the bejesus out of it because Richie knew how wretched it felt to fear losing it.

His condo—gleaming oak floors, 1920s twelve-foot ceilings, but a space-age kitchen, two large bedrooms, more space than he'd ever imagined having for himself—was one floor below the enormous illuminated red WESTERN AUTO sign on the roof. He'd chosen to live downtown, rather than in the trendier Plaza area or in the Kansas suburbs, where his married-with-kids colleagues lived, not only because it was close to work and work was mostly what he did but also because it overlooked the train yards. Growing up, trains had meant graffiti-covered subway cars, which he'd ridden from Brooklyn to Manhattan. Here it meant the freights and their mournful, middle-of-the-night whistles, somehow the loneliest yet most comforting of sounds, and Richie, at his core, was the loneliest of men. Although he disdained the sappy comfort of country-western music, he'd come to love the sound of freight whistles, the sustained sigh and rill, the fading in the night sadness, and he listened for the sound in his sleep, alone in his empty bed. Oh fuck, he thought. He felt all stirred up inside, no doubt Dave and Laura's news; he was happy for them. And what else? Bone-deep lonely. Without giving himself time to think, he dialed LaTisha, hoping five to eleven wasn't too late to call.

"Hey, Richard." Barely a whisper. "How you been?"

He'd called Monday, the day after what he now thought of as their first date, then everything got crazy at work. "I didn't wake you?"

"Nah." She yawned. "I'm lying in bed."

"I did wake you."

"I'm glad you called."

"I'm glad you're glad." He let himself fantasize about her bed and what she might or might not be wearing. On Sunday she'd asked to be dropped at the intersection of Sixty-eighth and Ruskin, near, she said, but not in front of her apartment. "I was wondering if you'd like to see me again. Or maybe you're too busy at school."

"I think you know."

Know? He knew nothing. "A real date. In the dark."

Did he just say, *In the dark*?

"What kinda date?"

"After dark. I meant to say, 'After dark.'"

"I bet."

Flustered, and therefore talking fasterandfasterandfaster, Richie continued, "The kind where I pick you up and take you out to dinner. I ate tonight with my friend Dave, the one I told you about?"

Call-waiting—*damn*—bleeped in the background.

"That's why I called so late. This really nice place near the Plaza. Then maybe a movie at the Esquire?"

Bleep.

"I'd like that."

"I'm sorry, I have a call coming in."

He pressed FLASH. Pammie said, "Richie, how are you?"

"On the other line."

"Who're you talking to this late?"

"I'll call you back."

"So who was that?" Tisha asked.

"My sister."

"Richard, you a playa?"

"What?"

"Sister or sistah?"

He took a moment to understand. "My big sister Pam, in Florida." He looked down at the sleeping city. Not a soul moved nor the lights of a single car. "How about Saturday?"

After he hung up, Richie walked around his apartment turning on lights. He should have suggested Friday. He should have said tomorrow! But he didn't want to seem desperate, even if he was, and he'd probably work late both nights. Still, Saturday was a long way away. He wondered what movie she'd like. Where'd he leave the paper? Oh yes, the bathroom. He walked from his living room to his bedroom, headed for the john, and glanced at the photo of his parents on the wall, the one from a long-ago cruise: Hank in a tuxedo and Marilyn in a green strapless gown, setting off her red hair. The phone rang.

"Richie," Pammie said. "You off yet?"

"I was just about to call."

"Who is she?"

He wondered how much to reveal. "How'd you know it was a woman?"

"Who else would you be talking to this late?"

"Saturday's our second date."

"Tell all."

He told almost nothing. Not how they'd met, the missing ID's, Tisha's race, or anything about Jada. A student. Studying to be a nurse.

"Baby bro, you robbing the cradle?"

Pammie, who had a fondness for adult beverages, sounded as if she'd sucked down several.

"Tisha took some time off. She's like five years younger than I am, twenty-four or five."

"Sheesh." Fourteen hundred miles away ice rattled. "I keep forgetting how young you are."

"How about you?" Richie asked. "Seeing anyone?"

"You're asking about my life?" Her voice rose on *life*. "I may fall down dead."

Richie wanted to ask, "Have you been drinking?" But that seemed rude. "Yeah, I am."

She didn't answer. He leaned back on his leather recliner,

raising his gray-socked feet until they obscured the window and the view of the dark train yards.

"A real question? Gordons don't do that."

"For Christ sakes, Pammie, I just asked if you're seeing someone."

"I'm not, okay?"

He heard the clatter of ice, the death of a cocktail, and saw Pammie as he remembered her. Voluptuous eighteen, blonde hair pulled back, shirttails tied off above her navel. Chasing him around the front yard with a spurting garden hose.

"You want to know how long it's been since I got laid, Richie?"

"Not really."

"Ten months. What about you?"

"I'm not saying."

"More than ten months?"

"I'm not saying."

"Poor little bro." She didn't say anything else and then, though he was half a continent away, he thought he could hear her moving around her white tiled condo. She kept trading up; the newest one had three bedrooms, granite counters, spa tubs. She was pouring herself another drink. She said, "Maybe we should just sleep with each other and keep it in the family."

"You're drunk."

"Your point is?"

"I'll tell you why I called."

"Not my love life?"

"I need my original birth certificate. I thought maybe it was mixed up in the papers you got when Mom died."

More ice rattle. Richie stared at the tops of his gray-socked feet, while somewhere in South Florida his sister drank.

"Why would you want that?"

She heard him out, no wisecracks. Then she said, "I'm not sure you really want the original, Richie."

"Without it I can't get a new social security number."

She didn't answer. Richie yawned, pushed down on the footrest, and stood up. In the distance he thought he saw the approaching lights of a train, traveling east, coming toward him.

"I'll do what I can," she said. "You still coming at Christmas?"

"Planning on it."

"Why don't you bring Tricia—"

Tisha, Richie thought but did not say.

"—if you're still seeing her. Maybe you'll get lucky in the sun."

"Maybe I will."

Two minutes after his head hit the pillow, he was dreaming of Project Turf and his blonde sister, her ponytail shining in the Brooklyn sun.

THREE

Saturday, when he found himself ready an hour early, Richie sat himself down on a high stool in front of his kitchen counter for a little chat. *Stop being an idiot. She's happy to go out with you.* Then that nasty voice in his head chimed in. *A single mom, poor and black? She's not just happy, she's lucky to have a free meal.* Well, if she's so happy and lucky, Richie thought, hopping down and circling the counter, why am I so goddamn nervous?

He reached into his fridge and popped a Sam Adams. He survived the next hour with a second Sam. Brushed his teeth twice, successfully resisted the siren call of a second shower, then drove south from downtown, jogged east around the Plaza and the university, then continued south on Troost into a part of town he'd never been to before driving Tisha home the first time, a neighborhood where every face on the wintry streets was some shade of black. He spied what looked like an old synagogue, although the sign on the brick facade announced the First Apostolic Church of Mayfield. Tisha had warned him to look out for it—*Turn left the next corner*—and he was paying close enough attention that when his headlights swept the darkness from the stained glass front he could swear there was a Jewish star and an eight-stemmed menorah underneath.

He turned left on Sixty-ninth. Houses lining both sides were ochre-colored brick, wrapped in wooden porches. Most, but not all, were well maintained and showed signs of architectural elegance, especially as he left Troost farther behind. There were multiple front doors and multiple cars in graveled driveways. *Not bad,* he thought and tried not to add in his mind, *for an allblack neighborhood.* What had he expected? The answer, as he

39

braked, looking for 1850, was he didn't know. Mayfield was in every way uncharted territory, although he'd been told that a generation or two ago it was the Jewish part of town.

Tisha rented the back second-floor apartment of 1850. She led him up a dark staircase that began inside the left of two front entrances, passing an apartment door marked with a big black *A*, from behind which hip-hop blasted: *ka-thump, ka-WHUMP.* Cooking odors both enticed and repelled him. Something spicy, something sweet. Tisha's round bottom preceded him up the stairs, and he hung back for a better view, her cheeks bumping side to side then disappearing when the stairwell bent sharply right. He hurried to catch up, spooked by the staircase, which was lit by a single bare bulb just inside the front door. He turned the corner—no one waiting, no ur-Richie or anyone else, pointing a gun, *you racist jerk!*—and entered Tisha's living room through the open apartment door. An overstuffed couch, green chair, a student desk. The hardwood floors glistened; the ceiling was ten-feet high, with crown molding. An archway on the right opened into a small kitchen. The opposite, street-facing wall contained two curtained windows. A doorway at the far end led to what he assumed was the bedroom corridor. Patchouli incense had been or might still be burning somewhere. The apartment was lovely. What a schmuck, he was so relieved.

"Hey." He produced the green tissue–wrapped bundle from behind his back. "I hope you like them."

LaTisha unwrapped the mum and sunflower bouquet. "How'd you know I love yellow flowers?"

"The yellow blouse you were wearing last time?"

Her eyes moved over his face as if maybe she were seeing *him* for the first time and not some white guy. "That's really thoughtful." She hugged him, and her hands and the flowers grazed his shoulders; her cheek pressed his. Stepping back so that she could see his face and he could see hers—dark plum lipstick, large glowing eyes—she answered his unasked question. "Jada's not here, she staying with the neighbor lady."

There it was, that awkwardness again. Tisha set the flowers in a vase, and they were ready to go.

Walking toward Yip's Cafe from where they'd parked, Richie longed to take her hand but didn't. This failure so dispirited him, he couldn't find anything to talk about, not even the weather. Wake *up*, he kept thinking, as if she'd cast a spell, though he knew what had bewitched him. She had to do *something* with Jada, didn't she? But he couldn't help thinking Jada wasn't there because Tisha didn't trust him. For God sakes, he was Richie Goody Fucking Two Shoes, Dave and Laura's welcome wagon. He tugged his coat collar tight against the wind, shivering as the low sky spat winter's first dry flakes. He didn't see how this would ever work. Too much distance: personal, racial, and probably cosmic. And he was such a loser. Good at work, sucked at life. He wanted to ask her about Pleasant Street again, if she knew who had lived there, so he could stop worrying. Then she'd really hate him.

Inside Yip's, however, with the first Chivas warming him and a second already ordered (Tisha sipped Merlot) and a glassed candle guttering buttery light on her cheeks and lips, he took her left hand, which was closer to the wall and thus hidden from view. Her eyes, though she did not look down, seemed to register the impact of flesh on flesh. Her thumb pad circled his. Finger sex. He was certain that's what it felt like to Tisha too. Their first real intimacy, simultaneously public and hidden. She placed her hand, palm up, on the table, and he traced its length with his second finger, starting at the base of her pinkie circling the mound of Venus below her thumb then up and over her wrist, his eyes never leaving hers. When the waitress arrived with his second Chivas to take their order, he slid his hand off Tisha's. *Coward, why do you care about the waitress?*

41

"Would you give us another minute?"

The waitress drifted away. Richie leaned across the table and kissed Tisha gently. "Thought you were shy."

"I am." *Or else I'd ask you to come home with me right now.*

"What should I order?"

"Anything you want."

When the movie ended, more than anything he wanted to ask her back to his apartment. But when they reached the street, snow had coated the sidewalks and parked cars. In the theater they'd never stopped touching: hand to hand then his fingertips stroking the bump of her stockinged knee. When he slipped his arm around her, nervous as a virgin, she lay her cheek against his shoulder. Now, under the illuminated marquee, their merged breath white as the falling snow, he felt timid again. One thing to play finger games in the dark, quite another on the streets of Calhoun City, M.O., named for the eloquent racist who had famously declared that slavery was not just a necessary evil but a positive good. He couldn't help noticing, as the stream of exiting moviegoers parted around them, that there were only two other African Americans and no mixed-race couples.

"What would you think?" He squeezed her gloved hand. "Of some ice cream?"

"Awfully cold, Richard."

It still felt different to be called Richard.

"What are you in the mood for?" *Did that sound too forward?* "Or do you need to get home?"

"Maybe"—she gazed at the steadily falling snow, large flakes descending without wind or sound—"you should take me home." She turned toward him, and the marquee's bright neon leached all color from her face but not her eyes.

Driving toward Mayfield, she asked where in New York he was from, and Richie remembered, with a jolt, how very little they knew about each other.

"Brooklyn."

"I see."

As if, to her, Brooklyn explained something, and he wondered what that could possibly be. He wondered if she would ask him up? If she didn't, should he offer to return Jada's picture? Second date, good-bye at the door? It's not like she believed in long courtships, pregnant after six months with Reece, that grievous motherfucker. Richie was still hassling with the identity theft paperwork, months from fixing his credit. Tisha directed him down the Promenade, a better route, she said, in bad weather. Snow didn't worry him; his CRV had four-wheel drive. He worried what would happen in her apartment, if he even got there. Had she ever been with a white guy? He certainly had never been with a black woman. And he couldn't help wondering— yes, he knew how stupid and racist this was; why did he have every one of these stupid ideas in his head, as if his cerebrum were the above-ground storage facility for centuries of racial garbage?—if she would think his penis was too small, by comparison to what she was used to. And what would her breasts look like? What color would her nipples be? But most of all he wondered what had she meant by "I see."

The Promenade, two empty lanes in each direction, passing houses that looked in worse and worse repair as they drove south, worked gradually up a hill. Brick homes, many of them substantial, eyed each other across the snow-cloaked street. The C. City Zoo was somewhere nearby, and there was a pocket community of mansions somewhere near here too; a marketing VP had invited him to a holiday party last year.

From the darkness of the passenger seat, Tisha asked, "You hear about the two young black men the police killed?"

What made her ask that now?

"The first was shoplifting, second died after a traffic stop."

He glanced toward her just as light from a street lamp briefly lit her face.

She added, "*Somehow* he got strangled."

"I'm sorry." As if it were his fault and all blacks were her family.

"His mother stays on my street. Her son, they called him Red, was a good guy. They said he resisted arrest."

"That's no reason to kill him."

"It's all bullshit. Only reason they stopped his damn car cause he black."

Richie kept his eyes on the road. The Promenade was still climbing and curving right. Snowflakes spun through the headlights.

"Left at the stop, then right on Beecher."

"In high school, believe it or not, I played football, and the coach, who also coached wrestling, made all the little guys try out and wrestle the lighter divisions."

"You played football, Richard?"

He glanced at her as he steered the CRV onto Beecher.

"My father played in college, and he'd died the year before I started high school. I thought he'd like it if I played."

"That must have been hard, your daddy dying so young."

More than I can tell you, he thought, and wondered about her parents. "Anyway, the high school I went to wasn't in my neighborhood."

"Why not?"

"I rode the subway to a science and math school in Manhattan."

"Smarty-pants."

He grinned. She'd mentioned his pants. "I knew kids from all over the city, and my junior year there was a wrestling tournament in the school I would've attended if I hadn't gone to Stuyvesant. And this friend of mine from the football team—"

"Sixty-eighth's the next right."

Richie flipped on his blinker. "Greg Laughinghouse, mostly black but part Indian, tall, really good-looking guy, drove to my neighborhood to watch the tournament."

He turned carefully onto Sixty-eighth, where there were no longer tracks to follow.

"Greg's father was a doctor, and he was driving his dad's new Cadillac, with MD plates. He hits my neighborhood, and *bam*, the cops pull him over to run his license and registration just because he was a black kid driving a nice car. That made me so mad."

And ashamed, Richie thought, as he pulled over.

"I wonder why you told me that story."

"Same reason you brought up the two dead black men?"

Their eyes met. When he leaned in to kiss her, she met him partway. For the first time, and he was still counting firsts, her tongue interrogated the hidden regions of his mouth, and he held it with his own. Then Richie hugged her and felt her heart beat, though it couldn't really be her heart, could it? through all their winter clothing.

"Let's go in," she whispered.

Up the porch steps, the dark staircase, past apartment A, and into her living room, where a stout older woman munched Cheetos in front of the television.

"Bertie, this my friend Richard."

Bertie heaved herself off the couch. Frizzled gray hair framed a face round as a pie plate. For a big woman she shook his hand without force, as if she feared she might contract a disease. A blue mu-mu draped her bulk, shoulders to knees; beneath it she wore gray sweats. Richie guessed she was sixty-five or seventy, medium-dark skin, pillowy breasts, heavy arms, a lap children must love to crawl up on. She eyed him with suspicion, or maybe the word that best described the scrutiny he felt was disbelief.

"This here the Richard I been hearing 'bout?"

Tisha nodded.

"Pleased to make your quaintance." Bertie turned to Tisha.

"I put Jada down an hour ago, but you know how much mischief she do."

Richie caught Tisha's eye. He hadn't removed his coat, hadn't even unbuttoned it.

"I hope she wasn't too much trouble."

"No more than usual, child."

Bertie still gave no sign of departing or finding a coat, while Richie, beginning to perspire inside his, felt as if he were laying siege, not so much to Tisha but to the old woman.

"You attending tomorrow at the A.M.E.?"

Tisha shrugged then asked softly, "Richard, want me to hang your coat?"

"Weatherman," Bertie said, "say we getting considerable cumulation."

"Richard's got four-wheel drive."

"Ooh." Bertie grinned, and against her dark face her teeth showed exceptionally white. Gazing at her, Richie felt his insides wobble. Black face, white teeth, so you can see them in the dark, all those awful jokes he used to hear growing up.

Bertie was saying, "So he won't have no trouble"—she watched him remove his topcoat—"driving home."

"Bertie," Tisha said. "I know where Jada getting her mischief."

With impressive grace for a woman her age and girth, Bertie started toward the door.

"Nice to meet you," Richie said.

"Nice to meet you, Richard. You treat her nice."

Bertie exited, with Tisha close behind, perhaps to pay her. Bertie hadn't put on a coat; she must live in the building. Richie could hear the women through the closed door. Bertie laughed. He wondered what was funny and suspected he was. A moment later, with the stairs creaking under Bertie's heavy tread, Tisha returned.

"What you think of Bertie?"

"I don't think she liked me."

"She just making sure you treat me right."

"I guess you hadn't told her I was white."

"You white?"

Kissing Tisha, he could taste her swallowed laughter.

FOUR

They spent two hours on her couch, then Richie drove home through the snow-whitened streets with an aching groin and a mind lit up with Tisha's promise to visit him tomorrow. In the half-light of her living room her nipples had shown nearly black above her upswelling breasts, and somehow that had excited him beyond reason. *Why,* he wondered, *why?* and felt a painful stirring in his crotch and squeezed the steering wheel harder. Tisha shared her bedroom with Jada. Hadn't been with a man in *so long*—how long was that?—but she didn't want to worry about Jada waking up and seeing them. Drunk on her taste and scent—he removed his glove and attempted to locate her funk again, *faint*, but yes, still there, no different from any other woman he'd been with, but her pubic hair felt springier, *kinkier*, and he felt that stirring again in his crotch, what's *wrong* with you!—he'd offered to pick her up.

But Tisha didn't want a ride; she preferred the bus, if he told her which one. Supine on the couch, her hand half-inside his pants, his under her skirt teasing the corner of green satin panties, Richie confessed he didn't know which bus served downtown and offered cab fare. Now behind the wheel at two a.m., the snow reduced to flurries with maybe three inches covering the streets and grassy median, he wondered if that was a mistake. He didn't want to be offering her money. *Just make my brunch tasty,* she'd replied, better sense than he had. And he wondered, too, when was the last time he'd endured such a night, hands under a woman's clothes, hers under his, but no release for either of them? God, but his nuts ached. Blue balls, or should he say, black-and-blue balls? *God, would you get off the race card?*

He turned onto Brush Creek and soon found himself stopped at a light in front of one of C. City, M.O.'s most famous landmarks: the concrete fountain with rearing stallions opposite the main entrance to the Plaza. He wasn't sure if the horses were meant to represent western mustangs or European coursers, probably the latter, given the clientele of the Plaza, which, he'd been assured by locals, was one of the oldest, classiest pedestrian malls in the country. It was thronged weekends and evenings, with every upscale national chain and lots of local boutiques and jewelry stores represented. This late, under its white pelt of snow, the Plaza was empty. It was pretty white the rest of the year too. Although the ghetto began just a few blocks away, east of Troost, he rarely saw black shoppers, and he wondered how that could be. *They know their place.*

The light changed, and he threw the CRV into gear. High school, he thought, the last time he returned home—to the house on Bedford Avenue—with his gonads knotted this way. No, junior year at NYU, his second date with Lianna Murray or maybe McIntyre; he was sure about Lianna. A New Age blonde, a vegan, Lianna had a high school boyfriend back home in Virginia. After she sobered up and retrieved her panties from one side of his bed and her brassiere from the other, she'd explained, weeping, she was so sorry and though she sure wanted to she was glad they hadn't because she could never forgive herself. She knew he would understand because he was so nice. Richie, who was nice and concerned that everyone think so, murmured, "Of course," and Lianna's eyes, which were the same washed-out blue of Sissy Spacek's, filled with tears while she thanked him, thanked him, thanked him.

He parked in the cold garage underneath Western Auto, hobbled to the elevator, and rose to his eighth-floor condo, a woeful creature from the throbbing blue lagoon. Jerk off? Take a hot bath? He couldn't remember which worked. He stomped the snow from his shoes and saw, across the room, his answering machine flashing 1, 1, 1. Still wearing his topcoat he crossed the room, stabbed PLAY, and Tisha's voice came on. "I wanted you to know, I can't wait till tomorrow"—a long pause—"to continue our conversation. Tisha."

She'd said noon; Richie was ready by eleven. Up at seven to clean then off to Thriftway for mushrooms, gruyère, sausage, bacon, chives. Anything she desired in an omelet, Chef Gordon would provide. He iced the bottle of Mumm's he'd been given two years ago but hadn't had an occasion special enough to open. Mimosas, he thought, and wondered if she'd know what that was, or maybe just straight up in the flutes he'd inherited from Hank and Marilyn: Hungarian crystal he never saw them use. He struggled to focus. He didn't know if it was last night's unconsummated fumbling or the year and a half since he'd made love to anything or anyone other than his palm. Or maybe it was because Tisha was black and he found that incredibly exciting. Was that wrong? Did his desire for her confirm he was the racist he already feared he was? Wouldn't not wanting to make love to her *because* she was black be even worse? Of course it was, and he believed what he felt for her was about more than race because when he thought of her as he sat at the desk chair in the second bedroom that was also his study it wasn't her color that rose before him but her voice. "Richard," she would say. And the way a smile seemed to burst like a sunrise from her face, fusing the hard angles into a bright whole, rife with intelligence, and oh he didn't know, kindness and, of this he had no doubt, riotous sex appeal. *Yes*, he thought. *You're an idiot.*

The downstairs bell rang, and he buzzed her up then forced himself to sit down at his desk rather than to wait at the door with his hand on the knob. In fact, he waited until the doorbell blew itself up not just once but twice then walked with measured tread from his desk in the study, clenching and unclenching his fingers while exhaling like the Little Richie Engine That Could. Stay calm, be calm, be fucking calm, she might not feel any of this. Richie snatched the door open, and there Tisha stood under the same purple hat she'd worn last night.

"Richard," she began, just as he'd imagined.

That was all he needed. He swept her in his arms and seized her plumy lips between both of his and gently then not so gently attempted to swallow them.

"Wait, I brought you something."

He released her long enough to close the door. If he didn't have her soon, his eyes were going to roll back in his head, but for now he forced them to focus on the Pyrex baking dish she held out toward him.

"Coffee cake." Her tongue parted and moistened her lips. "I hope you like it."

"I'm sure I will. Let me take your coat." He set the foil-topped dish on an end table and jealously watched her undo the red buttons of her car coat then slid his hands not only beneath her coat but her blouse, also red, and what felt like a lacy bra.

"That's not my coat."

"Those are my hands."

Without asking him to remove them, she slipped out of her coat then the blouse and brassiere. When he opened his fingers, her breasts were small brown birds with bumpy black beaks and throats.

"Your turn."

He tugged off his shirt, chosen that morning with such care. With his tongue teasing her nipples, he felt her undo his belt. His pants slid to the polished floor. The flat of her hand pressed against his boxers. Channeling too many nights of X-rated fantasies and actual memories of last night, her scent on his hands, the kinky black hair, Richie slipped to his knees, wrapped his arms around her waist, and blew where her pant legs came together.

Her fingers twisted in his hair. "You making me crazy."

He blew a second time then stood and wrapped his arms around her waist, his hard-on pressing into her. They were so nearly the same height when he looked for her eyes, which were the same deep brown as his, he looked dead on in and level.

"What you grinning at?"

"You look good enough"—he never knew where he found the courage—"to eat and drink."

"Richard." Her hand found his boxers again. "I wish you would."

He slipped his right hand behind her neck, his left under her knees, and although no one would call LaTisha petite, she swung up in his arms, light as light. Kissing her throat, he carried her to his bedroom, where they fell to the bed and had their way, he with her and she with him, not once but twice, with nothing to eat or drink but what they found there.

Later they would sit up in bed talking and eating the repast Richie prepared while LaTisha (sexy Tisha, he thought, not quite believing it had happened. Yes, there had been shyness and holding back the first time but not the second, first with Richie on top then Tisha, her cheekbones this high above him, her breath huffing like a drumbeat, *huh-HUH, huh-HUH*) explored the apartment wearing the dress shirt she had found in his closet. It looked so much better on her—pale yellow against brown skin, covering almost but not quite everything—he decided he'd never wear it again, and he certainly wasn't going to wash it.

"Can I help?" she'd called.

"Almost finished."

He folded the second omelet, ham and gruyère, this one for Tisha, so it would still be hot, flipped and slid it onto the plate beside a slice of orange and a strand of grapes. He'd planned the plate, and Richie excelled at planning. He wasn't a brand manager by mistake, although what his brand now seemed to be was Lover Boy. Carrying the laden tray, which included toast and two slices of her coffee cake, he found her in the dining room, still wearing his shirt.

"You want to eat here or in bed?"

She smiled, which is how they'd come to be back in bed, feeding each other toast and seedless grapes. When they'd finished the meal but not yet the champagne, she began her tale. Born right here in C. City, M.O., but raised in Mississippi. Her mother, Pearl, had moved back to be near her family when Tisha turned four. Pearl was also her mother's grandmother's name and the grandmother before that, back to slave times, every other generation. Before Richie could ask, not that he would have, "Why every *other* generation, and what happened to your daughter?" Tisha explained: Jada *was* named for Pearl, semiprecious and lovely. But giving birth with no last name to give her baby except her own (which she'd sworn she wouldn't do), unless it was the name on the ID of a man she'd never met (*Who turned out to be you*) she resolved to break with the past. Pearl was so old-timey, an Aunt Jemima name if ever there was one. And it sounded so, so (she'd hesitated then looked straight at him), so *white*, y'know? What kinda name Pearl, for a black baby?

Her mother Pearl was a big woman, five-foot-ten in her bare feet, tall and strong as most men. *Taller than this man*, Richie thought. She styled her hair short and natural, and most days before she left to clean houses, she tied on a red head scarf, so she even looked like Aunt Jemima but young and strong.

Head cocked to one side, Tisha paused but still looked straight at him in a way that meant, he thought, the houses she cleaned belonged to white people, and she wanted him to know it. But she didn't say, and he didn't ask. And sometimes, Tisha said, my momma painted houses with her brothers, Will and Too Tall, who could paint ceilings without no ladder. Tisha smiled, but there was scant joy in this smile, not like the one that burst from inside her, or her sexy one either, and Richie wondered what she was thinking about, Tisha who had an uncle named Too Tall.

Those were the only jobs I remember her having, cleaning

54

white folks' houses (*There*, Richie thought, *she'd said it*), and painting with her brothers.

"Why," he asked, afraid of her answer, "do you only remember two?"

"The winter I turned twelve, she was walking home one night, and a drunk old man ran her down then said he didn't know he'd hit her. How could you hit someone big as Pearl and not know? But because he old and sick and cried in court, and maybe because she just a dead cleaning woman, they didn't give him but three months."

What could he say that would make any difference? He looked away then back at Tisha sitting beside him in his rumpled, sex-smelling bed. There wasn't even the hint of tears in her eyes. "I'm so sorry," he managed, wondering, since she hadn't said, if the old man were white.

"Happened so long ago, I'm over it as I'm gonna be."

"My dad died when I was twelve too." She hugged him. He felt her chest rise and fall. "Was the old man who killed her, was he white?"

"That old nigger black as his heart when he said he didn't know he hit her. Why?"

"I don't want to feel, I don't know, *responsible*."

"Am I 'cause a black man killed her?"

He shook his head.

"Then how would you be if the old man was white?"

"I'm just glad because maybe you'd hate white people."

She looked at him, and he looked at her, feeling, oh he didn't know what.

"How you know I don't?"

"You're here."

"Maybe I just can't resist you."

"I can live with that."

"You know what? You full of shit sometimes, Richard, but awful sweet." She grinned, and he kissed her.

55

FIVE

Ten days later, the last full week before Christmas, Richie arrived home in the gray and grizzly dark to find a message from Pammie. He readied a Chivas. He sometimes thought that if he ever left C&M, it would be to market spirits. He was convinced there was a big move coming at the high end of the market, and while he didn't much care about single malts himself, he could imagine ways to sell them at huge price points: luxury whiskies as reflections of self. And not just scotch, which had established snob appeal, but something as unlikely, say, as tequila. Someday frat boys who drank rotgut shots would have money to spend on high-end tequila. Richie sighed and sipped his Chivas. *Enough.* He'd been working twelve-hour days, not just because he was compulsive but because of the continuing dis-ease in C&M Land. There were rumors of fifteen-year VPs being coached out. Smaller bonuses were the rule—that was no rumor—more fallout from Vanderwohl's resignation. Between arriving early and departing late, many days Richie didn't glimpse the winter sun, what little there was, and he felt stressed out and worried all the time. It wasn't just Richie but the entire C&M universe, as if every assistant brand manager, brand manager, and VP had come down simultaneously with seasonal affective disorder. They were cranky, depressed, pissed-off, stiff-necked, not with pride but from looking over each other's shoulders.

Richie drank half his Chivas, re-brimmed his glass, then drained the undiluted top half-inch. *Shika*, he remembered, hearing Hank joke with Marilyn, I'm turning into a *shika*, on the evenings he returned from the dealership and knocked back several Seven & Sevens. Hank was a sales manager, first at a Pontiac and then, before he died, at a Buick dealership, and Richie had loved visiting him at work. All the salesmen and service guys—grease monkeys, Dad called them—treated him like the crown prince. *Hey, Hank,* or *Hey, Mister Gordon, he's sure getting big.* And the secretaries: *Mister Gordon, he's got your smile.* Returning from his kitchen, where he stored the bottle, the delightful burn numbing the back of his throat, the boggy peat taste stinging his lips, he remembered being eleven or twelve, when he still confused *shika,* which Jews weren't supposed to be, with *shiksas,* girls Jewish boys weren't supposed to marry but who, because we aren't *shikas* and don't beat our wives, the *shiksas* are always after. Then Hank would wink and fake punch his arm. *I'll tell you about that later.*

And the *schvartzes?* Another word from back then. Lazy, no-account *schvartzes.* Good thing Tisha couldn't hear what played inside his head. He sometimes wondered what she heard in hers about him. He dialed his sister. When her outgoing message ended and she could hear his voice—Pammie was a call screener from way back—she picked up.

"Hey, little bro, how you been?"

"Working too hard."

"Same old, same old." He could hear what sounded like Pammie lighting a cigarette, the inhale and release. "How'd it work out with that girl?"

"Pretty well."

"How well is that?"

"Pretty damn well." He wondered how much to tell her then added, boasting, but as low-key as he could manage. "I'm meeting her daughter on Saturday."

"I take it you're sleeping with her?"

Was that any of Pammie's business? But Tisha was such a miraculous change in his life, and there were so few people he could tell—he'd told Dave and Laura, who seemed miffed it wasn't one of their assistant professors but were pressing to meet her anyway—that he almost answered, "As a matter of fact, and the sex kicks ass." But before he could, Pammie asked, "Or is meeting the brat the final test before unzipping her pants?"

"You've always been remarkably crude."

"*Remarkably crude.* Who shoved the broomstick up your ass? Try sounding like you're from Brooklyn sometimes."

"Fuck yourself with that broomstick, okay, Sis?"

"That's my baby bro. So you fucking the girl or not? What's her name again?"

"Tisha. And I am."

"*All right.*" Pammie's voice softened. "I'm happy for you. Does she have a brother?"

If you only knew. "I don't think so."

"Why don't you bring her when you visit me?"

"I'll let you know." Richie wondered what that would be like, taking Tisha to meet Pammie. And Jada, what would they do with her? "So what's up?"

"I found your birth certificate."

"Great. FedEx it."

"I want to give it to you in person."

"What's the big deal?"

"Trust me."

He wondered if a third scotch was in order, decided it was, and started toward the kitchen. "You're being pretty damn mysterious."

"Big sister's prerogative. How old you say Tisha was?"

"Twenty-five. Her daughter's almost five."

"What kind of name is Tisha?"

"Beautiful."

"Then bring her. When are you coming?"

"It's supposed to be January, but if we could get down the week after Christmas?"

"What's the rush?"

"I'd like to get out of town."

"That's the only reason?"

They both knew he wasn't telling the whole truth and nothing but, but she'd started, with all the mystery about his birth certificate. "Yep."

"Just let me know."

Richie hung up and poured himself that third scotch. He inserted a bachelor's special in the microwave—frozen beef and bean burrito—and when it dinged, striped the burrito red and white with salsa and sour cream. In an hour or so he could call Tisha. She'd asked him to wait until she put Jada to bed, and this being finals week, she wouldn't have much time to talk. It was disconcerting, he thought, savoring the first bite, to be dating someone who was both a parent and a student, which placed her both ahead and behind him on any flowchart of life. But his heart raced every time he thought about her, and a feeling of *bienestar* came over him as if his heart and head were in the middle of an endorphin rush.

Tisha, he thought. *I've just met a girl named LaTisha.*

He could imagine singing that, or really he could imagine Hank singing it. In addition to movie star looks, Hank had been blessed with a fine tenor. He knew dozens of 1940s love songs, which he belted out in the shower. Hank's singing was one more reason Richie believed his parents were a love match, that and how they looked together. And danced, he thought, abandoning his burrito and carrying his scotch to the hall to gaze at the picture of his parents on that long-ago cruise. Hank and Marilyn Gordon looked so right together it made his chest ache. He would never look like that with any woman. And a black one? He remembered watching his parents at some Gordon wedding or bar mitzvah, when they still attended such events. He must have been four or five. He could see himself on Pammie's lap, then he was dancing, legs wrapped around her waist, while in the center of the floor Hank and Marilyn swept past, every eye on them.

Now it's my turn, Richie hoped, to feel what they felt, to be that couple, though if everyone's eyes were on them, it wouldn't be because of how perfect they looked together but what a sensation it would be. (He still couldn't quite imagine bringing Tisha to a C&M office party, not in Calhoun City. Maybe in New York but not here.) Or was he getting ahead of himself? Okay, he *was* getting ahead of himself. He hadn't even met Jada. They hadn't met each other's friends. But he'd never felt like this before and hoped Tisha hadn't either. He felt happy just thinking about calling her. Happy he had the right to be thinking about calling her, and he believed she felt it too. Saturday night, lying in his arms in his bed—he drove her home at two because she wanted to be there for Jada when she woke up, she was such a good mother, another thing that thrilled him—she turned, eyes reflecting the moonlight pouring in through the window above his bed.

"If you want to meet my Jada."

"You know I do."

"It's time."

They were so nearly the same height everything lined up. Lips. Knees. Toes. His chest, her black nipples. His stiffening cock against the V of her thighs. He shifted, and the tip pushed inside her, her lips swallowing him as her mouth did his mouth.

"Richard." Her lips drew back, no, not those lips. "You're so hongry."

"Hungry for you."

He pressed the mattress on both sides of her head. She shifted, moved something, and everything moved. "So." Her breath coming hot. "You'll meet my Jada?"

Richie returned to the kitchen and his tepid burrito.

They decided to take Jada to the C. City, M.O., Zoo. Richie had never been. Zoo-ing meant a family or, at the very least, the sort of lighthearted lover he'd not had since he moved here—

definitely not professors focused on the Oversoul or postcolonial outrages—but he knew about the annual Festival of Lights because every year the *Star* ran a cover story in *Weekend* showing illuminated pathways between cages, metal lampposts, and leafless trees strung with lights. One year there was a grinning orangutan in a Santa's hat. That's what Richie felt like parking in front of Tisha's: a jolly monkey. He climbed past apartment A, which was pumping out its heady mix of hip-hop and soul food. Barbecue, he thought, C. City's specialty, spicy-sweet. When he entered the apartment, Jada stood behind Tisha in the living room, dressed in pink corduroys and a white turtleneck. Her hair was tugged back in pigtails tipped with pink and white plastic balls. Her skin, much lighter than Tisha's, retained the lemony cast of the newborn photo Richie still carried in his wallet. The child's nose was narrow, but her eyes were the same deep brown as Tisha's. For a little girl her jaw seemed square and set, as if the mannish lines of her mother's face lay inside hers, waiting for time to reveal them.

"Jada," Tisha said. "This my friend Richard. What do you say?"

How you doing, Honky?

Jada executed a quick half-curtsy. "Pleased to meet you."

"I'm very pleased to meet you too." Richie wished he'd brought a present, although Tisha had forbidden it. "Your mother's told me all about—"

"Can we go to the zoo now?" Then, as if intuiting what she'd prevented him from saying, she demanded, "What she say about me?" She turned toward her mother. "Momma, you always say, 'Don't talk behind people's backs.'"

"I wasn't."

"Your mom was just bragging what a smart little girl—"

"And how you talk all the time."

"Oh." Jada looked from Tisha to Richie. "Can we go now?"

"Tisha?"

62

But Jada was already running toward the couch for her coat. And if she'd noticed Richie was white or even purple, she gave no sign.

She loved the hippos and polar bears but dissed the lazy lions. She wouldn't leave the white tiger habitat until Richie hoisted her onto his shoulders to glimpse the famous and famously reclusive cat sleeping under a bush at the far end of its enclosure halfway down a hillside. She consumed blue cotton candy and dipping dots ice cream then asked to ride the train. Before Tisha could say no, Richie rushed off for tickets.

"You gonna spoil her," Tisha announced when they were seated on the little red train with its wooden bench seats, Jada on the outside, Tisha between them.

"If you let me."

Tisha grinned, and he had to resist kissing her. She wore her favorite floppy purple hat, brim molded around her face, and the red wool car coat with square buttons. The fingers of her left hand, sheathed in leather, brushed his thigh, circled his knee, then settled on her own lap as the train chuffed out of Penguin Station. With every whistled toot Jada's smile brightened. Wintry air buffed her cheeks as the Zoo Express executed its oval. "Whoo, whoo," the whistle screamed. Richie could see families seated in the rows in front of them as the train negotiated a curve. Maybe everyone would think they were a family too. Jada looked like she could be his, she was so much lighter than Tisha.

"Look, Momma." Jada pointed as the Zoo Express crossed onto a section of raised track spanning a lake alive with waterfowl. "Big birds!"

There were black birds and white ones, long necked and thick feathered, gliding in circles.

"They's swans," Tisha said.

"They big," said Jada.

They're black and white, thought Richie.

In the gift shop Jada picked out a snow leopard. It was eighteen inches long and exquisitely constructed: bright blue eyes and black spots on white fur so soft it felt real but couldn't be. The plush animal was just the right size for an almost five-year-old to hug. Richie decided to spring for the thirty-five dollars. A tag around the snow leopard's neck announced ten percent would be donated to the World Wildlife Fund to protect endangered species.

"That means," Richie said, kneeling beside Jada, "there aren't many in the world so we have to take good care of them."

"It's too much," Tisha said.

"Please, Momma!" Jada clutched the leopard to her cheek and squinched her eyes.

"The first time I picked her up was to look at the white tiger."

"Richard, it's a leopard, not a tiger."

"It's the closest they have."

Tisha looked from Richie to Jada, who was hugging the white leopard, then back to Richie "It's your money."

"I get to keep it?" Jada asked, sounding as if she didn't quite believe it.

Richie nodded, grinning as if he'd gotten the present.

"What do you say to Richard?"

"Thank you so, sooooo much."

He knelt and Jada wrapped her arms around him, pressing her cheek against his, the snow leopard tangled in their embrace. *Best thirty-five I ever spent,* Richie thought when they were leaving the zoo, headed toward his CRV with Tisha, Jada, and the snow leopard she'd named Stripes.

SIX

They flew to West Palm December twenty-sixth, the first ever plane ride for Tisha and Jada. He'd reserved three seats on the left side of the aisle, and although Tisha ceded the window, it clearly cost her. When they were taking off, Tisha craned to look out, her face pressed nearly as close to the glass as her daughter's.

"Jada," she said when the jet's wing dipped and the plane banked east then south. "Look how little the city is."

"Momma, I see our house."

Tisha turned and smiled at Richie over her shoulder. "No way. It'd be too teeny tiny."

Jada pressed her snow leopard to the window. "Stripes sees it too."

He slipped his hand onto Tisha's black-skirted leg, where flesh met cloth just above the knee. Without glancing back at him, Tisha joined their hands. Richie checked to see if Jada noticed, but she was busy at the window. He remained cautious in front of Jada, while Tisha, now that she'd let him in, didn't seem to care. His whole life Richie had shied from public displays of affection, and this past week with Tisha and Jada—they'd been out to dinner twice—he'd been torn between wanting to walk with his arms around both of them, *Look, look!* and not wanting to attract attention in C. City, M.O., one of the most segregated cities in the country. Was he being paranoid? In this new century, Y2K, so full of hope?

"Stripes sees my school."

"Jada Reece Gordon," Tisha murmured. "You something else."

When they reached cruising altitude, passing through clouds that obscured the world as they knew it—even from a sharp-eyed snow leopard—Jada hunted down the *Big Cats* coloring book he'd bought her from inside her pink backpack. Tisha attached herself to the Diskman that had been her present, closed her eyes, laid her head on his shoulder, and began to hum. Maybe the presents were too much too soon. He'd also bought LaTisha, who loved all things yellow, citrine and sterling earrings. While the presents pleased the girls, large and small, it absolutely thrilled Richie to have someone to buy presents for. The voice in his head whispered, *That's what she likes about you, what you can buy her, not your skinny white dick.* He decided not to believe the voice, which he'd been hearing his entire life. Tisha and Jada seemed genuinely to love their gifts, Richie loved the shirt she'd given him, and he was pretty sure he loved Tisha, though he hadn't spoken the word yet. And it wasn't just the idea of being in love, which in itself was pretty heady, or being in love with a black woman—he no longer cared what they said about black women, and who were *they* anyway?—but this black woman, LaTisha Nelson. Small-breasted, big-bottomed, mean-streaked, killer-smiled Tish. And he loved her daughter too, loved how people assumed he was the dad.

Richie Gordon, he thought, *you're just going to have to accept being happy.*

When their plane touched down, Jada and Tisha couldn't get over how warm it was. What bright colors! "And all the old people," Tisha whispered, "with such nice tans." Every other visit he'd had Pammie pick him up: the adult son flying home, though he wasn't her son, and Florida had never been his home. This time Richie rented a car. He planned to sightsee with Jada and Tisha, maybe even drive to the Keys for two nights. The words *Disney World* had been uttered, though they'd quickly been withdrawn—not during Christmas week. And there was this. Though Pammie had seemed happy in her generally miserable way that he was bringing Tisha and Jada and though he knew he should have told her in advance, he'd decided the color of LaTisha and Jada's skin wasn't any of Pammie's damn business.

What if she said, Don't come, and he'd already invited Tisha and Jada? Another voice said, *Don't be an ass. You should have told her so she'd have time to get used to the idea.* But why should she need to get used to it? A third voice whispered, *Putz, you should have told her. But since you didn't, you should have arranged for the first meeting to be in a public place.*

Too late now, Richie thought, standing opposite an Avis agent named Flora. *It's not like I can sneak into the men's room, call on my cell phone, and say, "Oh by the way."*

"Yes, full coverage." He always took full coverage on company rentals, and though he was paying this time, he liked to feel safe.

When Flora, whose thick blonde bangs fell within a quarter-inch of her eyebrows—she looked like one of those impossibly cute lapdogs—offered to upgrade him to a convertible for six dollars a day, he nodded.

"That ho thought you was hot," Tisha announced, when they were driving out of the airport in a red Mustang. She leaned across the bucket seat and kissed him below the ear. "She right."

In the back Jada chanted, "Palm tree, palm tree, palm tree!"

Richie glanced in the rearview. Jada was on her knees in her booster seat, bouncing and chattering to Stripes. Her pigtails and the snow leopard's ears—hers black, Stripes's nearly white—blew back in the breeze generated by the open car. Richie nudged Tisha's leg, indicating Jada with a backward nod of his head.

"Jada," LaTisha hissed, "get your black butt on that seat, and I mean now."

"But, Momma—"

"Don't Momma me."

He found Jada's eyes in the rearview. "It's not safe. Sit down."

Jada's mouth pursed like an old woman's. But after a moment she said, "All right!" and settled on her fanny. Richie grinned; he even found Jada's outrage charming. And in this way, with the top down, his girlfriend beside him, the little girl in back with Stripes the white leopard, they drove thirty minutes south from West Palm to Delray Beach in sunlight, exiting I-95 at Atlantic, driving west to Jog Road, then turning south again. At the third light—Tisha was in charge of the directions Pammie had e-mailed him—he turned left onto Dorado Drive, the entrance to Pammie's gated community. Richie braked in front of the pink pastel gatehouse and waited for the security guard to get off the phone. In the right-hand Members Only lane—they were stopped in the Guest lane, closer to the guardhouse—a white Lincoln slowed to a rolling stop in front of a yellow traffic gate. The gate's tongue rose, and the Town Car entered. The Guest gate remained down while the blue-uniformed guard, who seemed in no hurry at all, chatted on. Finally, the white-haired guard, who was six-two or three with jowls that hung from his ears like shower curtains, shuffled toward them.

"Richie Gordon to see Pamela Gordon."

The guard's rheumy eyes moved from Richie to LaTisha, where they lingered a beat too long. Then he dragged himself back to the guardhouse and flipped through hanging files for the guest pass Pammie had told him she'd left. Every gated community she'd lived in followed the same procedure, but this guy was molasses. A car pulled up behind them.

"Don't have one," called the guard.

Richie could feel Tisha's eyes on him. "Would you call my sister, Pamela Gordon? She's expecting us."

In super slo-mo the guard paged through a phone directory then picked up a black receiver. A third car pulled up behind them.

"Sorry about this," Richie said.

Finally, the guard slumped back toward them, bearing a Guest Parking pass. "Keep this on your dash at all times. And welcome to Dorado Palms."

The yellow-tongued gate rose. A left at the first stop sign took them past an unnaturally blue pond, then palm and golf cart–fringed fairways; on every green red flags snapped in the breeze. Two rights, and they entered the residential quadrant, passing large houses with negligible yards built around an outdoor pool and tennis complex that had Jada back up on her knees chanting, "Pool, pool, pool!" Richie pulled into the driveway of 689 Seahorse Lane—no one parked on the street in these places—and switched off the engine.

"It's beautiful," Tisha said, and he supposed it was. One tall story, a steeply pitched roof, large windows punched in its beige exterior. Pammie's mirrored identical houses across the street and across its own driveway; its only distinguishing feature was a red-flowering hedge outside the front door. Pammie appeared at the mouth of the hedge wearing white Capri slacks and a blue blouse tied off above her navel. Blonde hair was gathered off her neck, and though she'd emerged from the house—he'd barely turned off the car when she appeared—Jackie O sunglasses hid her eyes as she flew across the driveway to greet him. So there was no gauging what she thought when she glanced past him to Tisha and Jada, who bounced out of the car pleading, "Please, Richie, can I go to the pool? Please, please, please?"

"Oh," Pammie said, after she'd kissed and hugged him, he thought, without much warmth then extended her small, be-jeweled hand to shake Tisha's much larger one. "You must be Tisha. And you"—she half-knelt and extended her hand again—"are Jada. Who's your friend?"

Jada hugged Stripes to her pink and white collared T-shirt, twisted one finger around his ear and stared big-eyed at Pammie.

"Cat got your tongue, Sweetie, or do you have his?"

She looked good, his older sister, like maybe she'd been dieting. Which explained the tight slacks and midriff shirt showing off her shape, the large breasts and flat belly.

"Tell her, Jada," Tisha said.

"That's all right." Pammie came up out of her crouch. "She can tell me later."

But Richie feared it wasn't all right. He hefted Jada, who was still hugging Stripes and acting as he'd never seen her act before—her face buried shyly on his chest—until she was level with his sister's sunglasses.

"Jada," he said softly, "I'd like you to meet my big sister, Pam."

Pammie, who was only five-two or so in heels, pushed her sunglasses down her nose. "I'm pretty little for a big sister, aren't I?"

Maybe it was Pammie's eyes, which were their father's pale blue and hence irresistible, at least to Richie. Or maybe Jada had simply gotten over her shyness. She lifted her head off Richie's shoulder. "Pleased to meet you." She released Stripes from her stranglehold and dangled him by one hind leg. "This here Stripes."

"What a nice name!" Pammie smiled, first at Jada and then at Tisha, who'd come around the car. "Did you think of it yourself?"

Jada nodded and wiggled to be put down. "You know what?"

"No, what?" Pammie fell into step beside Jada.

"He has really good eyes."

"Would he like to see my house?"

"He'd like to see the pool."

"If you let me hold your hand, Stripes has got it made." Jada held out her hand, and Pammie led her toward the red-flowering hedge. "Richie," she called without glancing back, "get the luggage."

A moment later, wheeling the two largest bags up the driveway, with LaTisha beside him pulling the smallest, he asked, "You all right?"

"She kinda scary."

"I'll protect you."

Tisha laughed. "Who's gonna protect you?"

Later Richie reclined beside Pammie on a chaise lounge. They weren't at the Olympic-sized pool, which had first thrilled Jada, but a satellite pool closer to Pammie's house. A green canvas awning shaded one end of the patio. Under it four women played bridge, while two kibitzed. Just past the women's game two tables had been pushed together for poker. Average age of the gamblers, Richie thought, fifty-five or sixty. From what he could hear—he and his sister sunbathed in front of the shaded area at the deep end of the pool—the cardplayers were New Yorkers. Five years in Missouri, with its flatter *A*'s and slower speech, had only sharpened his ear. These were his people or had been, he thought, speaking his first dialect.

At the shallow end, wearing red floaties on her arms, Jada shouted something he couldn't quite make out. Two other children, considerably older—dark-haired, Jewishy-looking brothers nine and ten or so—played catch with their father. The rest of the crowd around the pool were either residents—Pam had explained this wasn't a senior community, which signified fifty-five and up, but an adult community, minimum age forty-five—or their Christmas week guests. What there wasn't, Richie thought, except for the balding dad, whose athletic-looking boys clamored, "Dad, Dad, throw it to me!" was anyone around Pammie's age, midforties, or a single male of any age. And of course, in this village of transplanted New York Jews, there were no other black faces.

In her yellow bikini against the powder blue pool liner, Tisha looked astonishingly dark, her skin the blackest thing for miles around. What an aberration, a true trompe l'oeil: sunshine, clear water, all the white faces. In C. City, M.O., Tisha wasn't especially dark, while Jada, with her yellowy skin, narrow nose, and light eyes looked mixed race, so much so that strangers seeing them together regularly assumed he was Jada's father. But in this light, on this pool patio, with the large Jacuzzi bubbling behind him, Tisha looked very black indeed. He strained to hear the cardplayers. Were they wondering if someone had invited her cleaning girl and daughter for a holiday swim?

"You could have told me," Pammie said.

"What?"

"Don't start." She pushed her dark glasses down her nose.

"Told you *what?*"

"Tisha's black."

Richie turned toward the pool. Jada had worked herself into the game of catch. "She is?"

Pammie grinned. She wore a form-hugging one-piece, black except for stripes of color—yellow, orange, and red—descending diagonally from her left shoulder to her right hip. "Date whoever you like. Black, blue, or white. But not to tell me makes me feel dirty." She seized his wrist, turning him toward her. "As if you couldn't tell me. It's not like I didn't suspect. I mean, her name's *LaTisha.*"

After a moment, although it wasn't the complete truth, which would have required examining his own complicated feelings, he admitted, "I guess I wasn't sure what you'd think."

"That's what I'm saying. You think I'm a racist."

"Why would I think that?"

"*Because* you didn't tell me. And because of Daddy."

"What?"

"For Chrissakes, you don't remember? With Daddy it was *schvartze* this and *nigger* that."

He saw Hank at the dealership talking to a deferential black janitor. Is that why he remembered everyone respecting Hank so much?

Jada rushed up, Tisha trailing her, calling, "Stop running."

"Richie, come in, I want to show you."

"He'll come in later," Tisha said.

"I wanna show Richie my tumblesault!"

Happy to escape Pammie, Richie allowed himself to be led to the shallow end then glanced back at LaTisha, a wet, big-boned vision in a yellow bikini. He grasped Jada's hand and stepped into the pool, heated to a very senior eighty-six degrees. Jada demonstrated somersault after underwater somersault, holding her nose with the fingers of one hand while windmilling herself around with the other until, happy and spluttering, she rose for air.

SEVEN

Pammie took them to Porfino's for dinner. Exhausted by an afternoon in the pool, the early flight and exciting day, Jada was balky as a donkey. She insisted on TWO MEATBALLS! although the waiter assured them the meatballs were jumbos and one would be enough. Jada sobbed, "Two, I want twooooooo," tears and snot streaking her cheeks until Pammie snapped, "For Chrissakes, get her two."

Richie turned to Tisha, who'd been holding firm to ONE MEATBALL! What a nightmare. "Twooooooooo meatballs."

"Jada Reece Gordon," Tisha hissed.

Pammie's eyes locked on his. "*Gordon?*"

"Stop that crying," Tisha whisper-shouted, "or I'm gonna warm your bottom."

"I know." Richie signaled the waiter. "Only one meatball because your mom and the waiter say one's enough, but how about chocolate milk to help you feel better?"

He glanced from Tisha to Jada to Pammie. No hostile boardroom had ever looked so tense. Then Jada, with fat tears still plopping down her cheeks, said, "Okay, Richie."

Tisha nodded. Pammie shrugged, as if to say, *Fuck the meatballs. Why is her name Gordon?*

The waiter approached. "Yes sir?"

Richie wondered what would happen if the restaurant didn't serve chocolate milk. But the sweet dark elixir arrived. Jada drained her glass and fell asleep on Tisha's lap, without touching her one and only meatball.

They returned to Pammie's apartment, where the first mystery to be resolved was whether Jada would sleep alone in the front bedroom. Richie hadn't worried about this—he was no parent, not yet anyway—but Jada had shared Tisha's bedroom her entire life. In C. City that was an inconvenience to be skirted, which they did by making love at his apartment then returning to Tisha's. They'd doze in her living room, then he'd drive home before first light, so Tisha could wake up in the room beside Jada. But at Auntie Pammie's, as his sister wanted to be known, Jada would have her own big-girl bed in her very own room. While Tisha waited, back against a ruffled bolster beside her daughter to see if this new world order would prosper, Richie and Pammie repaired to the living room. She fetched snifters and a Baccarat decanter of Courvoisier XO from a mirrored bar front, set everything on the black granite countertop. She poured three inches in each and clinked Richie's snifter with her own.

"*L'chaim.*" She knocked back an unladylike gulp then sat on the couch.

Richie wasn't sure he'd ever sampled an XO, although several BMs who traveled to Asia were always saying the Koreans and Japanese loved it. The liquid in his snifter, pale amber, not only lit up his tongue but a web of neural pathways triggered by scent and taste. Austere yet complex, all harshness distilled out—*you even think in marketing-speak, you schmuck*—except for a gentle burn at the back of his throat.

"That's good."

Pammie smiled. Through her thirties she'd kicked around in graphic design. Now that she'd thrived in old folks real estate, she liked to spend money, she'd once told him, conspicuously and well.

"I buy a bottle, sometimes two, after every sale."

Pam's snifter rose, obscuring the center of her face. For a moment, positioned below her pale blue ones, the snifter's base resembled a third eye. Then Pammie lowered her glass. Half her cognac—a good inch and a half—was gone.

"Don't you *sip* fine brandy?"

"Maybe you do."

Richie sipped and reexperienced the austere head rush.

"Besides." And maybe it was the alcohol smiling at him as Pammie used to when he was Jada's age and she was watching him after school, but she looked like that girl again. "This will go better if we're fucked-up." She threw back a glass-clearing swallow then tongued golden drops veining down the rim. "Trust me, I know what I'm talking about."

She started across the marble-tiled living room on her stack heels. Without breaking stride or even noticeably slowing, she stepped out of them, and the effect was like watching her descend a staircase. He sometimes forgot how small she was, how top-heavy her figure. Boom-Boom, the boys called her in high school, and she hated it.

She disappeared in her bedroom; Richie tried but found the XO too intense. When she returned with a faded white envelope, his snifter was still nearly full.

"Thought I told you to drink up." She paused at the dark granite counter, which divided her living room from the kitchen, refilled her snifter, then sat beside him. "Do it. Bottoms up."

His eyes watered. His throat burned, then it didn't. Heat rose from his gut until a sweet numbness filled his brain.

"Okay?"

She nodded. "I'm sorry for not telling you."

She passed him the envelope, which contained a birth certificate, black on white. The document felt brittle, and the border—beyond the actual document—had yellowed with age. "Richard Allan Gordon. Date of birth: May 8, 1970."

"What?"

Pam slammed another cognac. "Read everything."

Time of birth: 3:40 a.m.
Weight: 7 pounds, 3 ounces
Length: 21 inches

Place of birth: Brooklyn, New York
Mother: Lorraine Rachel Gordon
Father: Unknown

"What the fuck?"

"You asked for your *original* birth certificate." She set her snifter down and folded her arms. "The one you've seen was issued after Mom and Daddy adopted you."

Lorraine Rachel Gordon. "Who?" Then he had it, and a faint, the faintest of images, whether from memory or a picture he'd seen in his mother's purse, rose in his mind. *Oh, that's Lorraine—we don't know where she is.*

"My sister—" He tried to make sense through the curtain of cognac. "—is my mother?"

Pammie nodded.

"And Mom and Daddy?" He saw them, so beautiful, reddish hair, white faces, forever dancing. "My grandparents?"

Pammie nodded again.

"I'm going to be sick."

And he might have been, on Pammie's couch and white tiles, and on Pammie too, but just then Tisha's footsteps announced her return.

"Richard, Jada was . . . *Whoa,* everything all right?"

He shook his head.

It was a comfort, a very considerable comfort, to sit on Jada's white-sheeted double bed and contemplate singing "Summertime," as Hank had sung it to him.

"Roll on your side," he whispered, and she did, tucking Stripes against her chin and curling away from him.

"Summertime," he began, hearing Hank's tenor, which was so much sweeter than his own. "And the living is easy."

No wonder he didn't have Hank's voice.

"Fish are jumping, and the cotton is high."

So much made sense now, for instance, the dark hair he still had. No law of follicular inheritance had been broken. Marilyn's bald father wasn't his maternal grandfather; Hank was. He rubbed Jada's back through her pink jammies, remembering someone's hand rubbing circles on his own.

"Oh, your Daddy's rich . . ."

He gazed at Jada's profile, lemony skin set off by the white pillowcase, her hair, released from its pigtails, springing to life.

". . . and your Momma's good-looking."

Under his hand Jada's breathing quieted.

"So hush, little baby. Do-on't—."

He lingered beside the sleeping child then repeated the first verse, the only one he knew. When he was certain she was out, he slipped away. Blinking against the uncomfortable light, he entered the living room. Tisha hurried toward him.

"Oh, Richard." She embraced him, her lips near his ear. "I'm so sorry."

His eyes sought Pammie. His sister—no, his effing aunt—looked as if she needed someone to hug her too. She saluted him with her snifter then poured it down.

"I guess you hate me."

"I'll leave you two alone," Tisha said.

"I wish you'd stay." He grasped her warm solid hand and led her toward the couch. "Pammie, you have scotch? I'm more of a whiskey drinker."

"So was Daddy."

What was Dave's expression? Better than a poke in the eye with a sharp stick? That's what *Daddy* felt like. Richie filled a rocks glass from the Glenfiddich bottle in Pammie's bar.

"What else was Daddy?"

"I already told you."

"Tell me again."

Pammie twisted toward Tisha to indicate she didn't want to discuss this in front of her, but Richie didn't care.

"A racist," Pammie said. "Like lots people were back then."

"Like lots of people still are," he replied, while the voice in his head screamed, *Like you, like you!*

"But not me," Pammie said.

Richie tossed down an inch of scotch, but instead of calming him, it seemed to amp him up. "I want to know why no one told me."

"My older sister." Pammie turned toward Tisha. "It was nineteen-sixty-nine. Free love. Acid. Mescaline, speed, you name it, Lorr took it. And Mom and Daddy, especially Daddy, always wanted a son. You remember what a jock he was, Richie, navy boxer, a halfback in college when they sent him home for officer candidate school."

Richie had heard the stories. "What about it?"

"When Lorraine got pregnant and wouldn't say who the father was, and maybe she was telling the truth and didn't know. But by the time she admitted she was pregnant, there was no one waving his hand, saying 'Me!'" Pammie's eyes were becoming unfocused. "And you popped out all curly-haired, big brown eyes, they were like, '*We'll* be the parents.'"

Tisha asked, "What did Lorraine think?"

Pammie set the snifter on the coffee table, closed her eyes, and kneaded her temples. She drew a long slow breath and, when it was fully expelled, rubbed her temples again. "At first I think she was grateful. She liked hanging out in the Village. Even in high school, Mom and Daddy couldn't make her do much she didn't want to. Then, when Richie was almost two, she began to see how messed up it was."

Pammie unstoppered the Courvoisier and attempted to refill her snifter. Cognac sloshed over the rim. Pammie adjusted her aim, filled her glass, then clunked the bottle back on the coffee table.

"Maybe you've had enough."

"Don't start, Richie. Don't fucking start."

XO dripped from the glass table onto the white tiles. Tisha disengaged her hand—he'd forgotten he was holding it—and started toward the kitchen. He watched her bottom under the tight black skirt then turned to Pammie, who grinned in a way he didn't like.

"Nice booty," she said.

Tisha returned with paper towels and a sponge. She wiped the glass top and started on the floor.

"You don't have to do that, the girl's coming tomorrow."

Richie thought Tisha would pitch the sponge at her. Then her expression changed. This, he realized, was her face for White People.

"Richard, I'm really tired. I'm going to check on Jada and go to bed." Her eyes met his then skittered away, as did her lips when he tried to kiss her. "Talk to your sister long as you want."

Richie watched her out of the room then turned toward Pammie, who was chugging XO with such gusto she seemed determined to say everything she wanted without being able to remember what she'd said.

"Don't hate me, it wasn't my secret."

Richie fetched the Glenfiddich from the bar and filled his glass. "Now," he said, diving into it and feeling its force break over him. "Tell me everything."

In the morning Richie's head throbbed too much to move it, which didn't prevent Jada from bouncing into their room at 7:30 and demanding to be taken to the pool.

"It's too early."

"Tell him, Momma."

"Sh-h-h, let Richie sleep."

Next he knew the clock read 9:30 then 10:45, and he was alone. Sunlight licked his cheek. His own tongue felt enormous, his mouth as if someone had died. From the pain in his forehead he suspected that once he sat up, he was going to wish that someone had been Richard Allan Gordon, or whatever his name would have been if his mother wasn't his sister and his parents weren't his grandparents. Near as he could calculate, he was his own fucking nephew.

Richie slung his feet to the floor. Pammie had constructed a Roman bathhouse in South Florida, tile floors, statues everywhere. He walked past their open suitcases and entered the marble bathroom: gilded hot and cold water pulls, golden toilet handle, black onyx sink. He commenced a long, long, long pee in the black toilet. No wonder his head ached. The scotch and cognac—Pammie must have downed nearly a full bottle, he had this half-in-shadow recollection of a second Baccarat XO materializing—had dissolved his brain, which was exiting through his member.

He showered then dressed in shorts and a T-shirt, sucked down four glasses of water, trimmed his mustache, and brushed his hair. When he emerged from the bathroom, he didn't feel nearly as bad as he thought he would. Pammie sat at the kitchen counter, sipping coffee and reading the paper. She swiveled on her stool, one blonde eyebrow rising in the heart-shaped pool of her face.

"Morning, Richie."

He recalled hurling something—a glass, a candy dish?—in a paroxysm of self-pity. The room was immaculate again.

"Where's Tisha?"

"Took Jada to the pool." Pammie's eyes met his. He'd stopped maybe ten feet from her. "Cute kid."

Richie walked past his sister, no, his aunt, to the kitchen, found a sugar bowl and mug set out beside the coffeemaker. "Cream?" he asked.

"Just two percent." She turned the page of her newspaper. "You read *Boondocks*?"

Richie opened the fridge, found the plastic half-gallon. Normally he wouldn't bother; two percent was a terrible thing to do to good coffee. But after all the scotch he wasn't sure he could take it black. "What's *Boondocks*?"

"A black comic strip. Pretty radical and really funny." Pammie looked up at him. "About a grandfather raising two grandsons."

Richie added two percent. It barely lightened the coffee. He raised the cup, wondering if he were imagining it, or were his hands really shaking? "Do the kids call him Grandpa or Dad?"

"Gramps."

"If it's radical, they wouldn't run it in Calhoun City. They like their comics and their black folks pretty tame." He dared Pammie to say something. When she didn't, he added, "They only run *Doonesbury* on weekends, and not the political ones either."

"So," Pammie asked, "how'd you two meet?"

Richie wondered if he'd missed the segue. Black? Raising kids? Or was Pammie simply changing the subject. "Through a friend." Then, changing it himself, he asked, "So what am I supposed to call you, Auntie Pammie?"

"What does it matter?"

"Lots of grandparents help raise grandkids."

"If I'm not mistaken," Pammie said, "it's pretty common in the black community."

"What's that got to do with anything?"

She grinned. "You'll fit right in."

"But mostly they don't lie and say they're Mommy and Daddy."

"Are you saying black people are more honest? What kind of reverse racism is that?"

"I'm saying Mom and Daddy were big fucking liars. And so were you."

"All right, call me Auntie Pammie. But you shouldn't say that about Mom and Daddy, they loved you."

"Then why didn't they tell me the truth?" By now his hands were rattling so badly coffee was splashing out of his cup. "For Chrisssakes!"

"I already told you. With Daddy it was *schwartze* this and *nigger* that."

"Are you saying my father was black?"

"Do you look black? Do you have a big dick?"

"You changed my diaper. You should know."

Pammie grinned. "Lorr would never say who your father was."

Richie set his cup down and glanced from Pammie toward the entrance to the living room area from the front hall. *Tisha*, in a white beach wrap over her yellow bikini, large sunglasses in her hair. From her expression—eyes narrowed, lips pursed— he was guessing she'd been there for some time.

"Hope I'm not interrupting. Jada's hongry."

Unless he was mistaken, and he didn't trust his perceptions right now, her pronunciation was different than usual. More like *hoooongry* than *hungry*. "Where's Jada?"

"In the bathroom. She's all wet."

Pammie asked, "Do you need more towels?"

"No, ma'am," Tisha said. And if Richie hadn't been clear about what she was feeling, he soon knew. "We's fine."

Jada ran in, pigtails swishing. "Richie, Ri—*chie!*"

"Don't run," Tisha said.

"I dove in head first. Like you showed me."

"That's good." He scooped her up and hugged her wet body. "That's really, really good."

EIGHT

It took two days, but Pammie convinced them to go off for a night alone. She'd determined Jada's favorite foods were pepperoni pizza, Goldfish Crackers, and fruit roll-ups and promised her they'd eat nothing else. Momma and Richie would have their adventure. Auntie Pammie, Jada, and Stripes would have theirs: a visit to Lion Country Safari, where there would be real lions for Stripes to see just outside the car. Not that Stripes wasn't real.

"Please, Momma, please, please, please!" Jada said Thursday night for about the tenth time. "Can't me and Stripes stay with Auntie Pammie?"

Stripes and I, thought Richie.

"You'd be doing *me* a favor," Pammie said.

That was too much. Sure enough, on the far side of the couch, Tisha's face hardened. "How would I be doing you a favor?"

"For one, I didn't know what to get Richie for Christmas, so this will be my present. For another, I've always wanted to go to Lion Country but never had a child to take." She smiled wide as wide. For the past two days she'd been nothing but smiles and had drunk only wine. "I'll take really good care of her. You and Richie? You'll take good care of each other."

She managed to make it sound both peachy keen and lewd. Richie could see now how she sold all those condos. Big Sis, no, Big Aunt, was a terrier, with her teeth sunk in her prey's neck. Tisha's eyes found his as Jada climbed up on her lap. "Please, Momma?"

Tisha nodded, and Jada hugged her. Grinning, Richie wondered if he'd pay for this later. Pammie and Jada had ganged up on Tisha, and he hadn't provided much cover, but a night out with no child around?

"Great." Pammie reached for the phone. "I'll make the call."

When Richie and Tisha set out in the morning for South Beach, Pammie stood in the driveway holding Jada. Their faces, separated by only a few inches in bright sunlight, looked remarkably similar. Heart-shaped, mouths open on a plenitude of teeth, although Jada was missing one in front. Pammie's hair and Jada's complexion were complementary shades of gold. Their hands waved as Richie backed out, cut forward, and pulled away.

"If anything happens, I never forgive myself," Tisha said to her window. After a brief pause, she added, "Hell, anything happens, I never forgive you."

"Should I turn back?"

"She gonna be five, and we never spent one night apart."

A sob sailed from Tisha's lips, and the next thing Richie knew, she was crying.

"We'll go back, it's no big deal."

Tisha sucked her bottom lip between her teeth. "Jada would kill me." She brushed tears away as they rolled up to the gatehouse. "And what you mean no big deal, us spending the night in a hotel?"

"So, we're good?"

She nodded, and Richie turned onto Jog Road.

The Astor, a restored Art Deco structure, occupied a corner lot two blocks from Ocean Drive. It was Richie's first visit to South Beach, and though he'd had no trouble with directions, he felt disoriented when they pulled up. Maybe it was just the sunshine, but the off-white exterior seemed to glow.

"Looks nice," Tisha said.

Richie handed his keys to a valet and extended his arm to Tisha. For the first time in his life Richie wished he owned a Mi-ami Vice suit, but at least he had Ray-Bans, purchased the day before at Pammie's insistence. Arm in arm, they passed under brushed nickel trim, which arched over the main entrance. Inside he removed the dark glasses and saw: green-tinged white walls, marble floor, chrome elevator doors with frosted glass up and down lights. To their right mini-pendants illuminated a blond wood reception counter. On the left a murmuring fountain and the faint tinkle of piano jazz. The entire scene was so tasteful and restrained, he felt as if they'd stepped into a tableau vivant of *Architectural Digest*.

"Mister Gordon," said the young clerk dressed in a pigeon-gray suit. Blonde hair, severely tugged back, skirted her face. "Our manager would like to say hello."

Svetlana, according to her nametag, made a quick call then asked for his credit card. "Incidentals only. Your room bill is already paid."

A wraith-thin Latino, his good looks enhanced by the gray in his ponytail and the scar on his cheek, emerged from the hotel office.

"Mister Gordon?" Black slacks, open white shirt. "Ramon Hernandez. Pam told me you were coming. Quite something, your sister." Hernandez had just the whisper of an accent. "And this lovely lady?"

"LaTisha Nelson, pleased to meet you."

"Igualmente." Hernandez took her hand in both of his.

Champagne was icing in a pewter bucket in the sitting area of their junior suite.

"Oh, Richard," Tisha exclaimed after the bellhop departed, slipping Richie's five into his slacks. "Champagne! And look at those teeny bananas."

The welcome plate included a spray of fingerling fruit. She touched one then headed toward the bedroom.

"I think," he called, following, "this is Pammie's way of saying she approves."

Their room extended the lobby's color scheme. Off-white, green-tinged walls, blond furniture, brushed nickel fixtures. The king bed, set on an unusually high pedestal, was topped with a shimmering light green spread. Tisha climbed up and lay flat, arms extended from her sides. "Check this out."

"If I do, we may never get to the beach."

Tisha raised herself on an elbow and patted the empty space beside her. Richie dove on as if into a green pool. When she caught his lower lip between both of hers, he murmured, "Wait."

"For what?"

"Champagne."

He returned, already tumescent, to the sitting room, collected the champagne stems and ice bucket. Somehow—how did she manage so quickly?—LaTisha was naked when he got back. She lay against the headboard, hands behind her neck, small breasts pointed at the ceiling, nipples fully erect.

Later, dressed, they strolled to the beach. It was barely one o'clock, and they'd already made love and finished a bottle of champagne. Their faces glowed like heat lamps. This, Richie thought, was how it felt to be in love. This was what a couple with intimate knowledge of each other looked and felt and even moved like. A couple who, when glimpsed on the street, induced strangers to murmur, How wonderful! And perhaps remembering a similar moment in their own lives inculcated in them a desire to do something special. The best table, free wine or dessert, something to contribute to and to share in their glow. Somehow the shy white guy with dark hair and reddish mustache holding hands with the slightly taller black woman, who was good-looking but not beautiful except when she smiled, made everyone feel as if things were almost right in this fucked-up world.

The actual beach, when they crossed to it from the developed side of Ocean Drive, was broad and white, lined with row after row of dark blue umbrellas, so symmetrical it might have been painted. White sand, pale sky, royal blue canvas. They hurried across the burning sand, rented an umbrella and two chairs near the water. Tisha confessed she'd never swum in an ocean, had never even seen one up close before. They discarded tops and shorts, Tisha emerging in her yellow bikini. Richie broke out Pammie's bottle of NO-AD and coated his nose and cheeks.

"Want me to do your back?" Tisha asked.

When she'd finished, smoothing it from his neck to his waist while he stood white and still as marble watching blue-green waves roll toward shore, he asked, "You want some?"

She didn't answer until he turned around.

"Why would I want suntan lotion?"

"Don't black people burn?"

"Only when white folks light us on fire." She pointed with her chin toward the water's edge. A black man, a really big and really *black* black man, wearing a tank top and a tiny red Speedo, his skin so dark it seemed to burn with an absence of color, strode past, moving with a weight lifter's pigeon-toed strut. "Think he needs NO-AD?"

"I doubt it." The voice inside his head whispered, *Deepest, darkest Africa.* "But I thought you might. Skin cancer? To keep from getting burned? How would I know?"

"That's right, how would you?" She brushed her fingers across his cheek. "I thought you were telling me to put on lotion so I wouldn't get no darker."

"You think I care how dark you are?"

"Most do, white or black. Why not you?"

His whole life he'd excelled at taking tests, and he was pretty sure he knew the right answer for this one. "'Cause I'm in love with you?"

"Oh, baby." She cupped his chin with her large hands and kissed him bang on the mouth. "I love you too."

A moment later they dove in. It was icy, which explained why the other bathers were little kids and parents jumping waves or teenage boys in shorts and tank tops.

"I miss Jada," Tisha said, after they'd returned to their umbrella.

"Let's bring her this summer when the water's warm."

Rewarded by her smile and exhausted by the swim, by their lovemaking, midday champagne, and who knew what else, he fell into a deep and troubled doze in the sun. When he woke— where was he? Wait, Hank and Marilyn weren't his parents?— a wind had kicked up, and LaTisha was gone. He scanned the water's edge, no girlfriend. Shielding his eyes, he looked back toward Ocean Drive through row after empty row of blue umbrellas. The sun, slipping toward the roof of the tallest Ocean Drive hotel, looked like a pumpkin head on Art Deco shoulders. If Hank and Marilyn weren't, who were? And if Hank had hated *schvartzes*, did that mean Hank had hated whatever he was? How could he, when all Richie remembered was Hank loving him? For a second Richie thought he might cry, and he closed his eyes, pushed it all away. After a moment he opened them. Even with his hands pressed perpendicular to his forehead, the light hurt his eyes. He turned back toward the chair for his Ray-Bans and spotted LaTisha striding up from the water's edge in her yellow bikini. She said something to the tall black man beside her, who peeled off in the opposite direction.

"So, Sleepyhead finally woke up."

"Who was that?"

She seemed surprised he'd noticed. "He didn't say his name, and I didn't ask."

Later, showered and changed, they drank mojitos in the Astor lobby bar. LaTisha wore a white cocktail sheath he'd bought her on their stroll. The dress exposed a brown isthmus from her neck to her cleavage and a second island of flesh from an inch or two above her knees to the ankle-clenching straps of her heels. The bar was crowded, close, and warm. Jazz swung from a Steinway with its lid propped open. Beyond the plate glass walls dusk slipped toward night. The piano player, a youngish black man named Andre, had Cherokee cheekbones and reminded Richie of Greg Laughinghouse from high school. Everyone else in the bar was white, except Tisha, who had been matching him mojito for mojito. Placing his lips just below her ear, where a lacquered curl glistened, he whispered, "You look good enough to eat."

"I'm hongry too."

"How about room service?"

"I've never had no room service."

"I've never had room service"—his hand settled above her knee, her hand covered his—"with such a beautiful woman."

"Richard." Her eyes laughed. "You a slick white devil."

Was that good? Didn't sound so good. "I am?"

"Not really, but you slick when you wanna be."

He ordered another round and settled the bill. Carrying drinks, they started out of the bar, flushed and tipsy, passing the piano. Richie paused long enough to stuff a bill in Andre's tip glass.

"Good-looking sistah," Andre said, smiling, or Richie thought he said. The correct response? He didn't know. Andre glanced at the keys, and the music moved from a melody Richie didn't recognize to one he did. He hurried after Tisha, who was almost to the lobby doors, as a syncopated riff of "I Heard It through the Grapevine" broke from the open black Steinway.

Richie proposed another bottle of champagne and asked what she wanted for dinner.

"I'm so ignorant. You order."

But she wasn't ignorant, and it made him uncomfortable she thought so. Or maybe she was ignorant about fine dining, but that didn't imply anything else about her; she simply hadn't eaten in fancy restaurants. He ordered a duck breast appetizer, seared tuna, a filet mignon to be safe, chocolate mousse, and tiramisu. He liked teaching Tisha about food and wine, a little bit of Pygmalion and Galatea, Henry Higgins and Eliza, and he was drunk enough not to worry what it meant, how insecure it might mean he was. Tisha played with the tuner. "We should have brought some discs," she called.

He was in the bedroom.

"But I didn't know it would be like this."

He returned to the sitting room. Tisha stood, bent over the tuner, her white-sheathed bottom waving like a flag in the wind.

Boom, he popped an erection. "I didn't know either." He came up behind her, thinking he'd grab her hips, maybe press against her. The tuner dial she'd been spinning through, salsa, easy listening, salsa, classic rock, landed on hip-hop, and before he could reach her, she pumped the volume, straightened up, and turned around.

"Wanna dance?"

Yes, he wanted to dance, but it had been years and never to hip-hop, *thump, thump, b-thump,* the singer's accent so ghetto he couldn't understand half the words. One song ended, and another began.

"Here," she said, grinding from the waist down, pink tongue out for a ride on her plum-colored lips. She moved his hand to her waist and backed her bottom against him.

"Tighter." She craned backward, lips slightly higher than his own, her ass and hip grinding against his thigh and groin. Now, who was teacher, and who was pupil?

Yo sistah is a twista
Yo Mister is a trigga
Bang, bang, Niggah
Ooh, dawg you missed her

Tisha led him around the small sitting room, her back to his front, leading with her body's discreet and not-so-discreet pressure. Richie struggled to follow and struggled to relax. He struggled. After a few moments she turned to face him.

Bang, bang, Niggah!

"Hey, Richard, this is fun."

It was? Mostly, he worried he couldn't keep up. And he wished the singer would stop dropping the *N*-bomb. He knew they were allowed to launch it any time they wanted, like a secret handshake, but man oh man it made him nervous with Tisha rolling first one bare shoulder then the other as if she were connected to the music in a way he would never be, a drop of sweat rolling down her neck over her bare clavicle toward the bodice of her dress.

"This just you and me." She looped both arms around him, pressing against him from their chests to their knees, in and out–ing, out and in–ing, getting their mojos and mojitos working. He moved his mouth to hers and with every limb and nearly every opening conjoined, he felt as if they fucking fully clothed.

Sistah is a twista
Mister is a trigga
Bang, bang, Niggah
Bang, bang, Niggah!

She danced him from the sitting room toward the elevated bed. The beat made him feel twisted up inside, the singer and that awful voice in his head, locked in a fierce duet. *Ooh, ooh Niggah, bang, bang, sistah.* Tisha pushed him onto the bed and fell on top of him, his legs dangling almost to the floor. She whispered, "Now, we really dancing," as her mouth moved the length of his body, nipping at his belly. Then her hands were at his belt and zipper, his hard-on springing upward as she dropped from the bed to her knees, pulling his pants off as she fell.

Bang, bang, Niggah, Niggah,
Bang, bang, sistah, sistah!

"Wait."
"*Wait?*" Her face rose from between his legs.
Richie pushed himself up on his elbows and pulled her toward him. "You're going to think I'm crazy."
She smoothed the glistening curls on her cheeks.
"You ever think bad words about me? Like, when you said, 'White devil?'"
"I was playin'."
"I know."
The receiver in the front room blasted, "Bang, bang, Niggah, Niggah, bang, bang, sistah!" and he watched it register on her.
"Do you?"
"It's not like I *think* them. It's like I hear them in my head."
"Like what?"
"Like in that song."
"Say it."
"I don't want to."
"Yes, you do."
"Like nigger," he whispered. "Like, you're a nigger lover."
"What else?"
"No, you."
"How do you know I—?"
"I want to know."
In the front room the music shifted to something softer, sweeter, more obviously sensual.
"Pale face, Snow Bunny, Casper. Your turn."
"I hate this."
"Then why'd you start?"

"To get it out." He reached for her, but she withdrew. "So there'd be nothing between us."

"There wasn't, not for me. So call me another one, Honky. Snowflake, White Devil."

"Jungle Bunny," he said. "Shine."

"De Enemy, De Savages." She cupped his cock and, looking right at him, squeezed till it hurt. "You'll like this one. Pink toes."

He pushed her hand away. "Coon. *Schvartze*." He pushed his hand up the front of her dress, between her legs, until he found her panties. "That's Yiddish for black."

She squeezed his balls through his boxers. He groaned, in pain, and then her hand moved inside the cloth. "Oh, yes," she said, lying on her side beside him. "We've got our nice words for Jews, don't worry. Stalagmites, Shirley Temples, Syna Gouges."

He pulled her panties down and pushed a finger inside her, didn't have to force it, she was already wet.

"Israel Mights." She rolled above him, moved her finger to the edge of his bottom, then poked it inside him. "Caesar's Pet."

"Ow."

"No more words?" She worked her finger.

"Nigger."

"That's always what it comes to." Her face hard. "Fertilizer. Jesus Killer."

"I love you," he whispered.

"Grab my titties, niggah lover."

He did. Then her finger, which had felt like it was halfway to his chest, withdrew. She fumbled at his cock and pushed it inside her. "Da Enemy." She pinned his hands above his head. "Da Savage, da Other. Pink Booties. Da Muthafuckin Man."

With Tisha on top, then Richie, then with Richie behind her and Tisha's white dress bunched around her middle, they fucked until they collapsed on the bed, and he rolled her over, said to her face, "I love you, LaTisha Nelson, I really do."

"If you love me like that—"

He wondered what she'd say next, *It don't matter that you white?* But he'd never know because they suddenly heard the knocking and realized they'd been hearing it for some time at the edge of carnal consciousness, not their heads or body parts banging as they might have thought but room service trying to serve their meal.

NINE

They didn't speak of what had happened or the things they'd said. Richie didn't know if that was good or bad. They made love a second time before falling asleep, the third time that day, and once more in the morning before departing for Delray Beach. Nothing like this had ever happened to him. Was it because she was black, what one of the assistant professors, he couldn't even remember which one, had explained, after they'd watched *Bodyguard* together, was properly referred to as the racialized female body or some such crap? He didn't think so. His desire for Tisha only seemed to increase with his satisfying that desire. The only remotely similar experience he knew of was eating chips and salsa; only another salsa-dipped chip could extinguish the burning the previous one had ignited and then only momentarily before a third was required. Driving north on I-95, he wondered what Tisha would think of being compared to hot salsa then decided to save it for some moment when he needed a compliment. But she caught him smiling and worked it out of him.

"If I'm the salsa, what are you, the corn chip?"

"I'm the corn dog."

"Nah, you the horn dog, white boy."

How'd he get so lucky? "No." He struggled to keep his eyes on the road, traffic whirring past on both sides. "I'm the Lay's potato chip. 'Bet you can't eat just one.'"

Jada and Auntie Pammie had loved their mini-vacation too, and when it was time the next morning to drive to the airport there was much hugging and kissing amid promises to do it all again.

"Next time," Jada declared, holding Pammie's hand as they walked toward the red convertible, "me and Auntie Pammie are going to Disney World. Aren't we?"

"Auntie Pammie and I," Richie said, walking behind them.

"No! Only me and Auntie Pammie." She tugged Pammie's hand. "Right?"

"That's right."

Pammie scooped Jada into her arms, and the child turned toward Richie, dark eyes gleeful. All that was missing was her sassy tongue poking out between her lips.

"Richie was trying to tell you the right way to say it is 'Auntie Pammie and I,' not 'Me and Auntie Pammie.'"

"But we still going?"

"If you say, 'Auntie Pammie and I.'"

Just then Tisha, who'd gone back inside to make sure they hadn't forgotten anything, emerged waving a pair of Jada's pink cotton panties.

"Auntie Pammie and I are going to Disney World next time!"

"I haven't heard you thank her for this time."

"Oh yes, she has," Pammie said, enjoying a throat-clenching, legs-around-her-waist hug.

"Thank you, thank you, thank you," Jada chanted. Pammie set her down, and she swiveled to face Tisha. "See, Momma?"

Pammie said, "Why don't you get in the car and get your seat belt on?"

"Stripes wants to kiss you too."

Pammie accepted Stripes's kisses, bestowed a few of her own on the snow leopard, then Jada climbed onto her booster seat in back.

"Thank you for everything," Tisha said.

"No, thank you," Pammie replied. "I've never seen my brother so happy."

Richie was struck, as he had been all week, but especially now as the women embraced in front of the top-down convertible, by how opposite in appearance they were. Little and big, light and dark, buxom and small breasted.

"I was going to say, if Richie doesn't treat you right, let me know and I'll come up and beat some sense into him." Pammie grinned. "But I have the feeling you can take care of yourself."

"Richard always treats me right."

"You guys are disgusting. If you ever want to put Jada on a plane to visit me, I'd love that."

Tisha looked shocked then smiled her high-wattage smile. "Thanks for everything."

She climbed into the car. Richie said, "I haven't seen you look so happy in a long time either."

"Once an aunt, always an aunt." Pammie's blue eyes held his. "If you want to get in touch with Lorraine, let me know."

Why hadn't that occurred to him? He nodded then kissed his sister. He still couldn't think of her as *Aunt* Pammie. He climbed into the convertible, and they drove to the airport with the top down. It was going to be cold for a long time in C. City.

A week later, Friday night, he was walking south on Market to meet Laura, Dave, and Tisha at La Table, Calhoun City's landmark five-star restaurant. He was finally getting them together. It had been unusually warm all day, sixty-two and sunny in January, but he'd grown used to meteorological abnormalities in C. City. His first winter it had snowed just once; the temperature rarely dropped below freezing; and Richie concluded he'd moved not to the edge of the Great Plains but to the South. The very next year, after three ice storms in January and a blizzard in March, he bought the CRV.

Now in this, his fifth winter in C. City, M.O., he'd grown used to the temperature swings and had learned to anticipate a January thaw. Their first few days back had been bitter, with a mustache-crunching wind, a weather pattern the Channel 8 weatherperson called an Alberta Clipper. Wednesday the cold broke, and today was a miracle: soft, springlike air, like a warm embrace, even now, long after dark. He'd decided, on something of a whim, to walk to La Table rather than take his car. After dinner he'd ask Dave and Laura to drive them to his office to retrieve it, or maybe he'd treat Tisha to one of the horse-drawn hansoms available this time of year. Horse cabs were a C. City, M.O., Yuletide tradition, along with a temporary skating rink, Christmas tree, and Chanukah menorah set up across from the Plaza. There was also something every year about the Ku Klux Klan petitioning to erect an illuminated cross there too. The city fought it, though the ACLU, which he'd always thought of as a Jewish organization, supported it. But he'd been so busy at work and his heart was so full of Tisha and Jada, he couldn't remember if the Klan had been allowed to set up the cross this year or not.

He'd started walking at Twelfth and Market, a few blocks from his own office; he'd scheduled a late meeting with Seitz and Van Nostrand, a direct-mail firm he'd used before and was considering bringing aboard for the Folgrow launch. He felt comfortable with Dave Seitz and Scott Van Nostrand if for no other reason, initially, than that his parents' house—it was still impossible to think of them as his grandparents—was a few short blocks from Nostrand Avenue in Brooklyn, and it delighted him to encounter a familiar name in a strange place. Seitz and Van Nostrand were no better than several other firms, and they were sometimes more expensive. Still, there was a comfort level, and Richie liked attending meetings at their office—they would have come to his, if he asked—a converted loft on the site of C. City's original downtown market. A Calhoun City Historical Society plaque hung on the red brick facade, and something about the late-nineteenth-century warehouse's connection to an even earlier time now housing the twenty-first-century phenomenon of market testing appealed to the dormant but always present part of Richie that could stand outside himself and marvel, *You do what for a living?*

At six-fifty on this Friday the streets and sidewalk were deserted: white flight; a dying downtown—that sad, familiar American tale. C&M employed uniformed security guards twenty-four/seven and guaranteed cab rides home for employees working late. The only white people on the streets this late in this part of town—like the bum slumped against the building on Richie's right, a plastic Arthur Bryant Barbecue cup at his feet—were probably homeless. This guy was what, forty? Wore a red and white Chiefs hat tugged over his face. Richie didn't slow to drop change in his cup. In fact, he sped up until he spotted a circle of young African American males on the next corner. Now what, cross the street? What were they doing, just standing around? Then he realized the kids were waiting for a bus, and he cursed his knee-jerk racism.

He continued to walk. When he reached the corner of Race, there were suddenly more and better-dressed people on the street. Late model cars, several SUVs, what was that really huge one? Oh yes, an Expedition. He crossed Race, and through the open window of a white Eldorado stopped at the light, he spied a silver-haired couple in evening attire. Probably headed to Music Hall or the new Sprint Center. A few blocks made a huge difference in street life, and once again he felt happy to be outside walking in this January break from winter.

At Twenty-third he turned one block west to Promenade. He didn't think it was possible to feel this happy. Thirty years of living had taught him this sort of happiness wasn't in the cards for little Richie Gordon. But LaTisha had gotten two A's and two B's, good enough to be admitted to the practicum at Good Samaritan Hospital for the spring quarter. At Wednesday's BM meeting he'd been singled out for praise by Haddy Horstmeyer, senior VP of new business development, and at a follow-up with the senior and regional VPs, he'd been given a firm rollout date during the April-May-June Walmart module, with a shelf date of April eleventh. He was not only in love with a beautiful black woman who seemed, though he could hardly believe it, to love him back; he was equally in love with her daughter. Dave and Laura were having a baby, and he was going to be the godfather. He felt totally unlike himself, transported to some other plane of existence, where he was experiencing someone else's life, so light and so full of light that, walking the last half-block to La Table, he could see himself as he might look as a float in the Macy's Thanksgiving Day Parade. Tethered to the ground by a Lilliputian army, all red nose, white cheeks, and an ENORMOUS grin.

Oh God, don't let anything bad happen. When a movie soldier felt like this, he told his tentmate what he was going to do after the war, and in the next scene or in the one after that a bullet opened his chest. In a heartbeat a dirge was playing, and his friends or maybe a young lieutenant was pulling off his dog tags to ship them home to his girl.

But the girl was never black, and she was never named LaTisha.

Richie stopped in front of La Table and squared his shoulders. He avoided the uniformed valet who was rushing forward to assist an arriving Audi and checked his watch. *Seven-oh-four.* He was probably first. But when he stepped through the heavy door held by a gray-cloaked, gray-haired African American doorman and let his eyes adjust first to the flash of light and then to the generally dim anteroom, taking in the ornate drapery, the distinctive peach decor of the main salon visible through a half-drawn curtain, there was LaTisha beside Dave and Laura in front of the maître d's station. Tisha wore the simple black sheath he'd given her. For better or worse it was nearly identical to Laura's. That's where he'd gotten the idea, of course; he'd shared plenty of restaurant meals with Laura, and she always seemed perfectly dressed. The women faced each other so that Richie saw them in profile: two tall, strong-looking women talking passionately about something. In the moment before they turned, Richie thought, *Uh-oh, same dress, not good, and Laura's starting to show*. Then Dave caught his eye. Indicating Tisha with a quick nod of his head, he okayed his thumb and index finger, the last three fingers of his right hand pointing straight up, signaling that Tisha was A-OK.

Just then Tisha noticed him. The smile he loved, lips to eyes, transformed her face, like flash bulbs *pop, pop, popping*, and he stepped forward in the peach restaurant light to greet her.

BOOK 2. APRIL 2001

East of Troost

TEN

When Richie startled awake, he felt as if he hadn't slept, though he'd been traveling in the land of Nod for a solid eight. Through some hiccup in his REM cycle he'd tumbled from a dream at precisely the wrong moment. He was who he used to be, running to school, already late. Why hadn't Mom or Daddy gotten him up? Then his hand grazed something not of that world, and he came into himself as much as he ever would that Sunday: Tisha's arm laid casually across his chest, her fingernails connubially attached to his shoulder. And that? *That* was Jada bed-bouncing, chanting, "Richie, Richie, the sky is falling! Wake up!"

"What?"

"April Fools! April Fools!"

Tisha, who woke one limb and sense at a time, with speech often far in advance of cognition, muttered, "Jada Reece Gordon, what I tell you about waking us up?"

"It's April Fools'," Jada protested. "Isn't it, Richie?"

"I'll show you *fool*." Tisha tugged the sheet up over her face. "If you *mmphh, mmphh schnout grumphle*."

"But Momma—"

Richie put his finger to Jada's lips. "Let Momma sleep." He swung his feet to the floor, stood, and reached for Jada, who raised her arms to be carried. She'd hit a growth spurt in January and February and now seemed tall for her age, though she still weighed next to nothing. She takes after Reece, Tisha told him. "His family skin and bones."

With Jada's legs belting his waist and her arms strapping his shoulders, Richie slipped from the bedroom. He had to pee, and the pressure of Jada's knees increased that need. He still had a morning woody from whatever dream he'd been roused from, and Jada's legs below his waist felt morally as well as physically uncomfortable. He swung her up to his shoulders, where she perched, slim calves hanging down on either side of his face.

"Richie," she said when he stopped in front of the couch. "I'm hungry."

"In a minute." He swung her to the ground. "I'll fix breakfast."

He headed for the bathroom, awkwardly located on the far side of the kitchen, thus at some distance from the bedroom; before the house had been divided into smaller apartments, Tisha's bedroom must have been a dining room.

"I want pancakes."

"Okay."

"With worm syrup. April Fools!"

Richie often made Sunday breakfast to allow Tisha to sleep in. Her nursing practicum had started, and between coursework, her hours at Good Sam, and her part-time job, she was run off her feet. Months ago Richie had suggested that she quit the job. It would be better for everyone if she spent more time with Jada; he'd gladly give her the money (it wasn't like she earned much anyway). But she said, "No, thank you," and when he pressed her, added, "Mind your own damn business," with such a fierce and frozen smile he never mentioned it again. Instead, he fixed Sunday breakfasts, kept her fridge stocked, and tried to buy her and Jada useful presents so she wouldn't have to worry so much. His efforts seemed mostly to annoy her. Sometimes, he thought, the difference in their economic status was more problematic than their skin color. After five months she was brown, he was white, Jada somewhere in between. Weren't all couples different colors? No? How weird. "We're complementary," he'd said once when they lay in bed, spooning.

"Beautiful brown and pasty white?"

"No, Richie and Tisha plaid."

"You silver-tongued devil."

But money, he thought, as his morning pee kept going and going, the Energizer Bunny of Whizzing, what a successful ad that was, he must have already passed a quart and showed no signs of stopping. He had to be careful not to suggest too many expensive restaurants or to buy Jada too many presents. What was the point of making all this money if he couldn't give Tisha a hundred a week so Jada wouldn't have to stay in extended care every day after school? By the time Tisha paid for day care, she was netting four dollars an hour from her job. But no. She didn't want his damn money. Maybe if he wasn't white, the money thing would be different. Once, exasperated with him, she'd asked, "You want everyone think I'm with you 'cause you rich?" Behind that he could hear other voices, *Tisha boning that white dude for his bling.*

"No, because I make you happy."

"Then don't push me."

What Richie really wanted was for Tisha and Jada to move in, but after she refused his offer to quit her job, he'd been afraid even to mention living together except one time pretty early on, when she'd brushed the suggestion aside. "Oh no, you'd get so tired of us."

"Richie," Jada shouted. "Hurry up!"

He mixed batter from the box and laid bacon in the pan. For all her braggadocio Jada ate a single cake and two itty-bitty pieces of bacon then skipped off to watch Sunday morning cartoons. Richie poured a second cup of coffee and tucked into a Too Tall stack—eating, he wondered about Tisha's uncle, Too Tall, in Mississippi, if he'd ever meet any of her family—doused with maple syrup bought yesterday at City Market. Tisha would likely sleep another two or three hours; he should have brought some work to do. Instead, he finished eating and headed for the living room to keep Jada and the Princess Ponies company. An hour later, when the phone rang, she was on his lap. No one who knew Tisha well would call this early: ten a.m. on Sunday. He could let the machine answer. *Tisha, pee—eeace.* But if he did, the ringing might wake her. He snatched the receiver to his ear, and a male voice crooned, "Hey, baby."

"Who's calling, please?"

"Tish?"

Do I sound like Tisha? "May I take a message?"

"Who is this?"

"Who is this is what I'm asking you."

"Tish there?"

"She can't come to the phone."

"Cool." The voice was low-pitched and resonant, a smooth and stealthy baritone. "Tell her Reece called."

Richie brooded, not only while Tisha slept but while she was eating. Had she been talking to Reece all along, or did this call mean he was out of jail? They'd never worked out the whole Time Warner bill mess, he and Tisha, just let it drop. Now what? If Reece were out of jail, had she been seeing him on the sly? *Hey, baby?* That didn't sound like someone who was out of your life.

"Umm," she said, "this syrup's sweet as you." At noon she was still in her nightgown, untouched hair all around her face. "Thanks for getting up with Jada."

He nodded.

Tisha washed her mouth with milk. "You keep fixing pancakes, you gonna have one fat girlfriend." She smiled. "Now's when you say, 'Baby, you never be fat in my eyes.' Or 'Tish, I like a girl with some cakes on her booty.'"

"When you were sleeping, Reece called."

He thought he'd know everything when he uttered those two little words: *Reece called.* He realized now how ridiculous that was. Tisha's eyes narrowed, but whether from annoyance at him, at Reece for calling, or simply as an unfeigned marker of surprise, he couldn't say. She cut another wedge of pancake, dragged it through the amber syrup, and ate it.

"Reece say *where* he calling from?"

Richie shook his head.

"He leave a message?"

"I think he was too surprised to hear my voice."

"Maybe he wanted you to think so. Not much surprise old Reece." She tried to take his hand, and in a flash he realized just how upset he was, drawing back as if he'd been burned.

"Now what, you all angry?"

"No."

"I haven't spoken to Reece in months. Haven't seen him neither. You know what, Richard?" Her face a dark scowl. "I shouldn't have to defend myself. I been nothing but straight."

"I know." He leaned forward to kiss her, and though she kissed him back, he knew he'd messed up. "I love you, you know that too."

"That's the only reason I ain't pissed. Maybe Reece let out the County. Maybe he calling about Jada."

"He asked for you."

"Would you rather he was calling for Jada? Me, he got no claim. But Jada, he's her daddy."

"Not much of one."

"In his way."

Richie wanted to ask, *What way was that?* She'd told him Reece rarely paid child support, not only these past five months but Jada's whole life. He didn't call or visit, certainly not since Richie had been around; then again, he'd been in jail. Richie had hoped Reece would never get out so he could feel like the father, not only in name—*Jada Gordon*—but in deed. Meanwhile, the voice in his head kept demanding, *What way was that again? Some totally fucked-up, absent black father kind of way?*

Richie himself might have answered, *A father is the person who helps raise you, not the one who shot the jizz,* but he knew enough not to bring his own issues into what was already too complicated for him to work out on this first day of April, April Fools', not with the week they had lined up. On Friday Tisha was taking him to Dreams, the hottest black dance club in C. City, M.O., the first time they'd go out like that, sort of his coming-out party in her world. Sunday night was Passover, and he was making his first seder. Dave and a very pregnant Laura were coming. So was Pammie, flying up Saturday from Florida, a plan they'd conceived in the afterglow of the December visit. Then a few days ago, out of the deepest, darkest blue, Pammie had called.

"What would you think if Lorraine came to your seder, how would that be?"

"Just like that?"

"Just like that."

"She's not going to call me first?"

"Have you called her?"

Pammie had given him the number months ago.

"I didn't know what to say."

"Maybe she doesn't either."

She's my goddamn mother, she should call me.

But he hadn't voiced that, just as he didn't enumerate Reece's failures as a father. Who was he, really, to chide an absent parent, never having been one? He'd answered Pammie, "Sure, tell her to come." And now he uttered not one more word about Reece, instead headed home claiming he had work to do, though no one was fooled.

Late that afternoon, going over recipes for a Passover shopping list, the phone rang, and a voice he could swear he'd never heard before, said, "Richie, this is Lorraine."

Holy fuck, he thought or maybe said.

"Yeah," the voice continued, "pretty fucking weird."

The voice, girlish and whispery, not at all what he'd imagined, still retained the street sounds of Brooklyn, more so than his own, though she'd been away thirty years.

"Look, I could understand you wouldn't want to see me, in fact I'm totally surprised, but Pammie said you invited me to a seder, for shit's sake, so I bought a ticket then realized I couldn't get on the plane unless I spoke to you first, because honestly I can't believe you do. I mean who could blame you, right?"

She paused, he assumed, to breathe then continued, "I'm shaking like a fucking leaf, excuse my French, maybe you don't think women should talk like I do, but when I'm nervous, you know, it's 'Fuck this, fuck that, fuck the other thing.' Anyway, Pammie said you turned out real well. She always sent pictures—it was really hard to stay away when Daddy died, but I knew if I came and saw you. Oh Christ, can you help me out a little here?"

"What should I call you?"

"Call me Pisher, just don't call me late for dinner. Like Uncle Sidney used to say."

"Who?"

"That's right, you didn't just lose me, you lost all the Gordons. You sure you want me to come?"

He hesitated. He'd been slow-witted all day, never having quite recovered from Jada breaking into his dream. "I'm sure."

"Thank you." She laughed or maybe sniffled, he couldn't tell. "Took you long enough."

Took *me* long enough? Richie thought, but did not say, this time he was sure. *Took you thirty goddamn years.*

"I'm one to talk. *Thirty goddamn years, right?* Hey, don't worry, it's just something I can do sometimes, probably all the drugs I took."

There was an increasingly awkward pause. He tried not to think anything, lest she repeat it back to him, but all the time he was thinking, *She's a lunatic.*

The voice said, "You always this shut down?"

"Only when my mother, whom I haven't heard from in thirty years—"

"Don't call me that. It's disrespectful to Mom and Daddy."

"What should I call you?"

"When you were a baby, you called me 'Or.'"

"I did?"

"It was the last thing you ever said to me. 'Bye, Or.'" The voice stopped, and this time, Richie decided, she was sniffling. "Anyway, Pammie tells me you have a black girlfriend, or do you say African American?"

"Whichever."

"That's so cool, I just wanted to tell you. Do I get to meet her?"

Suddenly, standing at his living room window looking west into the vastness of the country, Richie felt so weary he feared he'd pass out.

"She'll be at the seder."

"And you're sure you want me to come?"

"Yes, I already said so."

"Thank you."

He mouthed a quick good-bye, hurried to his room, and dove onto his bed, where he lay, as if underwater, trying to remember how to breathe.

ELEVEN

Now that he had a life to distract him from his job, Richie found little time to be distracted. Folgrow would ship in two days, a week in advance of next Wednesday's official launch, timed to be on shelves in time for Easter weekend, beginning Friday the thirteenth. Not a good omen, Friday the thirteenth. He'd been fretting about the numerological implications for months, as he was fretting yet again at his desk on Monday morning. Official launch was Ash Wednesday, followed by Holy Thursday and Good Friday. What could be more propitious for the rollout of a product formulated to keep men's heads from getting holey? It was also the middle days of Passover, with its subtle echoes of *Comb-over*. All his people, whom quite frankly he no longer believed were his only people, would have just attended seders, yarmulkes covering male pattern baldness. It was the perfect Folgrow moment, *bubelah*. Everything was going to be fine!

He recognized he was an inch, a smidge, a micro snit, from hysteria. Twice that morning his redheaded secretary, Jeannie, who tended to mother him even though she was three years younger than he was, happily married with two kids, had cautioned, "These next few weeks, maybe ease back on the Starbucks, Richie boss, know what I mean?" After the conversation with Lorr, Or, Lorraine, whatever he was supposed to call her, he'd needed several scotches even to contemplate sleep, and he'd nearly taken one of the Xanaxes Dave had given him at their last Havana Martini confab when he confessed how stressed he felt. "Perfectly understandable," Dave said. "It's your first launch, Cosmonaut," although Richie had no compelling reason to worry. Presell had gone well, initial placement four point eight percent above conservative projections. Not great but decent. And the print ads, first in a series titled "Why Worry?" had tested well and would begin running on Wednesday in select major markets. In the left foreground an early forties male, business attire, with a dark, splendid head of hair, left hand suggestively placed against the lower back of a sexy (but not too sexy) woman in a cocktail dress, extends his right to shake the hand of a second business-suited male, who not only lacks a woman but displays a male pattern bald spot, bare scalp clearly visible through his thinning hair. Subphoto text extols the effectiveness of Folgrow in slightly more than fifty percent of the men who used it. Of course, *Results may vary*. That's what results do; they vary. But the woman's slim waist and the male model's splendid cap of hair establish the ad's irrefutable subtext. *Why risk it?* Just twenty smackeroos to establish that genetics don't have to be destiny. Who would you rather be, Bud? A sad sack with a bald spot or the hunk with his hand above that honey's honeypot?

Richie gathered his things, waved good-bye to red-haired Jeannie, who was on the phone—she was on the phone a lot, maybe more than he was—and headed to the Monday morning BM meeting. Maybe he *would* cut back on the coffee, no more than two, well, three grandes a day. Everything was going great and would no doubt go greater and greater. But just in case, after the meeting he'd check with sales for updated figures and with logistics to make sure there was nothing else he needed to do.

He worked late Monday. Tuesday, too, though he'd arranged with Tisha to stop by for dinner and he had to cancel when a late meeting was scheduled. "Don't worry, Richard," she said, "we both got lots to do, it's fine."

But everything wasn't fine, not with Reece's uninvited ghost floating through their lives, or was it hanging over their heads? He wasn't clear about the best expression, but he certainly felt threatened, a free-floating, impossible-to-put-his-finger-on kind of threat. He'd received his new social security number, so there was no longer any danger of his identity being stolen. But except for Pleasant Street, Reece had been using his name, not his social security number: "I, Richard A. Gordon," he'd written on a medical clinic's business card that had been returned with Richie's wallet, "have no known allergies." The man was a career thief and who knew what else, and Richie was sleeping and sometimes living, though not nearly as frequently as he wanted to, with a woman for whom Reece must have, or certainly had had, strong feelings, his Baby's Momma, his BM. They were both BMs! Maybe a jailhouse code of honor or the pride of a black man whose woman had crossed the color line required said black man to beat the living shit out of the white guy? Complicating the equation was said white guy's declared love not only for the woman but Baby Jada Herself.

Richie was in over his head, out of his gourd! In uncharted waters! *Ad-speak*, he thought, *don't fail me now!* And that was before anything had actually happened. Reece might have been calling from jail, or maybe he was just around the corner. Tisha insisted there was nothing between them and hadn't been for years. Richie wanted to believe her. But he'd wanted to come by late after work to spend the night. Normally she would have agreed, but she had to get up extra early Wednesday morning, and she'd had a rotten day herself. Forgot to record a patient's BP at Good Sam, and while she knew that was wrong, she was beginning to think the nursing supervisor, a skinny old white woman, didn't like her because she'd written her up for it. To top off the pile of crap her day had been, she'd fought with a customer at work.

"You could quit that job."

"Richard, don't start. And Jada's being a brat. Soon as she's down, I'm gointa sleep myself. Why don't you just come by tomorrow"—he took them out to dinner on Wednesdays—"wouldn't that be okay?"

When he didn't respond she added, "Everything's fine, fool. I love you."

What could he say without seeming loony, jealous, and suspicious without cause, except *I love you too.*

On Wednesday he started work even earlier than usual; he'd been at his desk a full hour when Jeannie arrived at seven-thirty. No lunch date, so he worked straight through and left at four. He drove to Shawnee across the Kansas line to do his Passover shopping at Blinder's, a Jewish specialty store Steve Ross, a VP in sales, had assured him was the best place in town. He started with four bottles of kosher-for-Passover wine: two sweet traditional Manichewitz and two Israeli cabernets that might actually taste good. He considered how much Pammie drank, thought about Lorr-Or-Lorraine, and added four more bottles to the cart. He selected a giant jar of gefilte fish; two bottles of horseradish, red and white; soup mandlen; matzo ball mix; a kosher soup chicken; apples and walnuts for charoses. For Jada he purchased plain and chocolate-covered macaroons, chocolate-covered matzo, and those brightly colored fruit jellies—neon orange, electric green, and stoplight yellow shaped like fruit slices—he'd loved when he was her age. He already had a turkey and a brisket at home. He stood in the aisle with his undersized, overflowing cart and tried to remember childhood seders, which, like almost everything else festive, had stopped when his father died. *Grandfather. Chopped liver*, he thought, and rolled toward the appetizing counter, took a number, and waited while a four-foot-ten crone ordered four ounces of every smoked fish in the case. When she finished, Richie ordered a pound each of chopped liver and pickled herring then hurried to the front of the store, where he stood in line behind the same ancient yenta, thought about the seder and Lorraine's visit, and added another four more bottles of wine to get the case discount.

He arrived in front of LaTisha's at half past five, an hour earlier than usual. After five months his Honda was a familiar sight, and so was he. *White guy, silver ride.* Sometimes VaShawn and Victor, ten-year-old fraternal twins who lived in the second-floor apartment on the right side of Tisha's building, and their posse of mini-hoodlums would run out and offer to watch his car for a dollar apiece to make sure "nothing bad happen." Once or twice, for grins, he'd hired them. Then Tisha told Cherisse, the twins' mother, that if anything *bad happen* to Richie's car, Bertie, who lived on the ground floor on Cherisse's side and watched the street, would let her know and something *badder* happen to Cherisse. Richie and the twins were friends now. They'd sometimes toss a football in the side yard—on weekends their father, Donnie, who worked second shift somewhere, would join them for two-on-two—so he wasn't thinking much of anything when the twins ran toward him except maybe he shouldn't bother taking the chicken up to Tisha's, it wouldn't sit that long in the car anyway. VaShawn, also known as V, the smaller, faster, and smarter of the boys, feigned a punch, while Victor, called V-Square, grabbed the chicken bag. The boys played keep-away until Bertie stuck her head out of her window and shouted, "V, V-Square, give Richie that bag!"

"You lame." V tossed Richie the chicken bag, which had smacked the sidewalk several times already and looked muddy and bloody.

"Watch your car for *five* dollars?" V-Square asked.

"Not today." Richie felt sweaty but pretty good otherwise.

"Watch your *chicken* for fifty cent," V said, and cracked up, socked his twin in the chest, and ran off, V-Square in loud pursuit.

Richie came up the front steps, fielded a look from Bertie, half-smile, half-what? before she dropped the blind. He unlocked the left front door with the key Tisha had given him months ago, walked past the thumping bass of apartment A, ran up the stairs still carrying the chicken bag, which was beginning to ooze chicken juices, and let himself in. *Whoa.* Tisha and Jada sat on the couch beside a very light and very good-looking black man.

"You must be Richard." The stranger stood and smiled. "I been hearing all about you."

"Richard." Tisha looked strained around the eyes. "This Reece."

They faced each other, Reece four, maybe five inches taller. His long forehead rose above ironically arching eyebrows—*Who you and what the fuck you doing here?* they seemed to ask—toward cropped hair lighter than Richie's: birch-brown with reddish highlights. White blood, Richie thought, not far back. His skin color wasn't much different from Richie's, but the pigments had started from a different mixing point: deeper as much as darker. His eyes showed hints of green; his nose, though wide at the nostrils, was the narrow bridged, straight one Jada had inherited. What he thought of the minutiae of Richie's appearance—that is, if he'd gotten past the obvious: *white guy*—Richie couldn't guess. Reece wore a small diamond stud in his left ear. His upper lip showed several days' growth, again more reddish than black. He was otherwise clean-shaven, wore sweats and Jordans, extended a narrow-wristed, long-fingered hand.

"My bad for using your cards. No hards, bro?"

Richie took Reece's hand. "Depends what you did with them."

"Nothing much." Reece initiated a complicated handshake Richie struggled to complete. "Just the name."

"You want to tell me about Pleasant Street in C. City, Kansas?"

"Nothing to tell."

"Really?"

Reece met Richie's angry glare with a grin. If he was lying, he was skilled. His eyes, which were almost creepy, not so much green as brown with green *under* the brown, gave nothing away. "That's right."

"So, you didn't open a Time Warner account with my name and social security number last year?"

"I never stayed in Kansas."

Richie could feel the ocular weight of Tisha and Jada on him. What was he going to do, call Reece a liar to their faces? "Just so you know, I changed my social security number."

"Most prudent." Reece grinned again. "I hear you familiar with some of my things too."

"Reece," Tisha said, "none of your things here."

"Richard A. Gordon knows what I'm saying."

He did. A glance at Tisha showed she now took Reece's meaning. "By the way, I don't know your last name."

"Woodson. Seems like you ought to be happy I used them IDs. Hell, you should pay me a finder's fee."

Richie glanced again at Tisha and at Jada beside her. Tisha shook her head emphatically *No!* and Richie grasped two facts as one: (a) he would gladly pay Reece almost anything if he would go away and never come back; and (b) in his left hand he still held the bloody chicken bag. He dropped it to the floor. "I don't think so."

"Is that *No?*"—oh those green-tinged eyes and arching eyebrows, the resonant radio announcer's voice—"or *I'd like to think about it?*"

"It's no."

"Too bad." Reece turned toward Jada. "Come kiss your daddy good-bye."

After a worried glance at Richie, Jada climbed down from the couch and stepped into Reece's long arms. "Mind your pretty momma." He bussed her cheek, smiled at Tisha. "Catch you." He ambled out, long limbed, loose jointed, half-glide, half-strut, the crown of reddish hair his coxcomb.

Tisha said, "I didn't invite him. He on the porch when we got home."

Richie moved to the couch and kissed Tisha, *bam*, right on

the mouth. "I never thought you did." He hoisted Jada, kissed both her cheeks and the tip of her nose, then tickled her belly till she squealed. "How about dinner at Dino's?"

"Yay, Dino's!"

Dino's was Jada's favorite restaurant and pizza her favorite food, but there was something false in the way she shouted. Poor little kid, not even five but already worried what he thought of her for kissing Reece.

"Richard," Tisha said, "what's that dirty bag doing on my clean floor?"

That night Richie dreamed what he came to think of as the dream of blackness. He and LaTisha enter a club. She wears a polka-dot top. He can't see what he's wearing, can't see himself at all, but the rest of the club is dressed to kill. Super-fly suits, purple, white, and green. Gold chains, snarky shades, backless dresses, crotch-high skirts. They step onto a glass block strobe-lit floor, reverb rocking neck to knees. His dream-self thinks, *Oh shit, everyone will know.* Then the boogying begins, and no one notices. He leapt like Baryshnikov, clapped his hand to Tisha's butt, and woke murmuring, "The dream of blackness." It was the first dream he'd remembered since he can't remember, and he understood in the chasm between wakefulness and sleep that it wasn't the first time he'd dreamed it. To dance in a black space and have no one care or notice. He dropped an arm over Tisha and tried to hip-hop back to sleep.

On Friday, after a workday that included his launch presentation to an NBD group meeting and reports from Cincinnati about shipping delays, he arrived home at seven-thirty to find a message from Pammie. "Would it be all right if Lorraine and I stay longer?" Pammie wasn't home, nor did she answer her cell. He didn't even consider calling Lorraine-Lorr-Or so left two identical messages for Pammie, one at home and one on her cell. Why not, though it was a particularly busy workweek, so they might be on their own some of the time. Then he shaved and showered and thought about taking Tisha dancing tonight at Dreams. Since they'd danced in their South Beach hotel room and he felt, *I can do this,* and Tisha said, "Just you and me, Richard," he'd been building it up in his mind into who knew what? What if someone insulted him? What if they insulted Tisha after they saw him dance? If white guys couldn't jump, could they boogie? Was there a dancing gene? A gene for rhythm? Would he be the only sodden white log in a grooving sea? Sometimes he hoped to be the only white face, sometimes the prospect scared him half to death. *Idea.* Convince C&M to develop a product he could market as *Dance like a Black Man.* Didn't matter what it was, he'd sell a million units a week.

Richie stepped out of the shower, toweled off, slipped into new silk boxers—he needed to feel sexy tonight—then ran his fingers through his hair. Oh my god. He'd forgotten to wash out the Pantene. *Gordon, you are such a* yutz. He reentered the shower and rinsed his hair. Then he dried off a second time and laid out the club clothes Tisha had picked out. Lapel-less Italian-cut black suit, lavender wide-collared shirt, some sort of exotic leather boots with two-inch heels. He'd understood everything else, but why the heels? "Wait," she'd said, "until you see what I'm wearing."

And wait he would because when he pulled up in front of her house at nine-fifteen and let himself in, Jada popped out of the bedroom to say Momma wouldn't be ready for at least an hour, why didn't he pick up a bucket at the Colonel's if he was hungry? Then she grinned.

"You look *nice,* Richie."

"Really?"

"And extra biscuits, please."

He drove to the KFC six blocks away. He didn't know what it was about African Americans and fried chicken. He didn't know if he was allowed to ask such a question or if it was a thought he needed to attribute to the voice in his head, the mouth-piece of four hundred years of cultural prejudice, but in fact he believed it was his own question, the innocent inquiry of a white male very much in love with a black woman who wanted to know what he was getting into. *Question.* Were there inno-cent questions? Just think of the shit storm that had erupted when someone, he can't even remember who, suggested that the champion's meal Tiger Woods should select after winning the Masters include watermelon and fried chicken. Maybe that was different. The image of black people, moist red flesh, and black seeds that needed to be spit set everyone's teeth on edge. Maybe if the menu had been chicken and Georgia peaches there wouldn't have been such a stink.

Now what about this? If you went into Burger King or Mc-Donald's, which he tried never to do, yes, there were black people, but the clientele, except in all-black neighborhoods, was mixed or white. (He was sure there was extensive mar-ket analysis, broken out by race, gender, age, and income if he cared to look it up.)

But blow into the Colonel almost anywhere—just then the light he'd been waiting at changed color; he crossed Mitchell and pulled into the lot—and almost everyone, regardless of the rest of the demographic, was black. Families. Teenagers. Court-ing couples. When Tisha asked him to pick up fast food, which happened maybe once a week, it was always the Colonel or a local chicken and ribs place, believe it or not, named Richie's, a few blocks farther away. Even sides at the Colonel—collards, macaroni salad, corn bread—appealed to black taste buds. Was it just marketing? Exiting his CRV and clicking the remote, which chirped twice, he reminded himself he shouldn't say "just mar-keting" because marketing had paid for his car, the ridiculous-ly expensive club clothes and boots he was wearing, and had probably even bought him his black girlfriend (would she have gone out with him if he didn't have money? he didn't like to think about that), and hence his concern with the black folks–fried chicken conundrum. *Just marketing?* Life was just marketing. Identify market segments and give them what you'd made them believe they wanted equaled success, and African Americans, perhaps because of their historically southern roots, wanted fried chicken. Or was the explanation more sinister than that? A conscious attempt—if so, by whom? The whole idea was probably crap—to create a segregated, or mostly segregated, fast food universe.

Richie stepped through the swinging glass door. Everyone, including the teenager behind the counter, the fry chef in back, the gray-haired manager, and four customer groups—the woman with peroxided cornrows, tight pink sweats, and enormous ass; three middle school boys in hoodies; the mother, father, and two little ones under three; and the thirty-something professional couple in front of him ordering eight pieces, all white meat—everyone except Richie was African American. And while he waited his turn—ten pieces, half-spicy, half-traditional, mashed potatoes, corn on the cob, six extra biscuits, their standard order—he wondered what it did to his segregated food theory that the same fast food corporation now owned Taco Bell and the Colonel, with both outlets under one roof. Who ate Taco Bell tacos anyway? Was the consolidation an attempt to bring Latinos into the Colonel? To market Taco Bell to blacks? It certainly wasn't attracting any white trade. Richie stepped to the counter in his hip black suit, and Makeesha, who had waited on him before, big sweet smile, big hair, big everything, looked up from her cash drawer, seemed to recognize him, and asked with a conspicuous smile, "Welcome to the Colonel's, may I help you?"

LaTisha's dress, shaped from something silver-blue and sparkly, swooped between her breasts nearly to her belly button, or so it seemed to Richie when she emerged from the bedroom.

She wore a matching silver-blue cap fashioned from the same sparkling cloth. Half-moons of metallic silver shadow lidded her eyes, and her day-to-day plum lipstick had been replaced by a shimmering blue gloss. From her ears hung the topaz and sterling earrings he'd given her for Valentine's Day, around her neck its matching necklace. She looked like she'd stepped out of a Jazz Age poster or perhaps as if she were a dancer in *Dream Girls*, which, she'd explained to Richie, surprised he didn't know, was where she'd copied the dress from.

"How do I look?"

Bertie said, "Like you gonna fall outta yo top."

"Fabulous," Richie offered. "Better than fabulous."

He stepped forward to kiss her, and Tisha turned sideways to receive his lips on her cheek. "Bertie," she said, "don't wait up, we gonna be late."

"It already late."

It was nearly eleven.

"You can't make no entrance," Tisha said, "if you arrive first. Jada—" Tisha half-squatted, affording Richie a pretty complete view of her breasts. "I let you stay up to see us dressed, now you mind Bertie and go to sleep."

"Yes, Momma."

Tisha and Richie stepped toward the apartment door, her hand on his forearm. "I almost forgot." She opened her purse and handed the old lady a disposable camera. "Bertie, would you?"

Bertie snapped two, one just Richie and LaTisha and one with Jada between them in her PJs. Then they were out the door and on the stairs.

"You sure you can dance in that dress and those shoes"—even in his two-inch boots she was conspicuously taller than he was, so hers must be nearly three inches—"without falling over and showing everything you got?"

"Richard." She squeezed his hand. "You watch me."

Watch he did. He couldn't take his eyes off Tisha, though at Dreams, a two-story club off Race near City Market, there was a tremendous amount to attract his eyes. After they'd waited on line and paid ten-dollar covers, they entered a long dark hall that led to the bar, which in turn opened onto a large dance floor with elevated DJ tables in the far corner. Open staircases on both sides ascended to a balcony with a second bar and a smaller dance floor. After glancing upstairs, Tisha said, "Let's stay down here."

Richie purchased drinks: double scotch rocks and Tisha's favorite, rum and coke. The packed bar and dance floor vibrated with dancers of every size, shape, shade, age, and style of dress from sweats, sneakers, and do-rags (and what were those hairnet things called?) to men in ties and suits nicer than his own. Most of the crowd appeared to be in their twenties—"Dreams twenty-one and older," she'd explained, "and nice"—though there were couples in their thirties and single guys even older than that. Everywhere Richie's eyes fell on good-looking women, including two white girls on the other side of the bar, a long, straight-haired blonde and her friend, a brunette with a silver cross between pushed-up breasts. He couldn't help thinking, or was he hearing that nasty voice again—*We know what they're here for. Black dick*—a particularly ugly and self-incriminating thought because if that's what they were here for, what about you? Chewing the cubes of the scotch he'd chugged, Richie thought, *Good luck, girls, and you shouldn't have any trouble finding it* because there were black men everywhere, small, large, and larger. As far as he could tell, he was the only white male at Dreams.

"Richard," Tisha said, "let's dance. And don't let no one cut in."

She led him from the bar toward the dance floor, twining their fingers. Her dress fell loosely past her breasts but clung more tightly to her ass, as if she'd designed it for a figure more up and down than her own. He followed her shimmering silver-blue shape—the hem stopped several inches above the bend of her knees, the rear neckline exposed the wings of her shoulder blades—and realized he'd never been anywhere with so many black people—okay, there were two white girls too—and felt a stampede of pleasure. Tisha led him through the gyrating bodies, which slid out of their way like assassins in a video game. In the sweaty center of the floor she put her lips to his ears. "All right, Richard, show these niggers what you got."

Did his eyes pop like flashbulbs? Hands flat on her thighs, Tisha shimmy-shook, shimmy-shook, and the top of her breasts, how they wobbled. For a moment Richie couldn't move at all. Who was taking the bigger risk? She'd brought him into her world, so clearly she was, but no one would beat the crap out of Tisha. Just as her silver-shadowed eyes formed the question, *What's wrong?* he decided. This is just the physical manifestation of the emotional risk we take every day. He could feel the beat grinding in his head and legs, his groin, his arms, his big Jew nose, and shimmy-shook against her shimmy-shaking hip. Slipping behind her, he felt her push back against him, her bottom against his front, and wondered, *Can you do that in public?* He glanced around at all the gyrating, sweaty black folk—*they even smell different!* the voice cried, but they didn't; *they* smelled like Tisha, familiar and sweet—and saw that no one in the strobe-lit crowd, which sang as it danced—he'd never heard the song before, but they seemed to know the words—seemed either to care or notice that Tisha was grinding her hip against his groin or that the groin and hip in question were different colors beneath their insubstantial coverings, except for one short plump girl with straightened hair teased into a foot-high beehive, dancing several bodies away. She turned and shouted, smiling, *"Girlfriend,* how you been?"

When the song ended the short, big-butted girl and her beautiful, light-skinned friend, who wore strange yellow sunglasses, which made her eyes look like compound insect eyes, slid over to be introduced.

"Saundra," Tisha shouted over the beginning of the next tune. "Raelene, this my good friend Richard."

"Nice to meet you," Richie said.

Saundra kept her attention on Tisha. "Haven't seen *you* here in a long time."

Tisha answered something he couldn't hear, his attention distracted by Raelene the Insect Girl, who seemed to be checking him out.

Laughing, Saundra said, "That's white, girl."

No, Richie decided, it must have been, "That's *right*, girl."

After a moment Tisha's two friends moved off, and unless he was dreaming, Raelene trailed her fingers against his. Richie pulled Tisha close and danced as if it were a slow song, though it wasn't, so everyone would know she was his.

Tisha moved her mouth to his ear. "They both in my nursing program. That Raelene, she's a snake."

"With those glasses she looks more like a bug."

"I seen her looking right at you."

He kissed Tisha's buttery lips. "I've only got bug eyes for you."

"That the rightest thing to say."

Every time the music shifted or stopped, Tisha's friends would stop by to talk. Richie smiled but didn't try to join in. *How's it going?* was as much as anyone expected from the white guy. But they all smiled, and they were all female. Either Tisha didn't know any men, which seemed unlikely, or the men were less eager to make his acquaintance. When two women wearing the same red dress stopped to say hello then slid away, Tisha said, "Hey, Richard, how you doing?"

"I feel checked out, like the new Harry Potter book."

"You like it?"

He nodded and squeezed her bottom through her dress.

When the song ended, the red dress women dragged Tisha off the dance floor to the ladies' room. Richie tried to decide which need was most urgent, booze in or pee out? Then Saundra and Insect Girl appeared at his side. Saundra, who couldn't have been more than five-two though her hair went up another foot, began to bounce her medicine ball booty off his thigh, not so much suggestively, he thought, but to see what he'd do. Pressed to defend the rhythmic honor of the Semitic and Caucasian races and Tisha's honor too—he wouldn't want word to get out her flake boyfriend couldn't dance—he scooched down behind Saundra, knees bent like a limbo dancer. What he was getting down to and partially under, however, was Saundra's big round butt, which she banged against his crotch as if ringing a dinner bell. Next thing he knew, Insect Girl, whose name, Raelene, popped back into his head as the fronts of her long, long, long yellow legs, her smooth belly, and the tips of her breasts slipped underneath him, propping up his back, her hand wrapped around his chest for balance. For two, five, eight, long beats the three of them danced, six legs, four breasts, big trouble.

When the rhythm changed, they separated, air again coursing between their dancing limbs.

"*All right*," said Raelene, red, blue, and yellow lights reflecting in her compound lenses. "Very much all right."

"Pretty fly." Saundra laughed. "For a white guy."

Richie floated high above the dream of blackness, *Pretty fly for a white guy!* until he noticed Tisha a few feet off, looking angry.

"Hey, baby." He pushed through the sea of dancers.

"Don't, 'Hey, baby' me." She knocked his hand away. "Why I find you Oreo-ing with those nasty hos?"

He'd thought *Oreo* meant someone who looked black but was white inside.

"You shame me, Richard."

"We were just dancing."

Tisha's silver-lidded eyes, which had swollen double, shrank back to normal size. "We just playing. Saundra, Raelene?" The girls were at his side again. "What you think of my man?"

Saundra said, "Had you going." She bumped hips.

"Had *you* going," Richie answered. "Who wants a drink?"

They all did, and he climbed to the balcony bar.

"Why look here," a voice said.

Before Richie turned around, he knew it was Reece, who sat, legs splayed beneath a table overlooking the dance floor. He wore red warm-ups, two chains that may or may not have been gold, and tinted glasses over which he peered. Beside him sat a fine-featured, shorter, and much darker man wearing a suit much like Richie's, but he also wore a tie. Richie guessed the stranger was Reece's age, twenty-five or twenty-six, but closer to Richie's height; if anything, he was shorter, with chin-length dreads fringing his narrow face.

Standing with the insouciant grace he managed to impart to every movement, even those not normally larded with irony, Reece said, "My man Byron Black, this here Richard Gordon, Tish's new mister."

Byron stood and shook Richie's hand, leaning into him for an interrogative shoulder bump.

Reece said, "Bet you didn't know they more black people named White than Black. My man Byron the exception."

Mister Black fought a grin.

"That so?" Richie answered.

"Think I'm lying?"

I think you're lying about Pleasant Street. "Why would I think that?"

If Reece intuited Richie's meaning, he ignored it. He asked, "How you think that happened?"

Richie didn't answer, certain Reece would enlighten him.

"White muthafuckers think they funny give us their names. Let me axe you something else. You think black men like being called 'Mister White?'" Reece edged his glasses down his narrow, almost white nose and peered over them at Richie. "You think that's funny?"

Richie glanced toward Byron Black to see if he thought it was funny. Below them, at the corner of the dance floor, the DJ was cueing up "Gangsta, Gangsta" by NWA.

"It may be one of the great ironies of American history that so many black people are named White, but no, I don't think it's funny."

"Well, I think it funny as shit."

Reece and Byron slapped hands.

"I'll tell you something else," Reece said. "Black men *do not like it*, and they would change they names to something more suitable, like Mister Black here or Mister *Rufus*. You know why they don't?" Reece spread his large, pale palms. "Because you have to stand before a judge, and you *know* he going to be white too, and pay your money to one white man to get rid of a name some other white man gave you."

"Or," Richie said, "you can just find somebody else's name you like better and use it."

"Well, now." Reece looped his long arm around Richie's shoulder. "That wouldn't be legal."

Richie pushed Reece's arm away. "Or *Pleasant*."

"Let me tell you one more thing," Reece said, "then you best be gone 'cause Tish be wondering where you are. And I know, that girl gets jealous. Black men don't appreciate looking like white men either, 'cause some white man raped some sistah—"

Possibilities other than rape entered Richie's mind.

"—but there ain't no judge can undo that crime no matter how much you pay, unless you that twisted bitch, Michael Jackson, who thinks lightening up makes you white."

"*Reece*," Byron Black said.

"But hey," Reece continued, "some sistahs like they men light. I mean, look at you and me and tell me our girl Tisha—"

"*Reece*." Byron pushed Reece away then stepped between them. "Enough."

Richie glared at Reece, who slowly flexed his long neck and arms the way a horse ripples its skin to shoo a fly. Then he squared his shoulders and pushed his glasses up his nose. Richie wondered if Reece was trying to goad him into starting a fight? Like that was ever going to happen, the one white guy for miles around. But he had a feeling he wasn't finished with Reece and turned his back on the image of the much smaller Mister Black standing between them. *Fuck him*, Richie thought, then walked slowly, with dignity, *slowly*, across the balcony to buy drinks for himself and the girls. When he turned around, drinks in hand, Reece and Byron Black were gone.

Tisha and her friends weren't where he'd left them. He found them at a table at the far end of the club, but only Tisha and Saundra, Raelene having hooked up, they said, with other friends.

"What took so long?"

Richie glanced at Saundra then back to Tisha. "I ran into Reece."

"That must have been interesting," Saundra said. "What you all talk about?"

"Mostly Reece talked."

Saundra added, getting up, "I think I'll find Raelene. Nice to meet you, Richard." She hugged him and whispered, "Be nice to my girlfriend."

"I will." Her sweaty dress pressed against his own damp clothes. "Nice to meet you too."

He watched Saundra's big blue bottom disappear in the crowd. "Have I told you," he asked, sitting down beside Tisha, "how absolutely fabulous you look in that dress?"

"Tell me again. How fabulous do I look?"

"*So* fabulous that if I died tonight and an angel guarding the pearly gates asked the most fabulous sights of my life, I'd say Tisha in her silver-blue dress at Dreams was number two."

"What's number one?"

He leaned across the table and kissed her. "Tisha naked on the bed in South Beach. I never knew how you got naked so quickly."

"I was motivated."

He felt her hand find his knee beneath the table, felt it inch up his leg then stop.

"And now you turning on so much silver-tongue, Mister Marketer charm, I guess you don't want to tell me what all you and Reece was discussing."

"Those really are my one and two."

Her fingers continued their clandestine climb. His penis yearned toward her fingers.

"And Reece said?"

"He said, and I believe he was drunk."

"He probably high." Her fingers advanced another inch or so.

"'Black men don't like being called Mister White, although there are more black men named White than Black.'"

"Was Byron with him?"

Her fingers crept a tiny bit closer. Richie nodded.

"What else?"

"'Black men don't like looking like white men because of what it means some white man did to a black woman.'"

Her fingers brushed his penis, edged off, then climbed back on. In a frenzy of excitement heightened by fear Richie wondered what would happen to him if the hundreds of black men in the club, some of them extremely large and powerful exempla of the masculine form, knew what was happening under the table.

"I heard all that not once but twenty times. Poor Reece, never got over being light. What I want to know"—she ringed her thumb and second finger around his penis, moving them up and down and up and down—"what he said about me?"

Richie gazed into Tisha's silver-dusted eyes, while out of sight he pressed through the O of her fingers.

134

"He said, 'Some fine-looking sistahs,' and of course he meant you, 'like their men light.'"

"He said *that?*"

On the dance floor feet pounded.

"To be honest, judging from me and Reece, he might be right."

She stopped stroking him. "Reece picked *me*, not the other way around, and you and me, Richard, the way we got together was one in a million, nothing to do with color. Not everything does, that's what Reece don't see."

"I don't care," Richie said, "*what* got us together. I'm just glad we are. And that's no marketing man talking, that's me."

She gave his mister a parting squeeze. "Maybe we should be getting home."

"One last dance?"

But it took two then a third last dance before she could get him off the floor, so by the time they were walking up Race Street toward his car, it was nearly two-thirty. They crossed Twelfth and Race, headed west toward Vine, and turned north again.

They'd almost reached Thirteenth, when on their right they passed an alley that ended in a vacant lot. Richie was glad the street was still crowded—it felt safer that way—when a young black man wearing a red do-rag and pants so baggy he had to hold them up, and even holding them his boxers showed, tore past so fast he would have knocked them over if Richie hadn't put his arm out to stop Tisha. The runner cut down the alley, crossed the empty lot, and mounted a six-foot chain link fence, one sneakered foot halfway up the barrier, both hands on top, legs swinging as if he were vaulting a horse. He landed cleanly, softly, and, without breaking stride, raced on. *Looks like he's done that before*, Richie thought, then barely had time to turn and get out of the way of two white men, one soft and fat, the other tall and buff, both moving as fast as they could, which was nowhere near as fast as the black kid. The fat guy shouted something into a walkie-talkie—an off-duty cop?—as they turned into the alley, then the buff one climbed the fence with considerably less grace than the runner, who suddenly reappeared a block south of them, at the corner of Twelfth and Vine, running west. Richie got a better look this time. He looked young. He looked scared. He looked like he could run forever; the white guys didn't have a chance. And he looked, Richie thought, as the kid flashed past—red head rag, open mouth straining for breath but also grinning—as if he were enjoying this race he was so clearly winning. Then he disappeared from view.

"I hope he gets away," Tisha said.

"I wonder why they're chasing him."

"'Cause he's black."

No, Richie thought, *that's why they haven't caught him.* And he also thought, but did not say, *I wonder why they're chasing him rather than some other black kid*, realizing as he looked around that he and the chasers were the only Caucasians on the street.

He heard a faint *pop*, nothing more, a faint *pop*, a block or more away.

"Let's get out of here," he said.

Tisha nodded and took his hand. They hurried to his CRV and drove down the hill, back toward where he and Tisha dwelled.

TWELVE

Lorraine still can't believe she is flying east to rendezvous with Pammie in Florida, a state she associates with the very old and infirm. Great-Grandma Zollie, whom she remembers as a round-faced old woman with a plume of white hair, lived in Miami until her brain dissolved and the extended Gordon family brought her north to expire in a nursing home. For Lorr that's the not-so-secret truth of Florida, a place where the elderly go to lose their minds, and Pammie's far too young, but what does Lorr know? She hasn't been east of Denver in twenty-seven years. Maybe there's a new Florida. There sure as hell is a new Pammie: dueling cell phones, a prodigious career, and now, she says, a new shape. Lorr hasn't seen it yet—she hasn't seen Pammie since her last trip west, almost a year ago—but Baby Sis had the surgery she's been talking about for years.

"How's it look?" Lorr asked.

"Smaller."

But if it is a new and less buxom Pammie who will meet her plane in Fort Lauderdale, it is the same Lorr zooming east. She remains so terrified of little Richie, who, of course, is no longer little, she had to beat herself up for days to leave the heavy-duty Xanax and Ambien home. She's flying all the way to Florida to ensure Pammie will be with her when she deplanes a day later in Calhoun City, although it would have been a much easier and cheaper itinerary than the one she's paid for: San Francisco–Fort Lauderdale, Fort Lauderdale–Calhoun City, Calhoun City–San Francisco. To make this morning's flight she rose at five; fed, watered, and exercised the dogs boarded at her kennel, Woof Time (which her friend Patty will tend while she's

137

gone); drove three hours south from Redwood Valley; crossed the Golden Gate; parked her pickup in the long-term lot at SFO; and arrived at the gate with time to spare.

Even now, at thirty-six thousand feet, she remains in frantic motion. By this Lorr doesn't mean the cross-country flight but the spinning map inside her head. She's lived in Redwood Valley almost twenty-five years, arriving in time for the whole Master George scene; she can still bring to mind those slap-eyed girls Master George led around in dog collars out on Colony Drive. And she was there in 1978 too, when Jonestown was on the front page of every newspaper, and still there when the movie came out a few years later and tourists would drive up to gawk, maybe leave flowers at the big red, tin-roofed People's Temple. She knew those kids, and even now when she drives past the church, which has a different name but is otherwise unchanged, she hears their souls cry out to her. All those meaningless, stupid deaths, and she might have been one of them—she'd been invited to Guyana—but she's always loved life, sex, and drugs more than easeful death, even when she was at her lowest: after learning she and Bobby couldn't have kids and he left her for someone who could. It took years to accept what happened. She'd had no trouble conceiving little Richie; shit, it had happened easy as shaking hands, and no problems with the delivery either. One of the arguments Mom and Daddy made, may their memories be a blessing, was that she was so young she could have more kids when she arrived at a place in her life she could take care of them. But if Lorr's learned anything from her voyage on Spaceship Earth, it's that once you break certain rules, there are no controlling forces, no gravity, so to speak, so there is nothing left to work out or not work out. It's all free fall. It took years to understand that. Through her twenties and half her thirties she berated herself for being a bad person, for bringing on her own problems, before deciding what had happened was karma. You give up your kid, become his sister not his mother, and what do you expect? You can't be a mother. Another part of Lorr believes the karmic explanation is sentimental crap, a socially acceptable form of self-pity, and if there's anything Lorr hates, it's self-pity. She's known quite a few girls, more than you would think, who gave up their first babies then knocked out a gaggle later on. What about *their* karma? But when she tried with Bobby, nothing happened. It wasn't until his father, a Ukiah lawyer, paid for an infertility workup that she learned the Dalkon Shield she had inserted after Richie was born because she kept forgetting to take the Pill, which was how it all happened in the first place, had somehow gummed up the works. Talk about a punishment fitting the crime. The only child she would ever conceive was the one whose mother she wasn't, and so she stayed away and away, self-exiled in northern California. Half her life slipped past, and Mom and Daddy died while she learned to grow dope on the westward-facing slope of the land purchased with the good-bye money Bobby gave her when he left. Though he has been back from time to time because he still loves her, he says, and she has allowed him into her bed but not her heart, which she keeps locked up tighter these days than an old nun's pussy.

Oh Lorr, she thinks, *get over yourself.* It's weak, it's disgusting, it's self-pitying, still to be regretting something that happened thirty years ago, and it's not like you can magically return to eighteen and live off your genetic gifts from Hank and Marilyn. It's not quite the same at forty-eight, when the thick, dark hair is neither quite as thick nor dark, and your body is starting to sag, just a little, where it never sagged before. In fact, it is sagging in places it never had before, a development that at long last has brought her sagacity. *Oh, you're so funny.*

But attracting men has never been Lorr's problem, or maybe attracting men has always been her problem. Even at forty-eight, forty-nine a week from this Sunday, she can still turn heads, although many of those heads are gray or balding, though she had a phase not that long ago when she was sleeping with men ten and sometimes fifteen years younger, until she thought, *For shit's sake, they're almost young enough to be your son.* Several of the younger ones were notably empty-headed, and though it's true they could get it up more often, they didn't know what to do with it once they had. She didn't find the role of sex instructor a turn-on, and several of the young ones were awfully slow learners. And if she were long past settling down and marrying, at least she could show a little self-respect and stop wasting time with guys who were not only wet behind the ears but empty between them.

Lorr gazes out the window at the clouds thousands of feet below that look like conga lines of cotton balls. Lorr has known dozens of men in the biblical sense—how weird is that, equating fucking with the Five Books of Moses—probably more than a hundred if she put her mind to remembering, which she doesn't care to do. But as she hurtles eastward, riding her life's pendulum on its returning arc, she finds herself pondering one man in particular, as she has increasingly these past few years: the grown man who used to be little Richie.

Sunday morning Lorr fears she's stroking out. She sits in Pammie's kitchen, drinking her third cup of French roast, when her hands begin to shake. She often has three cups, hell, three large mugs, and she has ingested every sort of speed there is to ingest more times than she can remember, though she had the sense to stay away from crystal, so she can still think well enough to know this isn't right. It isn't right! Pammie clatters across the living room on two-inch heels. She appears in the kitchen, still click-clacking, dressed in black Chico travel pants and a silk blouse that drapes her substantial but no longer outsized bosom. She's slung a designer purse over one shoulder. When she mentioned the designer's name and Lorr didn't know it, Pammie shook her head. *You old hippie!* The purse matches her pink blouse. With her left hand Pammie drags a black carry-on over which she has draped a spring-weight wool coat.

"Let's go, the car will be here any minute."

"I can't do this." Lorr holds up her right hand, fingers spread. "Look."

"*What?*"

"My hand is shaking."

"Big fucking deal."

Later, when it's time to exit the Mercury Marquis driven by the eponymous Big Burt of Big Burt's Car Service, Pammie has to coax then berate her to get her skinny ass out of Burt's back-seat. They tip him an extra twenty, and Burt, a retired New York fireman, tall, thin, white-haired, and randy for an old guy, lugs their bags to curbside check-in.

"Sexiest sister act I seen in a long time."

"Thank you, Burt." Pammie winks. "Don't forget to pick me up Friday."

"I never forget you, do I, Pammie?" He turns to Lorraine. "Pleasure meeting you, big sis."

He returns to his Marquis, walking with an awkward hip-rolling gait; perhaps some old firefighting injury? Yes, Lorr realizes, we are sexy sisters. She doesn't believe she's ever comprehended that before, not that she's never thought of herself as sexy or conceded over the years that Pammie was too, just that she's never thought of them as *sexy sisters*. It's been so long since they spent time together, and when they lived with Mom and Daddy, may their memories be a blessing, Pammie wasn't sexy, and they didn't feel like sisters. But suddenly in middle age they are, and as they stride through the terminal, boarding passes in hand, Lorr has a vision of them as a forty-something Mod Squad, tall and dark, short and blonde, every eye on them.

It's not until they begin their final descent to the Calhoun City Regional Airport that the bright sister light winks out, and Lorr thinks again, *Holy shit, I can't do this*. She'd jump out the window if she could, she might as well, there's no air inside this plane anyway. If there were an emergency cord like there used to be on the subway, she'd yank it. Why not? She's going to be sick, her gorge has risen past the lid of her throat, and she fumbles for the airsickness bag in the seat pocket, as tears slip down her cheeks. Pammie takes her left hand in her smaller, softer, white ones, no weeding or cleaning dog runs for Baby Sis, and squeezes and keeps on squeezing until Lorr gives up searching for the puke bag and turns toward her.

"You can do this," Baby Sis says.

"For shit's sake, look at me."

Mascara streaks her cheeks, and she's pretty sure tusks of mucous hang from her nose.

"You *are* doing it."

"Tell me again what he's like?"

"Small, smart, kind of shy." Pammie's blue eyes, so like Daddy's, latch on hers. "He's going to love you."

A sob breaks from Lorr's lips, and she's only saved from further and perhaps terminal embarrassment by the arrival of the rat-faced stewardess who's been shooting her death rays the entire flight. Stopping in the aisle beside Pammie, she asks, "Is everything all right?"

Oh sure, Lorr thinks, *everything's fine, you skanky bitch*. She releases Pammie's hands and dries her face. Soon enough, the plane touches down.

Richie asked Tisha again if she wanted to come to the airport to pick up Pammie and Lorraine.

"You sure you want me?"

"Didn't I ask you?"

Tisha pursed her lips. "Nah, you just being nice."

It had been like this all morning: swirls and eddies, undercurrents of every sort. Not only were Pammie and Lorraine-Lorr-Or arriving—he couldn't think of them as his aunt and *mother!*

without freaking out—he was hosting his first seder, a decision he now regretted. And if that wasn't enough, they'd heard last night, and it was all over this morning's *Star*, that on Friday night another young black man had been killed by the C. City police, most likely, though they couldn't confirm it, the kid in the red do-rag they'd seen being chased down Twelfth toward Race. Tisha had been staring at the paper all morning. When he asked about it, she turned toward him, eyes glistening.

"I hate them so much."

"Who?"

"White cops."

He wanted to say something about power corrupting and absolute power, etc. etc., but he didn't want to upset Tisha more than she already was. It felt as if the dead man, Timothy Thomas, nineteen years old, unarmed and wanted for traffic violations, was in the living room with them, jumping the chain link fence again and again.

"I'm so sorry." He hugged her, and for a moment she clung to his shoulder.

"Why do they hate us so much?"

"I don't."

"I didn't mean you, Richard."

So maybe he hadn't wanted her to come to the airport. He already had company. For weeks Jada had been promised she could help pick up Auntie Pammie, and she was at his side in her favorite pink jumper, her hair in cornrows, as he waited outside B19. At ten after the first passenger on Delta arriving flight 315, emerged, a tall brunette somewhere on the vast plain of middle age, and Richie wondered, *Is that Lorraine?* But she swept past, commencing a discomforting array of unfamiliar faces.

"Richie." Jada tugged his hand. "Pick me up."

He bent to lift her at the precise moment Pammie and Lorraine must have emerged under the illuminated B19. So when he turned back, it was as if they'd always been there, short, blonde Pammie pulling a black bag, Lorraine, the woman who must be Lorraine, half a head taller, lean in boot-cut jeans, dark hair showing strands of gray. Her angular face was surprisingly young looking. Then her eyes met his.

"Auntie Pammie!" Jada shouted.

Pammie came toward them, grinning, and he just had time to observe there was something different about her before Jada leapt from his arms into hers. Pammie raised her lips to his ears, whispering, "Go to her, Richie."

He stepped forward and led Lorraine out of the path of other arriving passengers. They were nearly the same height and had the same slightly hooked nose, maybe even the same color hair.

"I've been crying," she said, "I never cry." She brushed tears from her cheeks. On her wrists bangles shook. "I look like shit, don't tell me I don't. Help me out," she said. "I'm dying."

In a flash he realized he hadn't touched her. Hadn't shaken her hand or kissed her cheek. He slid his arms around her shoulders, and she leaned against him.

"It's okay," he said. "Really."

Then she took his hand, which freaked him out, although he told himself it shouldn't. Joined at the palm, they walked toward Pammie and Jada.

"Jada, this is my mother. Lorraine, this is Jada."

Lorraine shook Jada's hand. "I'm so happy to meet you. And please, call me Lorr. Everyone does."

They left the gate with Lorraine still holding his hand.

Laura and Dave Manning rang the bell right at six. Laura was in her eighth month and big, really big, big-as-a-barn big. When she stepped through the doorway, her face, much rounder than in years past, seemed to glow with the alchemic joy of creating life. Her arms appeared rounder too, possibly firmer. She looked better, Richie decided, kissing her, than she ever had. She no longer resembled Dave quite as much either. Dave seemed to have added a dab or two more gray at his temples, while Laura, despite or perhaps because of her belly, which preceded her like the prow of a ship, seemed somehow to have grown younger. Dave kissed Tisha's cheek and handed her a bouquet of mixed spring flowers.

Laura said, "Would you believe I had to stop him from buying Easter lilies?"

Tisha said, "Easter's not till next week."

"Wasn't the Last Supper a seder?" Dave grinned. "So why not bring the same flowers?"

"I've read," Richie answered, "lilies symbolize rebirth. Since Passover is a spring holiday and celebrates release from slavery, sure, why not?"

Richie glanced from Tisha, whose face looked shut down, impossible to read, to Lorraine, who stood a few feet away, waiting to be introduced. Was he showing off for her, trying, twenty-five years too late, to show Mommy how smart he was?

"The reason why not," Lorraine said, "is the lily is a Christian symbol." She shook Dave's hand. "I'm Lorraine. Richie's biological mom."

She smiled at Dave then seemed to half-glance at Richie to gauge what he thought.

"Richie's told me all about you," Dave said.

"I doubt it—he hardly knows anything."

She turned to introduce herself to Laura. Richie started toward the kitchen to check on the turkey, the brisket and gefilte fish, hard-boiled eggs and boiled potatoes, all the festival food.

"Wait." Dave caught up, whispered behind his hand, "You didn't tell me Lorraine was such a fox."

Richie glanced back. Lorraine was talking to Laura and Tisha, moving her hands in front of her face. She wore black boots, black tights, a black miniskirt. "You think?"

"What planet are you from? She must be what, fifty?"

"Something like that."

"You've got Tisha. But at our house, with Laura big as she is? Sex is pretty scarce."

"You're lusting after my mother?"

"I'm just saying you must take after your dad." Dave winked. "Whoever he was."

Richie headed to the kitchen thinking, *And this is my friend?*

Jada had helped him arrange the seder table: Haggadahs, seder plate, Afikomen bag, and ceremonial goblet for Elijah the Prophet, all the trappings of faith and family, purchased two days ago at the B'nai Israel temple gift shop. It was partially his sense of all that Lorraine had relinquished when she gave him to Hank and Marilyn—all claims on him and her place in the family—that convinced him to go ahead with the seder, for it was on Passover that he'd felt most like a Jew and most like he was part of some larger family; at least he did until Hank died. Lorraine had given all that up, though he doubted if when she made the decision she knew what it would cost her. So this was his way of giving something back because from the little he knew of her, the scatteredness, the insecurity, the drug use Pammie had hinted at, the powerful whiff of sexuality Dave had picked up on, Richie very much doubted he'd be who and where he was today if he'd been raised by Lorraine. And if he were someone else—not a businessman but a hippie love child—then he never would have moved to C. City, lost his IDs, and found Tisha. Which was the other reason he'd decided to stage a seder. He thought Tisha would relate to the story of the Israelites' release from slavery, and it would help bind her to him, make her see that Jews and blacks were historically linked, oppressed brothers and sisters under the skin.

You're an idiot, he thought.

Richie sat at the head of the table with Lorraine on the right side, opposite Jada, who, as the only child, had a special part to play. Pammie sat between Jada and Laura opposite Dave, who seemed pleased to have Lorraine on his left and Tisha on his right, at the opposite end of the table from Richie. It was the first holiday meal he'd hosted, and he couldn't help remembering the Thanksgiving feast at Dave and Laura's just this fall, how much his life had changed since then and how impossible it would have been to predict this gathering five months ago.

"We'll start on page one," Richie said, "on the right side of the Haggadah, which you'd normally think of as the end."

"It's backwards!" Jada shouted.

"Hush, Jada."

"No, it's all right," Pammie said, "Passover is all about kids asking questions. Isn't that right"—she grinned—"Poppa Richie?"

"That's right. And the book's backwards because Hebrew, the language of the Jews, goes from right to left, not left to right, like English, so the book is opposite too."

"Oh," Jada said.

"I'll read the leader part, then we'll go around the table." Richie cleared his throat, remembering being the youngest child, the *grandchild!* with Hank in the leader's chair. "Welcome to our seder! Tonight we observe a most ancient festival, recalling the Egyptian bondage of the Children of Israel and their deliverance by God. The seder, which keeps alive in us the love of liberty, has a significance for all people." He glanced at Tisha. "Freedom must not be taken for granted. If any people anywhere are exploited and oppressed, then nowhere is freedom really secure. The seder expresses the need for our eternal vigilance in the struggle to preserve and advance the cause of freedom and human dignity. May God grant that freedom become the lot of all His children."

"Amen," whispered LaTisha.

"Amen," said Lorraine, sister/mother, and Pammie, his sister/aunt.

"Hallelujah, sisters and brothers!" Dave cried, grinning like the fool Richie was beginning to suspect he was. Laura elbowed him and rolled her eyes as if to say, "This is why we waited so long to have a child—I already have one."

After reciting the blessing over the first glass of wine, Richie said, "Now it's time for the first of Jada's special parts. She's going to help me wash my hands."

Jada rose, her narrow face touchingly solemn, and walked to the sideboard. She placed the blue and white hand towel on her shoulder, carried the yellow bowl to the table and placed it near Richie, then returned for the yellow pitcher. She carried the pitcher two-handed, the pale yellow crockery nearly the same shade as her skin. Peering up, she poured the cold water over Richie's hands. He made a big show of rub-a-dub-dubbing.

"Thank you."

Jada kept pouring.

Just before the bowl overflowed, he added, "That's enough."

Jada set the pitcher back on the sideboard then handed Richie the towel from her shoulder. Still no smile.

"I don't think my hands have ever been so clean." He kissed Jada's forehead and glanced down the table at Tisha, who was smiling, full lips pursed with pride. On his right Lorraine regarded him through glowing eyes.

Dave asked, "Why didn't he wash before he sat down like the rest of us?"

"Dave," Laura said, "will you please shut up?"

Everyone laughed. Then Tisha helped Jada bear away the bowl of water, and they started to retell the ancient story of the coming out from slavery into freedom.

"Why," Jada would ask later, "is this night different from all other nights?"

And the answer, Richie knew, although it wasn't in the Haggadah, and therefore wasn't what the Leader was supposed to say, was that he finally had his family around him.

THIRTEEN

Not long after the pregnant couple departs, Richie drives Jada and LaTisha home; tomorrow is a school day, after all. Lorr and Pammie finish clearing the seder table then pour themselves fresh glasses of wine, and not that disgusting Manischewitz treacle either, settling in on the leather couch, which has been returned to its customary position overlooking the train tracks running west toward C. City, Kansas, and the prairies beyond.

"Well?" Pammie asks.

"Well, what?"

"Don't give me that."

Pammie cuts her eyes and takes a substantial slug of her wine. Lorr sips. There's no way she can keep up with Baby Sis. "Jada," she begins, "is a really cute kid."

"But if Daddy's up there, looking down—"

Or up, Lorr thinks.

"—he's shitting his pants about now."

"Kinda sweet to think so."

The sisters share a laugh. Lorr asks, "Now what?"

"You tell Richie the shameful secrets you came all this way to tell him."

Lorr suddenly feels in desperate need of a cigarette though she hasn't smoked in years. "When do I do that?"

Pammie pushes beautifully layered blonde hair back from her forehead, now as clear of blemishes as it was once peppery red. Lorr is reminded just how blue Pammie's eyes are, Daddy's eyes, and how pale her skin, like Mom's. What a shame she never had kids—she'd be so much happier.

"We're here till Friday, for Chrissakes, you'll find the right time."

"Do you have a cigarette?"

"You quit."

"I'm un-quitting while we're here."

Pammie pauses, trying to decide, Lorr believes, if it's any of her damn business anyway.

"Maybe," Pammie says, "we should walk to one of those nice little bars and buy a pack."

Pammie leaves a note. They take the extra key and ride the elevator down to the deserted lobby then strike out for the stretch of bars on Charlotte Street, a few blocks away, to see where this will lead them.

Richie turned left on J. C. Nichols Highway, planning to pick up Troost, which is just east of Prendergast. This revised route, which by now he knew well enough to follow without thought, established how long he'd known Tisha: long enough to devise a shortcut, not long enough to convince her to move in with him. Normally Jada would be bubbling about something or telling herself a story, but she had dropped off almost as soon as he'd started the engine and now lay facedown across the backseat clutching the silver dollars he'd given her for the Afikomen. He wasn't sure what Tisha thought about that singularly odd expression of Jewish culture: bribing a child to return a ceremonial matzo she'd been encouraged to steal. For that matter he didn't know what Tisha thought about the entire event. She'd smiled a great deal, but he'd learned long ago Tisha's smile was her GET OUT OF JAIL card. She praised the unfamiliar foods, helped serve and clear (all the women had, even Laura). But what LaTisha really felt about the seder and Lorraine's startling appearance in their life, he couldn't guess. It wasn't only that they hadn't discussed it. He sensed a new and terrifying distance yawning between them.

She said, "Must be nice to see your mom again."

Hers had died six months before she moved to C. City.

"I don't think of her that way."

"I'd give anything to show Jada to my momma."

"I was glad," he said after a moment's thought, "she could meet Lorraine."

"It's not the same, Richard."

"Of course not."

"I'm thinking I'll attend those hearings tomorrow."

Should he offer to go with her? There was quite a difference between celebrating a seder and protesting a shooting, but it could be argued protesting wasn't, or shouldn't be, exclusively a black issue, even if the only people getting shot were black. Then he considered his schedule—the official launch was Wednesday—and knew he wouldn't be anywhere tomorrow except his office. And when he did leave, he was committed to dinner with Lorraine and Pammie.

"I wish I could come with you."

"I know how busy you are."

They lapsed into silence.

Carrying Jada, who still clutched her Susan B. Anthony dollars, Richie followed Tisha up the stairs. While she fitted the first then the second key into her locks, he felt apartment A's bass in his gut. No home cooking smells tonight, just the faint stench of the stairwell. Then the door swung open, and he followed Tisha, crossed the living room, and set Jada down in the bedroom. The silver dollars he pried from her palm felt warm.

"*Mine*," she murmured.

"I'll put them on your dresser."

Jada lay on her back, only her eyes moving. Richie removed her Mary Jane's and sweater, sat her up, and hauled her dress over her head. He found the pink footsie PJs under her pillow, where Tisha placed them each morning, and helped Jada into them.

"Now run and pee."

"I don't have to."

"And brush your teeth." He set her on the floor, patted her skinny rump through its covering of fuzzy PJs. "And kiss Momma good night."

Richie waited; Tisha must be in the living room, tidying, or checking her schedule for tomorrow. He glanced around: Jada's new little bed beside theirs; Tisha's collection of hats hanging off her lamps; the spicy tang of her patchouli perfume. Jada returned, and he lifted her into bed.

"Night-night, Jada-kins." He kissed her cheek.

"Were Jews really slaves?"

"A long time ago."

"Chains and everything?"

He nodded, and Jada scrunched up her nose.

"White people owned them?"

"Some say the Egyptians were black."

"What you say?"

"Slavery is wrong. That's why God and President Lincoln freed the slaves."

"Yes, but." Once Jada seized a subject, she was a terrier with a bone. "What color do *you* think?"

"Brown."

"Like me?"

"Uh-huh"

"You coulda been my slave?"

"That's right."

"I woulda freed you, Richie."

"I love you, Jada."

"I love you too."

He kissed her and started for the door.

"And no ten plagues!" she shouted.

Tisha was waiting just outside the bedroom.

"How much did you hear?"

Tisha still wore her sweater. "I heard it all."

"They say Cleopatra was black, and she had slaves. So, my people *could've* been slaves to yours."

"It's been a long time, Richard, since black people had slaves."

"Except for you. I'm your love slave."

"Not tonight." She brushed her lips against his and led him to the apartment door. "Thanks for putting Jada to bed. She really does love you."

"What about her mother?"

Tisha pressed her lips to his again. "She does too. I'll call tomorrow."

He didn't hear from her all morning. After lunch he began on-site back-to-back-to-back meetings and didn't return to his office until almost four and found himself totally slammed: supplementary placement data; the ongoing distribution snafu in Cincinnati; preliminary analyses of ads running in the Pittsburgh, Minneapolis, and Jacksonville markets. By the time he emerged from under a shit-swirl of work, it was past seven. He phoned Pammie to announce he was on his way then tried Tisha's apartment but reached her machine. He roared home taking the curves as if he were driving Formula One. When he pushed through his apartment door, Lorraine and Pammie were sprawled on the couch, and the apartment stank of smoke.

"Sorry I'm late. Is something burning?"

"Lorr and I were burning butts, sort of old times' sake—"

"Though we were never bad girls together. Pammie was Goody Two Shoes."

Pammie turned on her. "You had Bad Girl all locked up. So it was either be good or be dead. I chose life."

"*I* chose life. You chose virginity. Biggest chest in Sheepshead Bay High, seventy to seventy-four, and she graduates a virgin."

"I didn't want to sleep with anyone you'd slept with, and since you'd slept with, like, the entire school—"

"Bitch," Lorraine said. "What will Richie think?"

"Whatever you tell him." She grinned and stood, rotating forty-five degrees each way, like a runway model. "What do you think of the new me?"

That's what's different.

"Look," Lorr said, "he's blushing."

"Nice," he managed. "Very nice—"

"Tits," Lorr said, and she and Pammie cracked up.

"I think," Richie said, "I'm going to change." He started toward his bedroom. "Did Tisha call?"

His big sisters? His aunt and mother? What trumped what? Nature or nurture? Biology or experience? They glanced toward each other, and a feminine force field crackled between them.

"Was she supposed to?" Pammie asked.

"She usually does."

On Lorraine's lean face a blossoming of . . . *motherly concern?* "I'm afraid not."

Richie said, "Save me some of that scotch."

In his bedroom he removed and hung his jacket and tie then dialed Tisha. Her familiar message, "Jada or Tisha. Pe-eace." Where could she be so late, and who was watching Jada? He wished again he'd bought her that cell phone, but she'd said no. He scrolled through the contacts on his, hoping he'd remembered to add Bertie to the dialer and discovered he had.

"Auntie Bertie," he said when she answered. "This is Tisha's boyfriend, Richard. Is she there?"

"No, child, but Jada right beside me."

After a moment Jada came on. "Hey, Richie."

"Hey. Are you doing everything Auntie Bertie tells you?"

"Yes. When's Momma coming?"

"Soon."

"Are you coming tonight?"

"I can't. I have to take Lorraine and Auntie Pammie out to dinner."

"Okay, bye."

She hung up. After a moment Richie called back. "Auntie Bertie, do you have any idea where Tisha is?"

"They was something on the TV 'bout that hearing. I tole her don't go, what good it gonna do?" Bertie sighed, whether in critique of Tisha or hearings he couldn't tell.

"Will you ask Tisha to call when she comes for Jada?"

Bertie snorted, or something like a snort, he couldn't quite distinguish.

Partly as a way to feel closer to Tisha, he drove Pam and Lorraine to Yip's Café. How long ago that first date seemed. He let the women out at the corner, across from the fountain, and circled to park in one of the Plaza's underground garages. He'd acquired this dropping off behavior from Hank: drop your womenfolk so they didn't have to walk, as if women's legs weren't designed for perambulation. Walking back toward the restaurant, he dialed Tisha's apartment. No answer. A moment later he came upon Lorraine and Pammie in front of Yip's locked door. *Closed Mondays.* He should have known. In fact, he did know—he just couldn't find what he knew.

"Now what?" Pammie demanded.

"They're a couple of Indians up the street. Do you eat Indian?"

"I prefer cowboys. What about you, Lorr?"

They chose Anwar India, the nicer of the restaurants located two doors apart, owned by the same family. Richie ordered, and maybe he was still showing off for Lorraine. He'd been eating Indian food for a decade or more, starting at the curry shops on Sixth Street in the Village, and he knew what he was about. This was his *mother*, after all, though he didn't know her, and his sister slash aunt, whom he didn't really know either, though he'd known her his entire life. How could he, when every moment they'd spent together was a lie? He ordered three pakoras

155

to begin. Raita and dal, yellow and brown, three kinds of pickle, three chutneys: Major Gray's, tomato, and mango. Three different breads: paratha, naan, aloo paratha. Three main dishes: rogan josh, chicken tikka masala, prawn saag, and three kinds of rice. As if he'd conjured a kinky Noah's Ark of a feast, the dishes came out three by three. He ordered three Tiger beers, and he would have ordered more; he would have ordered beer and three glasses of wine too, but Pammie tapped his arm: *Enough.*

He ordered for the anticipatory pleasure of watching the women eat. Not kosher for Passover but still a feast. He ordered so he wouldn't have to speak. He ordered because he could afford to, and he wanted Lorraine, especially, to grasp that. And he ordered because he knew how to and because he was scared. It was eight-thirty, and he still hadn't heard from Tisha.

Plates came and departed, more plates. The Gordon family ate. The Gordon three chowed down, but mostly, he realized, after some time had passed, he ate while the women drank and watched.

Lorraine said, "I guess you missed lunch today."

He swallowed then shook his head.

"Daddy," Pammie said, "could really eat too. He never gained weight either."

Richie wedged up the last smear of forest green saag gravy on a square of paratha. An armada of empty hull-shaped serving dishes sailed away from his side of the table through a sea of scattered rice pulao. He felt and found Lorraine's eyes: brown but not as deeply brown as his own. Hers were ringed in black liner. He wondered what she was looking for in his, and what this was like for her. He hadn't given that much thought, any thought really; he'd been too caught up in what it felt like to him, and how she could have done this to him, how heartless, and yadda, yadda, yadda, and so on and so forth, that he hadn't allowed himself to consider what it must be like for her. She hadn't had any other kids, at least that he knew of, but what did he know about her anyway? It all pressed in on him, this sense she'd had a life he knew nothing about, that this attractive woman sitting in front of him, raven hair shot with gray, neurotic and half-drunk much of the time he'd known her, really and truly was his mother, not just his *biological mom*. He opened his mouth to speak, and everything that was crowding in on him and the unconscionable, the truly extraordinary amount of distress-eating food he'd crammed through his piehole, the three pickles and chutneys, three rich sauces with three different animal proteins sopped up with three different kinds of bread and drizzled over three distinct rice preparations, it all caught up with him, and instead of *Lorraine, thanks for coming, I want to hear about your life*, a riotous belch escaped him, a boom so loud and redolent of South Asia heads turned at tables all around the dining room, and Richie turned a brighter shade of pink than the remaining stripe of tikka masala gravy on his plate.

"Jesus," Pammie said, "I thought I raised you better than that."

He mumbled an apology. A moment later the waitress stopped by to ask if they required anything else.

"Just the bill."

And just like that, the moment to say anything real to Lorraine, slipped past.

When the phone rang in the dark, Richie fumbled for the receiver.

"Sorry it's so late."

"Where are you?"

"My eyes are burning from tear gas. I was shot—"

"Omigod!"

"—beanbag pellets."

The red clock numerals glowed like eyes: 12:57. "Are you all right?"

"After City Hall, and there were hundreds of us, Richard, and

Mrs. Leisure, that's T. Thomas's mother, said, 'You took a part of my life from me, I demand to know why!' and they couldn't say nothing, what could they say? Most of the protestors, and soon there was even more, young girls with strollers, old folks, all kinds of people, we marched to police headquarters, you know, on Locust, chanting, 'Stop the killing. No justice, no peace, No justice, no peace!' shouting in the cops' faces. Cops on horseback, cops in helmets carrying those big black shields. I shoulda gone home, I know I shoulda 'count of Jada, but I was mad, Richard, if you coulda heard Mrs. Leisure talk about her son, and his new baby, how much dignity she had and how T. Thomas did nothing except drive without a license, that's all he did, and run away. If you a young black man, you'da run too—"

"I would."

"If it had been Jada, and someone shot her?"

"Don't even say that."

"Around midnight, and I shoulda went home before, I know, some gangstas starting chucking rocks, and one went *Bam*, through the glass door. The police started firing tear gas and beanbags, and we started running."

"Where are you?" *Fearing she was going to say jail.*

"Still downtown."

"I'll be right there."

He dressed, exited his bedroom, and headed for the door. In the animate dark he came upon Lorraine, smoking, on the leather couch. Above the black T-shirt she seemed to use for a nightgown, her face looked ghostly white, illumined by the cigarette's glowing end. On the tracks below them, approaching from the west, a long and mournful train whistle blew, once and then again.

"What the hell was that?" Lorraine asked.

"The one a.m. train, you get used to it."

Lorraine's eyebrows rose, as if to say, *I don't think so.*

Richie said, "I have to get Tisha."

"Would you like company?"

He shook his head, mindful she hadn't asked where or why, and he thanked her silently for her discretion. "Tomorrow." He bent, trying to recall his schedule. "Wednesday the latest, let's have dinner and talk, just the two of us."

"It doesn't have to be dinner."

He considered his performance at Anwar India. "But it does need to be a real conversation."

"I'd like that," she said.

The streets near police headquarters appeared, but did not feel, deserted. Instead, Richie sensed a desperate energy wraithing past the darkened storefronts, and the hair on the back of his neck rose like fur. Maybe he was imagining it, terrifying himself as he used to do in bed, his door half-open because he was afraid of the dark. But look! The streetlights' glow coming through Mom and Daddy's curtains. Ghosts! When he pulled up and spotted Tisha leaning against the corner of a building, her face crisscrossed in shadow, he was relieved to find her where she said she'd be and to discover she wasn't alone. The other figures, both male judging from their size and shape, one tall, one short, hoodies cinched around their faces, hurried off when he honked.

"Thanks," she said, climbing in.

"Your friends need a ride?"

"They just keeping me company till you came."

He leaned close to kiss her. She kissed him back, harder than he expected, her tongue compelled by some force he didn't understand to grapple with his own. Then she bit him. He bit her back, and she tasted like tears, or tear gas, a taste both metallic and rank. He broke off, murmuring, "I was so worried about you."

"Them motherfuckers wouldn't listen."

Which motherfuckers?

"Please, Richard, take me home."

Her cheeks and eyes looked swollen, as if she'd been punched. He glanced at the dash, 1:29, and calculated what time he'd have to wake up to get home, grab his things, and still be at work by eight.

She said, "I need to be there for Jada."

Richie put the CRV in gear and drove east to Brooklyn Avenue, a familiar name in a strange place, and turned south toward Swope Park and Tisha's part of town.

Reece waited out of sight with Byron until the silver CRV disappeared. Tisha's Mister had a sweet ride, no lie. Even before he got out the County, Granny Grace at long last paying his bail, he'd been hearing Tish not only found herself a white dude but a rich one, like there any other kind. Point of fact, Reece *knew* other kinds. His own father, whose name he did not care to admit he remembered, was several other kinds all by himself: poor, trash, deceased, and no-account, the greenest shoot of a Kentucky clan that had ridden north and west in a Cracker version of the Second Passage when the coal ran out or maybe there was no young cousins left to fuck. The Masons despised black folk, including their daughter-in-law and grandson, whom they barely acknowledged before the wreck and certainly not after.

"Dude must really dig her," Little B opined. "Come down here so late."

"His first taste of black pussy, now he's hooked."

"Reece, you gross."

They walked up Race Street, named originally, Reece had read, for some nineteenth-century contest to see which settler could grab the most land from the Indians in the new territory. 'Course, meanings changed over time, and it would be Race they were walking up this night of all nights, headed for Byron's place. Irony number one, the meaning of race. Irony number two, back in the day the local version of the Underground Railroad ran from Missouri, a slave state, across the border into the Kansas Territory, just like back east, it was across the Ohio River. Today, if the black man wanted to escape the segregation and racial profiling of C. City, M.O., he still had to get across the Kansas line, out into those lily-white suburbs. Some shit don't change.

"Huh," Reece said.

"What?" B asked.

Reece shook his head. Since his release, he'd been staying with friends, mostly B, trying to make plans for his own escape. He'd fucked-up big time. His Legal Aid lawyer, and he was lucky to have her, Caroline Something-Something, still good-looking though she must be forty, smart as all fuck and he wouldn't mind that, and didn't think she would either, but he'd been nothing but respectful, Reece Q. Woodson, nobody's fool but his own. Caroline Something-Something hoped to plead him down to twelve to eighteen months, less time served. Nothing like the dime the cops said they was going to drop on him when he was arrested for receiving stolen goods, a pickup full of TVs, but only if he stayed clean as a baby's sweet-smelling bottom until she did the pleading.

When pressed for connections, he'd given them an old friend he'd heard was dead and another doing a double-dime in the Jeff City super-max. That was no place Reece ever intended to see from the inside. Caroline Something-Something, long legs, tough smile, white freckly face, said he still young and smart enough she could hook him up with serious job training when he got out, maybe he could even take college courses inside, said she knew that lawyer Dawson who hired Malik Farmer, the brother who became an attorney after doing eighteen for murder; with a mouth and mind like his, maybe Reece could end up a lawyer too. It didn't hurt Caroline Something-Something's rosy predictions that no charges had ever been filed about those damn IDs he'd forgotten he had. But now with this shit about Pleasant Street blowing up, that could change. Damn, what a sorry-looking mutt Richard A. Gordon turned out to be. Who woulda thought they'd end up meeting and he'd be boning Tish? Not Reece, when he found the plastic sheath of IDs walking up Main, must be five years ago. He woulda tossed it except for the Franklin folded into the first sleeve, emergency money, he guessed, for *Richard A. Gordon*. High times for twenty-year-old Reece Q. Woodson, whose first-known forebear was Burrell Quarles, who Granny told him had been freed long before the Civil War. In whose honor Reece and all the family's men stretching back to slave days received the middle initial *Q*, which the whole time he was coming up his friends had said stood for Queer, but that was bullshit.

Reece thought about the scene at City Hall, all the angry niggers climbing on tables, the fear, yes, *The Fear*, on the white faces, even Police Chief Dog Snout Stryker, how the crowd only let the black councilwoman speak, demanding to know why. Why the cop shot him? *Why?* Everybody knew. Possession of a black face a shooting crime in C. City, M.O. No way that pig Bug would have used deadly force against an unarmed white man.

At the end of the meeting, when white Councilman Manzetti stood up, some were shouting, "Let him talk, Let him talk!" others trying to shout him down, but Reece cried "Listen!" in his deep speaker's voice, and the crowd hushed. Manzetti's eyes met Reece's across the room, and the councilman nodded, said he'd heard from *individuals* he trusted and believed should know, that Officer Bug mistakenly believed T. Thomas was reaching in his pants for a pistol and that's why he fired.

No, the brother just pulling up his trow and that's why Officer Bug murdered him, black man pulling up his motherfuckin pants.

"Reece, you hungry?"

Reece glanced at Little B, his best friend since fourth grade. B sold stereos nine to five at Best Buy, ran a DJ business on weekends. Reece had his own very different experience selling high-fidelity equipment.

"Nah."

A white-faced lie, but Reece was weary of letting Little B feed him. They'd come to the rally together. B still tried to keep things real, even though he wore a shirt and tie five days a week. Tish they'd encountered at City Hall. Surprised to see her too, but a great deal surprised him about Tish. How good she looked. How grown-up now, almost a nurse. How much, and he would never admit this to Tish or B, how much he'd missed her the months he spent in the County.

They veered onto B's dark street; the streetlights were burned out again. They always burned out east of Troost but never on white streets. Flake muthafuckers be calling up right away. *Send us new fucking bulbs. And I mean now!* On B's street it black as a monkey ass, the kind of dark some gangsta sneak up and shoot you, you never see him.

"I'm missing that march tomorrow," B said. "Got to work."

"Be some serious shit."

"I believe so." From inside his hoodie Byron fished the heavy chain and keys that hung down his chest. He opened three locks and stepped through. "Don't be no hero, Reece."

"Not me."

Little B triple-locked the door from the inside, and they headed up to his two small rooms.

FOURTEEN

In the morning, in the dark, they made quick and urgent love. Richie wasn't sure how they got started. One moment he was asleep, the next Tisha was whipping her head side to side, thrusting up at him while pulling him deeper inside. When they finished, gasping, she pushed him aside and hurried to the bathroom, a towel wrapped about her bottom so she wouldn't leak all over the floor. He glanced at the clock then closed his eyes. By the time Tisha returned, the bedroom was brightening enough to discern her shape but not her features. They'd come to bed so late his eyes felt as if they were filled with sand, as if he hadn't slept at all, but at the same time he felt too exhausted to wake up, consciousness this Tuesday morning a confused and confusing blur.

"Where did *that* come from?" he whispered to her shoulder.

"One moment, Richard, I was sound asleep. I rolled over, bumped this lovely *something*. Next thing I know . . ."

"Tisha"—he kissed the hollow at the back of her neck—"you fucked me awake."

"Guess I did." She sat up. "Now I need to see my baby."

Richie persuaded her to wait until six-fifteen. No one answered the first knock, and they stood on the cold porch wondering what to do, while at the eastern end of the street the sky lightened. Tisha knocked again with the flat of her fist; after a moment they heard movement. Then the door heaved inward, its security chain still fastened, revealing a slice of Bertie's pie-round face.

"Huh." She un-slid the chain. From the poles of her back a nightgown hung like a tent.

"I'm sorry, Auntie," Tisha said.

"Child still asleep." Bertie glared at Richie as if these nonsensical goings-on were his fault. "Come back later."

Tisha glanced toward him, apparently forgetting that nothing he could do or say would positively influence Bertie. "I'm sorry, Auntie, the demonstration—"

"Demon-*stration*." Her big eyes rounded. "Huh. Jada *your* child. If'n you don't care about her rest, I 'pose I don't neither."

Tisha stepped around Bertie and hurried down the hall. Richie had never been past where he now stood. "That poor child."

In a moment Tisha reappeared carrying Jada. "Richard, will you get her things?"

"*I'll* get 'em." Bertie started down the corridor glowing, in her white nightgown, like an angry ghost. She returned carrying Stripes, Jada's pink blankie, and a shopping bag of clothes. "*Demonstration?* I was here when C. City burned after they killed the Reverend Doctor King. I *know* 'bout demonstrations."

Safe at Tisha's, they lay down on either side of Jada, who slumbered on. This was unlike her, Richie thought, and he wondered how late she'd been up, and how worried about her mother? Tisha glanced at him across the pillows and Jada's small body in between.

"There's a march today. I'm gonna call in sick to Good Sam."

"Should you do that?" She was always complaining the head training nurse didn't like her.

"I *have* to."

"I'm stuck in meetings all day. Tomorrow's the launch."

"How's that going?"

He considered telling her about the distribution problems in Ohio and Kentucky and Horstmeyer's disturbing questions at lunch. "There's no way I can be at the demonstration."

She scooted toward him, bumping Jada, who murmured words wrapped in sleep. Tisha's lips compressed briefly against his, then she moved back to her own side of Jada. "That's all right, the only whites is gonna be cops."

"Would you want me to come if I could?"

"I'm just saying, it all right if you don't."

That sounded reasonable, but in her bedroom creeping toward full morning light, it felt terrible. Soon he kissed Tisha good-bye and drove home.

When he enters, Lorr is in the kitchen drinking coffee.

"Don't you sleep?" he asks.

"Not much. And if I do fall asleep, those train whistles wake me up."

"I'm sorry." He looks exhausted, the whites of his eyes filigreed with fine red lines.

"All this waiting around must be boring."

"Actually, there's so much going on in here"—she taps her forehead just below the band of gray she's decided not to color—"I can hardly keep up. You want breakfast?"

"Coffee." He starts toward his bedroom. "You know what? If you think you could find your way back, drive me to work. Then you and Pammie could have the car for the day."

When he reappears, dressed for work, Lorr has a half-awake but fully bitchy Pammie roused and sitting at the kitchen counter, her chin supported on her hand, her hair falling over her face. Lorr hands Richie a steaming mug.

"All he needs," Pammie mutters, "is a PB&J and a quarter for a cookie."

"All you need," Lorr replies, "is a shot in the mouth."

"She woke me because she can't sleep and doesn't want anyone else to. She's always been a bitch."

Lorr laughs. *Family.*

When they pull up in front of his office building, Richie asks, "What are you doing today?"

Lorr answers, "The zoo? The Jazz Museum? And Pammie read about this park out past Independence called Big Bone Lick."

From the back Pammie asks, "How can we pass that up?"

"Remember, if you get lost, call my office. Jeannie, that's my secretary, will straighten you out." He opens the passenger door then leans across the stick shift and plants a kiss on Lorr's cheek. "I'll call when I'm ready to be picked up, probably around seven."

She watches him walk away. He wears a black cashmere coat—it's sunny but cold for April—and carries a slim black briefcase. He looks successful and handsome; her cheek tingles where he kissed it. It seemed natural, as if the kiss weren't a one-time thing. Pammie clambers over the stick shift and tumbles into the captain's chair Richie just vacated. Behind them some asshole leans on his horn. Lorr raises her middle finger then slams the CRV into gear. Steel and glass business towers flash past. She turns right then right again. Unless she's mistaken, which she doubts, she's headed east, toward Richie's apartment. The traffic light at the next corner changes, and she clutches and brakes.

"You know where you're going?" Pammie asks.

"Where *are* we going?"

"Back to bed?"

"I don't think so." Lorr can still feel Richie's lips on her cheek and the impact on her heart of how grown-up he looked carrying that briefcase. Long suppressed emotions roil inside her. For shit's sake, it was just a briefcase

"Forget the zoo," Pammie says, "unless we take Jada."

"And I don't feel like the Jazz Museum. I want to be outside."

"That leaves Big Bone Lick. God, we're pathetic."

The light goes green. Lorr releases the clutch and screams through the gears. What does Pammie find pathetic? Middle-aged sisters lured to a park because its name includes *Bone Lick*?

Their inability to form lifelong connections? Look at them, all grown-up, no husbands. Pammie doesn't seem to have a man of any sort and no children between them except for Richie. Lorr spies a green overhead sign: *I-35/I-670*. She's always been good at getting places once she decides where she's going. She bears right then left and motors up the ramp, where their progress is halted by a necklace of brake lights. Stasis ensues, which Pammie eases by spinning through the AM dial: right-wing talk radio even this early in the day. Then the highway divides; they slip the yoke of traffic, and the sisters, in sunshine, head for Independence and Big Bone Lick State Park.

Whatever Reece expected, it wasn't this. By two o'clock, when he returned to the Jazz District, just around the corner from where T. Thomas was murdered, there was a crowd of maybe two hundred aggrieved sistahs and brothas sounding like they ready to do something. He recognized protestors from last night, City Hall and police HQ. Some carried the same signs; others waved new ones.

Don't shoot me!
No justice, no peace!
Racist cops KILL!

Today's crowd looked younger: lots of sixteen-year-olds ditching school, trying to look all hard. But there were marchers his age and older, even some old dudes with bullhorns, acting like someone put them in charge. It reminded him of an opposing gym when he was hooping it up for Ruskin. Everyone on this side for you, that side against, and entering you could feel it. *Something gonna happen.* Difference was, everybody on this street on the same side.

Gray-haired Bull Horn Man started up, "We tired a talking, talking. Tired a listening, being all reasonable, like back in '95,

169

when Emanuel Cleaver Two told us not to march on the Plaza, and we didn't. We tired of listening while young brothas get murdered. Tired of knowing our place, east of Troost and south of Race! Like Boss Prendergast Law still be in place, though it never a law and never be legal. Tired a asking and *asking* for justice. Two hundred years a asking and asking, we're not asking no more. We gonna take our justice. Take *our* justice. Take our jus-*tice*. Maybe then the mayor and his killer cops!"

"Yeah!" the crowd shouted.

As if a signal had been given, though there'd been none Reece could see, the crowd on the sidewalk and in the middle of Vine Street pressed forward. Reece tried to make up his mind: hang back or march. Why not, so long as he didn't get arrested and violate parole? Still a free country, wasn't it? Free speech and the right to assembly guaranteed, at least if you were white. Still, he hesitated and let the crowd surge past him, thinking there are right rights and there are wrongs, and he couldn't afford to be wrong again. He remembered Little B's advice: *Don't be no hero.* Then, no more than fifteen feet away in the crowd striding down the center of the street—Reece was watching from the sidewalk—Tisha marched past. In one hand she carried a large white sign held aloft on a length of two-by-four, its black painted letters shouting, STOP THE KILLING! With her other hand she led Jada.

What that crazy bitch doing here with the child? Reece pushed forward angrily and had almost caught up when the plate glass window of Lee's E-Z Market, against which he'd been leaning a minute before, exploded in a thousand glass stars. The next storefront and one across the street shattered too, fools chucking Hawaiian Punch cans, like that gonna do shit. Reece caught up to Tish just as the crowd started to run. He grabbed her shoulder, spun Tish around, and she windmilled her sign— STOP THE KILLING!—like she gonna kill him with it. Then she recognized Reece and lowered the sign. Kids started reaching inside the shattered windows, while all around them it sounded like the wind was blowing through ice storm–covered trees, as if there were thousands of glass bells tinkling.

"Tish, this no damn place for the child!"

Her eyes flashed with the anger he was accustomed to finding in them, and he could hear her thoughts. *You don't have no right to say one damn word. You had it, didn't want it, don't never say nothing again.*

Instead, she nodded and scooped Jada into her arms. "We're going home. Reece, you take care."

A squad of mounted cops cantered around the corner and started toward them. The crowd waved its signs. "Murderers!" they shouted. "Murderers! Don't shoot me!"

Just then, on the next corner—Reece, with his height, could see over the crowd—three or four kids pushed over a hot dog wagon. The vendor screamed in his own language, bashed one of the kids with a baseball bat. The other kids jumped him, and the cops fired a beanbag fusillade just like last night. One smacked Reece's shoulder and stung like a muthafucker. *Then.* Then, what was that sound? Jada, covering her eye. Reece had never heard a child scream so, as if the pain had started in some other universe, a sound that went on and on. He grabbed her from Tisha, shouted, "Let's go!" and with Jada still screaming, they ran from the cops, ran and ran.

When Richie entered the up elevator after a meeting on the second floor, he'd already heard about the rioting, and he was worried about Tisha. Rumors ricocheting around the building predicted the Eleventh Plague: rampaging Nubians headed downtown from east of Troost, destroying everything in their path. How high could someone throw a brick? Was the second floor safe? City Hall, someone said, was under siege; the mayor and his staff were trapped inside. Police defending them had been firing tear gas and rubber bullets.

"They ought to use real ones," said a male voice in the back of the crowded elevator.

"The problem"—Richie stared straight ahead at the bank of lit buttons; his floor was next—"is they have been firing real ones."

The same voice said, "If a cop with a gun says stop, you stop."

"If you're black when you stop, sometimes they shoot you."

The polished steel doors parted, and Richie stepped off. *Racist bastard.* He hurried down the cubicle-lined corridor. Folgrow news was mostly good; articles had appeared in several major business sections. Unfortunately, *WSJ*'s was subtitled, "Will C&M Corner the Snake Oil Market?" *Fuck them,* he had other worries. Though it was only four-fifteen, Jeannie looked as if she'd packed to leave hours ago.

"Richie, boss." She started toward him. "I want to pick up my kids. You heard what's going on?"

He nodded.

"Our neighborhood's mixed." She met his eyes. "Wayne's worried about our kids."

"See you in the morning."

"Thanks. There's messages on your desk." She started away then turned back. "A whole bunch from Tisha."

He almost shouted, *Why didn't you call me out of my meeting?* But why bother? Jeannie was streaking toward the elevator. Richie thumbed through the pink MESSAGES FOR YOU on his desk. Four from Tisha. Two-forty-five, three, three-thirty, and four, all with the same message. "Please call," and a number he didn't recognize. He took several deep breaths in an attempt to calm down, didn't calm down, then dialed. A strange voice, a male voice, answered.

"This is Richie Gordon," he replied, feeling like an ass. "Is Tisha there?"

For some time no one spoke, and he listened to ambient noise that could have been from a coffee shop or a bus station, anywhere and nowhere.

"Richard," Tisha said at last. "I'm so glad you called."

"What's wrong?"

"It's Jada." She started to cry.

"What about her?"

"Don't say nothing . . . I took her with me. I wanted her to see—"

"What?"

"And the cops—"

At least she didn't say white cops.

"—fired beanbag pellets and hit her eye."

Richie went cold. "Where are you?"

"Children's Mercy Hospital Emergency Room."

He hung up without confirming it was Reece who had answered, though he was pretty sure he recognized the voice. Nor did he criticize her for taking Jada to a demonstration, no, a fucking riot. Really, what was wrong with her? He grabbed his coat, crammed what he needed into his briefcase—he had hours, many hours, of work to do, he'd probably have to come back later—and ran to the elevator. He'd already exited on B2, PARKING, and was looking for the CRV, when he remembered. The women had it. He returned to street level and dialed Pammie's cell. No answer. He called home, hung up on the first syllable of his recorded message. Desperate, at least he felt desperate, but something else too, cold and desperate, he had the security guard at the lobby desk call Mann's Executive Car Service. Twenty minutes later he was seated in the back of a Mercedes. He heard sirens, police and fire, and as they sped south and east from his office toward the hospital, he was pretty sure he saw mounted C. City, M.O., police pursuing a crowd east on Eighteenth Street. But if the driver, an older black man dressed in livery, found any of this remarkable, he kept quiet about it, although once or twice he glanced in the rearview as if to confirm they'd both seen what they'd seen.

When they reached Children's Mercy Hospital, located just

north of the boulevard named for Martin Luther King, who, Richie thought, must be spinning in his grave, he asked the driver to wait and ran inside. Everyone in the ER waiting area was African American, except for the receptionist, whose bleached hair showed half-inch black roots.

"I'm looking for Jada Gordon."

The receptionist, who couldn't have been more than twenty, ran a long pink nail with an inset rhinestone along the register. She frowned then blew a bubble. "What's the name again?"

"Jada Gordon, five years old, eye injury. African American."

The girl shot him a look. *African American? Look around.* "She was taken up to a floor."

"Can you tell me where?"

The girl popped her gum. "Not unless you're family."

"I'm the father, Richard Gordon." Richie dared her to say one more fucking word. "Where is she?"

"217A. First elevator, then straight to the back."

Richie overtipped the driver and sent him away. Inside 217 he found LaTisha and Reece outside the curtained-off half of a semiprivate room, in conversation with a tall black man in green surgical scrubs. Tisha saw him, as did Reece; only Tisha smiled.

"Doctor Williams." She motioned Richie closer. "This is Richard Gordon."

Richie met the doctor's gaze. "Pleased to meet you." He shook the doctor's fleshy palm, which lacked the elegant bones of a surgeon. More like the paw of a power forward. *You racist pig,* he thought. What Williams had concluded about him, he had no clue.

"You're the father?"

Richie glanced at Reece, whose eyes, not green but not brown either, glimmered darkly. "She has my name."

Williams turned toward Tisha, whose face gave away nothing.

"You've probably explained already," Richie began, "but would you mind filling me in?"

"She suffered a fracture of the right orbital floor."

Williams spoke with a New York accent: *Orbital flawr.*

"When the beanbag hit her eye, it had nowhere to go. Eyeballs"—Doctor Williams pursed his substantial lips—"are sturdy and don't rupture easily. Instead, they're propelled backward toward the maxillary sinus and the weakest surrounding bone, which is the orbital floor, here." He dragged a finger across his own cheek. "In many cases, and the CAT scan my chief resident ordered confirmed that's what we're looking at, the inferior muscle gets entrapped in the floor, preventing the eye from moving normally, and we have to—"

From inside the curtained cubicle Richie thought he heard Jada. Then he was sure. "Momma," she cried. *"Momma!"*

He pushed the curtain aside. Jada sat up in the child-sized hospital bed, sheets drawn to her chest. Pale blue plastic banded her wrist, and he stepped toward her. Jada's face, above and to the side of her right eye, looked swollen and bruised. So did both her eyelids. Richie hugged her, and she wrapped her arms around his neck. When he kissed her, he made sure to kiss the left cheek. "I'm so sorry, Jadakins."

"It hurts, Richie. A *lot*."

He sat on the bed beside her. "You're being really brave."

"I cried. I wish Stripes was here."

"I'll get him for you," he said, aware Tisha and Reece were watching.

"For reals?"

"For reals."

There were a dozen things he wanted to ask the doctor, and he stood up, noticing as he did that Jada's swollen eye didn't track him as the other one did.

She wailed, "I see two of you, Richie!" She stuck out her hand but not directly toward him, to the side. Or maybe she was reaching for Reece. "There's two of Reece too." Her lower lip puffed out. "I don't like it." And now tears began to flow. "I *don't!*"

175

Tisha sat to comfort her. Richie and Reece followed Doctor Williams into the hall. Where, Richie wondered, recalling something he'd heard Hank say twenty years ago, were all the Jewish doctors when you needed them?

"As I started to explain," Williams began, as two orderlies pushing a child on a gurney passed them, "when the inferior rectus gets entrapped, it often prevents the eye from tracking normally, causing double vision. If the nerve is entrapped, there may also be numbness in the bottom lid and cheek. It's also possible that after the initial swelling goes down, the globe will appear sunken."

Richie glanced at Reece. Was it his brilliant idea to take Jada to the demonstration? Seeing Reece beside Tisha when he entered, closer than he had to be, clearly in her *personal space*, had convinced him Reece remained interested in her. And the stab of jealousy Richie felt? That ruinous, ruptured spleen sort of pain? Pain he wanted to inflict on Reece? But wait. Williams was saying something.

"In adults we free the entrapped inferior rectus and insert a piece of silicone to stabilize the shattered bone. With a child like Jada, with the bone still growing, we may not be able to. We may try mesh; we may not be able to use anything. I won't know until we get inside."

"When will you operate?" Richie asked.

"Tomorrow. I understand she had something to eat in the emergency room?"

"M&M's," Reece said, "and a Dr. Pepper. Then she puked it all up."

Reece and Williams grinned, as if they were in this together, not only the *brothas* but a sort of father and son, leaving Richie somewhere off in white field, although this motherfucker Reece had been farther away than that for years.

Williams said, "Nausea is often associated with entrapped inferior rectus muscles."

"It was associated," Reece cracked, "all over the floor."

Richie had to stop himself from associating Reece's neck with his hands.

Doctor Williams said, "So surgery can't happen until sometime tomorrow, which is probably best, regardless. Any other questions?" He glanced from Reece to Richie.

Richie asked, "Will she be all right?"

"Even with the CAT scan it's hard to know what we're looking at until after we're operating. But in most cases"—Williams pursed his lips again—"the double vision clears up when we release the entrapped muscle." He had a calm reassuring face; behind black-rimmed glasses his eyes were mobile and intelligent.

Reece asked, "That means sometimes it doesn't?"

"Rarely. Anything else?"

Richie considered asking in what percentage of such cases were there continuing problems. And what about the cost—he was pretty sure Tisha didn't carry health insurance. But both questions could wait. .

"I'll see you tomorrow," Doctor Williams said, "after the surgery. Don't worry"—he summoned a reassuring, professional smile—"she'll do fine."

Richie watched Williams proceed down the corridor then turned toward Reece, who regarded him through slitted eyes.

"Guess you be wanting to find out what all went down." Reece paused, as if asking a question, but there'd been no upward tilt of interrogation. "Tell Tish I'll be seeing them later."

Reece started down the corridor Doctor Williams had just pursued. He was so long-legged, Richie thought, he looked more gazelle than human. Stubby Richie, short-calved, pissed off, watched his double disappear around the corner then reentered the sickroom, stepping through the curtain surrounding Jada's bed. Tisha's eyes rose fearfully to his own.

FIFTEEN

The bones turn out to be from Ice Age mammoths: mastodons, giant ground sloths, and other outsized quadrupeds. The *licking*, which had so intrigued the Gordon sisters, is not in any manner sexual, instead references a salt lick that for millennia attracted mammals whose fossilized remains constitute the park's bounty. After they tour an exhibit of reconstructed skeletons, gawk at the mammoth castings set in a field adjacent to the Education Center and then at the herd of American bison Big Bone Lick State Park inexplicably maintains, Lorr convinces Pammie to hike up and over the park's rolling hillsides on a trail that winds through second-growth hardwood and scrub pine. As they stroll the morning wind gentles, the air warms, and although Pammie complains about how much she abhors nature, Lorr has heard more inspired bitching from her sister about almost every other aspect of her life. Near the crest of the second hill, just beyond the mound of an old foundation, they startle a hawk into flight from a low branch, blur of carmine breast and spotted feathers, the raptor so close Lorr feels the *whoosh* of air shunted by its wings. Pammie turns, eyes bright, looking for the first time this week like her former impressionable Baby Sis self.

"Goddamn," she says, "that was something."

Later, after descending from the ridge trail, they encounter a school group ogling the life-size mastodon castings. There must be forty or fifty little kids, holding hands in size-place rows. Some are the sort of blond crew cut boys she doesn't remember existing in Brooklyn but has since come to know in Redwood Valley. But there are also dark, curly-haired boys who remind her of Richie's school photos and little blonde girls who could be Pammie's.

"Ever think about having kids?" she asks.

"Just all the time, now that it's too late."

They treat themselves to a fancy lunch in Independence before getting back on I-70. And though the Buck Stops Here doesn't serve wine, nothing can dilute the joy Lorr feels. They drive west into Calhoun City, exemplar of the antebellum Midwest, windows open to the warm afternoon, sunlight's arrows glinting off their windshield. What a fabulous day, Lorr thinks. And tonight she'll have her talk with Richie.

Upstairs in his apartment they crack a bottle of red—it's half past four, after all—and wait for his call. And wait—well into a second bottle. Later, alone and bored—Pammie has perhaps enjoyed too much wine too quickly and opted to lie down, although she claimed the nap wasn't because of the wine but because she was woken up too early—Lorr switches on the news and learns about the riots: multiple images of a crowd marching down Race Street, windows broken out, trash can fires blazing. From a close-up of the shattered glass front of Bar C. City, the camera cuts to its white owner declaring, "I coulda been blinded!" More shots in front of the county courthouse, a black crowd chanting: "No justice, no peace! No justice, no peace!" At seven, carried simultaneously on several channels—Lorr is surfing one to the next to the next—C. City, M.O.'s mayor, former newscaster Malcolm Wilson, stages a news conference inside City Hall. Behind a spiderweb of microphones, light bulbs *flash, flash, flash*-ing, the producer crosscutting to helmeted police guarding the door, His Honor, who looks like a blue-eyed slaughterhouse hog who has already been bopped between the eyes with a hammer, calls for public discussions to replace violence.

"If we can't do that," he declares, and sipping her fourth glass of red, Lorr believes the mayor is blinking back tears, "then I'm not optimistic that the future will be that much better than the past."

The scene shifts to a squad of slow-marching white-helmeted cops knocking batons against riot shields then a handheld shot of policemen firing shotguns into the crowd. Next image is a fresh-faced African American reporter explaining that these shotguns only fire pellet-filled beanbags designed to subdue crowds from a distance. The reporter, who's out on the street, shoves her microphone at a white police lieutenant.

"The crowd's very young," says Lieutenant Osborne, whose name appears below him on the screen. "They're very mobile and breaking up into different directions. And the crowd sometimes helps the lawbreakers get away, so our arrests may be down."

When Chief of Police Stryker, a jowly white man of the sort Lorr has loathed and feared since the sixties, comes on-screen exhorting black leaders to urge their followers to *Stay calm*, she forces herself to watch. She wants to be able to tell Richie everything.

"First Amendment rights," Stryker declares, "we have no problem with that, until it turns unlawful, and then we have to intervene."

Stryker reminds her of Mayor Daly—"We are here to create disorder!"—back when she was in high school, and she douses the picture. She's called Richie's office for the past two hours, there's been no one there, and left half a dozen messages on his cell. She'll be forty-nine on Sunday, a mother thirty of those years, but this may be, in fact it *is*, the first time she's worried about her son's whereabouts. If for all these years she's been denied the satisfactions of motherhood, she has also been spared this fearsome anxiety. And then the phone rings.

By six-thirty, when a nurse's aide delivered her dinner tray, Jada's right eye had swollen completely shut. One-eyed, she picked at her food: cherry Jell-O, chicken soup, Saltines, choc-olate milk. Moments later the soup and Jell-O exploded from her mouth in a reddish blurt. After an aide changed the sheets and Richie and LaTisha cleaned Jada, changed her gown, and calmed her down—she missed Stripes; she wanted him now!—she passed out. Later still, on orders from the young attending physician, a nurse inserted an IV line in her left hand. While Richie watched from the foot of the bed, Tisha tucked the sheet under Jada's chin and turned down the lights, darkening the room as much as possible, which wasn't very much at all.

As long as Jada required attention, they'd barely glanced at each other. What would Richie have seen if he hadn't been afraid to look? *Why* Tisha had taken Jada to the rally? Proof positive she was back with Reece?

"Richard," Tisha said. "We need to talk."

They exited Jada's curtained-off area and sat on chairs flank-ing the room's other, unoccupied bed. The overhead fluorescent illuminated kid-friendly blue and yellow walls. He'd never seen Tisha look so disheveled. The curls, which normally sparkled against her cheeks, hung down, tossed and raggedy.

"I know what you're thinking. 'How could Tisha be so stupid and take Jada to that rally?'"

It *was* stupid.

"Admit it." Her eyes looked bruised. "You're thinking, 'That stupid ho took her child to the rally and got her—'"

"I'm not thinking that."

"You gonna tell me or let me think the worst?"

Richie gazed past Tisha out the plate glass window to the darkening street. On the corner a traffic light pulsed, red-yel-low-green. "It was pretty damn stupid."

"Lots of people had they children. Were we all pretty damn—"

"You prefer *misguided*?"

"You said *stupid*, like 'Stupid Nigger.'"

"Don't make this about race."

"If the crowd wasn't black, would the cops a been firing all crazy? And if you were, I wouldn't be explaining why I wanted her to see—"

She hesitated, while cognition blew back and forth. What an unfortunate choice of words: *to see.*

"—black people standing up for themselves."

"I want her to see that too."

He knew she didn't believe him. He reached for her hand, but she pulled away.

"And if you were black, you woulda been there, no matter how busy. Don't tell me different." She chewed her lips. But instead of the gesture appearing thoughtful, as it usually did, she looked as if she were trying and failing to hold herself back. "And maybe this wouldn't have happened!"

You're blaming me? I wasn't even there. But that was her point. "It would have been pretty damn crowded if I *were* there, you, me and Reece."

"That's what's in your mind? *Reece?* Not that my baby was hurt? What kinda stupid muthafucker are you?"

"Reece was with you."

"I was *with* Jada. After she got hurt, Reece helped us." Tisha looked hard as stone. "You should go. I can't deal with your shit right now."

He reached again for her hand. She scooted her chair away. Eyes interrogating the floor, she said softly, "Just go, Richard, I mean it."

Just go? She needed him. Jada needed him. He stood and stepped forward, arms wide to hug her.

"No."

Richie rode the elevator downstairs, hating her, hating himself, and exited through the main lobby doors. The cell phone in his jacket pocket began to vibrate. Eight missed calls, all from his home number. He pressed SEND twice and waited for Lorraine to answer.

She leaves Pammie asleep and sets out through the dark, unfamiliar streets in Richie's CRV. She doesn't scare easily and would like to believe she's no racist, but it's been decades since she lived in a city or around many black people, and the TV news has messed with her head. Richie said he would try to get a cab if she wanted—she didn't—then suggested a complicated route involving several freeways to avoid downtown, but she answered, sounding braver than she felt, "No big deal." She didn't want to upset him more than he already was. Jada needed eye surgery! *How was Tisha handling it?* He'd tell her later.

She follows surface streets, doors locked, and keeps an eye out for anything unusual but sees nothing. No fire, no smoke, no rampaging mobs. Twenty minutes after setting out, she executes the next to last of Richie's many directions. The hospital neighborhood looks sketchy and run-down. On her left aging six- to eight-story medical buildings; on the right funky row houses. She hasn't seen a white face in miles, not many black faces either. She's only doing twenty miles an hour but somehow fails to negotiate the left turn into the hospital driveway and has to execute a broken U to correct her mistake then nearly wets her panties when a police cruiser with its gumball lights flashing appears out of nowhere screaming toward her so fast it's going to ram her or at the very least arrest her. But the cop car flies past, and Lorr pulls into Children's Mercy trying not to hyperventilate. She goes ten miles an hour up the long drive, which ends in a circular drop-off area. The CRV's lights illuminate Richie in the dress coat she so admired that morning.

"Are you all right?" she asks, and immediately regrets the question because he doesn't look one little bit all right.

He doesn't answer. She changes seats. Richie adjusts the driver's seat and side-view mirrors, slams the CRV into gear, and peels away from the curb. Five minutes pass, and he still hasn't spoken. She doesn't know if he's just upset about Jada, not that Jada being hurt isn't enough, or if there's something else, but it's freaking her out. She has no idea where they are, it's completely black out there, but she's sure of one thing; they're not going back the way she came. And here's something else. He's driving way too fast for city streets.

Just then—they're racing down a long urban hill, and though the street signs whiz past too fast to read easily, she's pretty sure the street they're following is Brooklyn Avenue, which makes no sense at all to her—he runs a light, doesn't even attempt to stop, and though there are no squealing brakes, the car moving out from the corner on the driver's left swerves, and so do they, swerving, horn blaring, and just for a second she thinks they're going to crash, then they sail through the intersection.

"Stop the fucking car!"

"You don't want me to."

"Why not?"

But her question is not only stupid but rhetorical. Now that he's slowed down, it's easy to see *Why not?* Half the block's buildings are boarded up. Knots of young men man each corner. Fires leap in steel mesh trash cans. Smoke blows through their headlights like fog. A siren wails close by, and she realizes what Richie's done. Instead of skirting the riot, he's driven straight into it.

"What are we doing here?"

"Sightseeing."

She sees the brick flying toward them, she realizes later, from what feels like a long way off, a splendidly spiraling messenger of hate, headed straight for their windshield. She has time enough to scream or to shield her face, and she's still vain enough she covers up. Richie must have seen it too, or maybe he's just lucky. He veers right, and the brick *thunks* loudly off the roof.

For a moment he looks so unhinged, she's afraid he's going

to do something really dumb, like jump out and chase whoever threw the brick. Then he seems to come back into himself and motors on, neither too fast nor too slow, the baby bear of calamitous drivers. Five or six blocks later they reach Clay, where a cop stationed in the middle of the street in front of his flashing cruiser compels Richie to roll down his window. Shining an enormous black steel flashlight at them, he observes they are white and snarls, "What the hell are you doing here?"

Lorr's afraid Richie will answer "Sightseeing." Instead, in a perfectly kiss-ass tone, her son replies, "Heading home, Officer. We live in the Western Auto building."

"Then I suggest you get there."

Richie turns left. When they've haven't heard a siren or seen a cop car in several blocks, he says, "I'm sorry."

"You fucking well should be."

He pulls over and gets out. A moment later he's back inside. "There's a big dent in the roof."

"You're lucky it's not in your head."

"Still up for that conversation?"

She can't see his face, just its dark outline. "We should stop and tell Pammie, so she won't worry."

He turns on his blinker, pulls away from the curb, and drives home.

SIXTEEN

Pammie made it clear she didn't want to be abandoned, so they went out as a threesome.

"Tomorrow night for sure," he said, when he and Lorraine were seated in a booth at Gallagher's, which was two blocks from his condo. Pammie was in the ladies' room.

"Tomorrow night you'll be taking care of Tisha."

He looked into Lorraine's concerned eyes and wondered how much to tell her. "She doesn't want me anywhere near her."

"Of course she does."

"She says she doesn't."

Sitting down beside him, Pammie asked, "What did you do to her?"

"How do you know I did something?"

"Because I know Tisha," Pammie said.

Richie turned from his sister to his sister: his aunt to his mother under the new regime. "It's too complicated to get into with these riots—"

"It's a black and white thing?"

"Not just that."

"Then what?"

"I'm not going to talk about it."

"Another guy?" Pammie asked.

"No," Richie replied after the briefest of hesitations but long enough for something to pass between the women, who thought they knew more than they did.

"Whatever's going on," Pammie continued, "with Jada hurt your only job is to be there for her."

"Actually, my *job* is at C&M, and I have to go in after we finish dinner."

Lorr said, "I don't think you should go back there tonight."

"I have work to do."

"Go in early," Lorr said. "I'll get you up."

He looked from Lorraine to Pammie and back again. "My office is nowhere near the riots."

"Like that brick was nowhere near going through the windshield."

"What brick?" Pammie demanded.

"Have I ever asked you to do anything for me?" Lorr asked.

Richie wanted to say, *Women who abandon children don't usually ask them for anything*, but it seemed both too obvious and too cruel. "No, you haven't."

"You look like shit. Any work you do now, you'd have to redo anyway."

"What brick?"

"Pammie," Lorr said, "will you shut up?"

Their waiter, a rakish twenty-something with black hair and a goatee, started past their booth carrying a tray of dirty dishes. Pammie grabbed his free arm. "What's a girl got to do to get a drink here, get naked?"

The waiter's eyes popped, but he didn't miss a beat. "That would be nice, but all you really need to do is let me put down this tray."

"Three Grey Goose martinis," Pammie called after his retreating back. "Dirty." She turned to Lorr and Richie. "What brick?"

At five a.m. Lorr is standing over Richie's bed. She is struck by how dark his hair appears against the white pillow, how near her own shade or what her shade used to be, and she wonders, not for the first time, what happened to Ricardo Delgas? We were so young, what I now consider children, although we didn't think so back then. What would he do if Richie contacted him? In the fall of '69, when she found out she was pregnant, she didn't even tell Ricardo. She was too proud, too angry, and he was so gone, so full of himself, headed off, as her old friend Jackie liked to say, to Connecti-cunt, to find himself a blonde. Poor Jackie, dead at forty-two of breast cancer. She rattles Richie's shoulder, once then a second time, and his eyes startle open.

"What?" Understanding gathers, and he glances toward his alarm clock. "Thanks." He passes a hand over his lips. He still doesn't look completely awake, but he sits up, and she examines his face for traces of a young and vanished Ricardo or, for that matter, of Hank or Marilyn but finds none. For shit's sake, he's thirty. He looks like himself.

"I was dreaming. Something about Tisha."

"I don't know about your job, and you probably don't want my advice, Lord knows I don't have the right to give any." His eyes come to hers, and they're not angry, they're kind; she has a kindhearted son. She sits on the bed beside him. "But you really need to be with her when Jada goes in for surgery. Maybe she *thinks* she doesn't—"

"She doesn't."

"Or believes it's your fault for not being there when Jada was hurt or that it's impossible now for a black and white couple."

He looks at her as if she were pulling secrets out of the hat of his heart.

"But trust me, she needs you there. Later it will mean everything."

She thinks about saying more, something about how she and Ricardo let the world wrench them apart, but then she would have to admit she didn't even tell Ricardo she was pregnant, and that's more than she can cop to right now. Besides, it's only five after five, and she's already laid a lot on him.

"You're right," he says. "I should be there."

And still he doesn't move. She wonders if there's something more he wants her to say, or something else she should say, then recollects he was dreaming when she woke him. From her considerable familiarity with the male anatomy, she concludes he has a morning hard-on, too embarrassed to get out of bed while she remains in the room.

She kisses his forehead. "Would you like a cup of coffee?"

"Thank you."

For a heartbeat she thinks he's about to add *Mom. Thank you, Mom.*

Instead, he finishes, "For everything."

She exits and leans against the closed door, feeling for the first time since she left him in front of her parents' house twenty-eight years ago something like his mother.

Richie drove downtown in the dark, put in two and a half solid hours, drafting in that time three reports and several dozen e-mails, including one each to his division manager and senior VP explaining he had to be out of the office for the morning and possibly the rest of the day for a *family medical emergency*. He apologized for the timing, for the still unresolved distribution issues in Ohio and Kentucky, and was halfway to the elevator, where he encountered Jeannie, who was just coming in.

"How you doing, Richie boss?"

"Jada's having eye surgery. I'm leaving."

"Omigod." Jeannie's hand rose to cover her pretty mouth and briefly to touch her own eye. "What happened?"

He wondered how much to disclose, mindful Jeannie had been in a panic to pick up her kids yesterday because of her mixed neighborhood. "She was hit hard, by accident, in the right eye and broke the bone behind it."

"Omigod." Jeannie's own eyes filled with tears. "*That's* why LaTisha kept calling. Tell her how sorry I am, would you?"

Richie tried to recall if Jeannie and LaTisha had ever met and concluded they hadn't, but they must have spoken quite a few times. Jeannie had seen the pictures of LaTisha and Jada on his desk and remarked how beautiful Tisha was, how darling Jada was, what an "exquisite" little girl. What she thought about them being black he didn't want to know.

"When should I tell people you're going to be back?"

"Just take messages." Other support staff were arriving, and he didn't want to be seen leaving. Stepping toward Jeannie, he added, sotto voce, "The surgery's ten-thirty; if everything's okay, I'll be back this afternoon. And I'll tell LaTisha what you said."

Then he was careening toward the elevator through a line of arriving coworkers talking about the riots. He arrived at Children's Mercy before nine. He'd called Tisha's apartment several times on the drive without answer, other than her machine: *LaTisha and Jada, Pe—eace.* He assumed she was already with Jada and wondered if she'd spent the night. If so, she'd need clean clothes for Jada and a change for herself as well. He wished he'd started calling as soon as he'd gotten to work but had told himself that if she were home she'd be asleep and didn't want to talk to him anyway. But as he'd soldiered on in his dark office, he accepted what he'd known since Lorraine had sat beside him on his bed: Folgrow could wait. Jada's operation was happening right here, right now, and so he'd worked faster and smarter and knew before he let himself know it that when he finished he'd be doing exactly what he was doing now: hunting for a parking spot in the underground garage then racing to the C bank of elevators for the ride to the lobby then a second elevator to her floor, where he hurried down the hall and turned into Jada's room to find it empty.

At the nursing station he learned she'd been taken to surgery, and he rode yet another elevator up another three floors to the OR waiting area, a bright and cheery web of rooms that looked as if they could seat fifty or even seventy-five people on an eclectic mix of couches and chairs. A refreshment area behind a glass door at the far side of the suite of rooms held coffee and snack vending machines, even a microwave, but no Tisha.

It was past nine. If surgery were still scheduled for ten-thirty, Tisha had to be here somewhere, unless there were some side rail in the train station that was Children's Mercy, where Jada, terrified, he imagined, and most likely drugged up, was waiting for whatever was going to happen to her.

That she was close by and he couldn't see her enraged him; yet one more proof that his love for Jada was of the reptilian brain, lift-the-car-off-the-injured-child sort of love. Hands trembling, his mouth tasting of blood, he approached the Information Desk and convinced the matronly supervisor of his paternal rights and prerogatives. Within minutes she had determined where Jada was being held and summoned a teenage volunteer with purple rubber bands on her teeth and a name tag—GAYLE—pinned to her insubstantial bosom to lead him there.

"Richie!" Jada cried. "I told you, Momma."

He met Tisha's hard, hot gaze.

"Hey, Richard," she said softly.

He mouthed, "I'm sorry." Tisha, who still wore yesterday's clothes, did not respond, but at least she didn't say anything hostile, and he stepped, unimpeded, to Jada's bedside. Her left hand was connected to a plastic IV pouch suspended from a stainless steel tree. Her right cheek and eyelids, upper and lower, were even more terrifyingly swollen than last night.

"Jadakins." He kissed her forehead. "You're so brave."

She squeezed the middle fingers of his right hand. "I want Stripes."

"I'll bring him later, I promise." He glanced toward Tisha, who looked at once angry and scared but more than anything else exhausted. "And maybe another stuffed animal. A get-well bear or maybe a big old snake."

"No snake!" Jada's one good eye was both shiny and dull. "They nasty."

"I thought you liked snakes." He was playing this scene as much for Tisha, on the far side of the gurney, as for Jada.

"No Way, No How Dawg," Jada said. "Momma slept in the chair in my room last night."

"I bet she didn't sleep much."

"No, I didn't."

"Okay," he said, seeing Jada's eye start to close. "I'll get you a No Way, No How Dog, if I can find one."

The curtain opened. Two women in green scrubs, one tall and white, one short and black, entered the cubicle. The tall one glanced at the chart suspended from the foot of the gurney. "Hey, Jada, we're taking you for a ride."

"*Momma.*"

"You'll be fine," Tisha said. "They gonna fix your eye." She glanced toward Richie.

"And when you wake up," he added, "we'll all be here, Stripes too, and maybe Auntie Pammie and Lorraine."

"And my No How Dawg?"

"That's right."

The green-garbed women unlocked the gurney's wheels. The shorter attendant tugged it into motion, while the taller white one guided the IV tree.

"Mom and Dad," she said, "make yourselves comfortable in the waiting room. There're beepers if you want to go downstairs for something to eat. And try not to worry, Mom. Doctor Williams is one of our best surgeons."

Then they were gone—the women, Jada, the gurney—and into the sudden silence Tisha began to sob softly then louder and more violently, as if whatever strength she'd retained had rolled out with Jada. Richie hugged her.

"If anything happens, I'll never forgive myself."

"She'll be fine."

"You don't know that."

He kissed LaTisha's neck just below her ear. She smelled of sweat and worry. "But I believe it."

"Good for you."

"No, really." He hugged her close enough to feel her chest rise and fall. "I looked it up on online, it's not that serious."

"You don't know." Tisha stepped away from him. Tears streaked her cheeks, and her lower lip puffed out. "She might never see right from that eye, and you'll blame me."

"I won't."

"Hell, you will. Reece blame me, Auntie Bertie blame me, and when she grows up, Jada gonna blame me too."

"You're just scared."

Her head bobbed, then her lips disappeared under her teeth. "Richard, will you do something for me?"

"Anything."

"Pray with me?" She took his hands in hers, and though it was just the two of them, it felt as if they were forming a circle. "Dear Jesus."

Richie closed his eyes.

"Don't let anything bad happen to Jada. Help her to see right again. Help everyone in this damn city see right again. And have mercy on the soul of Tim Thomas and the bastard who shot him. Amen."

"Amen." Richie opened his eyes. "I bet you can use something to eat."

She nodded and followed him to the waiting room then down to the cafeteria like a person who'd done more than she could do, a person who was sound asleep though her eyes remained open.

SEVENTEEN

Reece woke late Wednesday morning on B's couch wondering if last night's fires still burned. Wondered, too, if this was this the day he'd fuck up big time, and instead of being booked and released like everyone else (fifty dollars and time served), he'd have his bail revoked and stay locked up until trial and likely some years after. So why march? Why not hide like a scared little bitch?

That's right.

He wondered what, and if there was any *what*, to do about Pleasant Street. He'd told Tisha's Mister straight-up; he'd never stayed there. But he had given Richard A. Gordon's name and social to Marshall King, an old friend he owed a favor. Nigger said he could afford cable, but his credit so bad Time Warner wouldn't switch him on. Been years since Reece had used Gordon's name or IDs, and he'd thought his ship coming in with all those TVs, though it turned out it was his shit not his ship arriving on the evening tide because he got popped with the whole load, though he didn't know that then. Marshall kept saying 'course he'd pay—"What, you think I can't afford no damn cable?" all the time flashing a roll big around as his fist. Now it turned out something had happened, or maybe you just can't trust nobody. If they made him for identity theft on top of receiving stolen goods, he wouldn't be getting off in no twelve to eighteen months like Caroline Something-Something said.

Reece sat up on B's couch and dropped his big feet on the rug. Last night after leaving Tish, the child, and that troublesome boob Richard A. Gordon, he'd made his way to City Market, scant blocks north of Byron's. Looked like Times Square after the ball dropped, except the sidewalk in front of the covered market was littered with glass not confetti. A dozen trash can fires burned and kids drinking 40s warmed their hands over the flames. Sirens exulted in the near distance, but none dared approach. The entire East Downtown, from north of the river and all the way out, had been declared a hot zone. Firetrucks wouldn't answer alarms without police escort, which the young kids thought was some big victory, like *We fucking showed them*, but which Reece knew reflected a decision made in another part of the city to let the *Niggers shit their own beds but nowhere else*.

Reece also knew because he was no fool that the last time there'd been rioting this bad was after they murdered Martin Luther King. And he knew from this old book he'd read, which confirmed a story from his Granny, who knew from her own Grams and on back and back, that when the first known ancestor on his mom's side came out from Virginia to Ohio, manumitted thirty years before Lincoln freed the rest of the slaves, he saw firsthand a race riot in Cincinnati. Reece needed to find that book again, which told how Crackers from across the Ohio River, and from the Ohio side too, broke up the printing press of an Abolitionist newspaper and dumped it in the Ohio River then attacked the homes and businesses of the free black community. Same as today's muthafuckers, those old-time Crackers couldn't stand to see the black man proud and free. It would set a bad example or shine a beacon of hope, depending how you looked at it, for all the slaves in Kentucky and farther south. The blacks defended themselves, and though the army and militia would later come down hard as hard *because they could*, what the black community did was brave. They heroes. Why didn't they put that in schoolbooks? Why'd Reece have to ferret out on his own proof of what everyone knew but wouldn't say? White man feared and hated the black man so he kept him down.

That's why, Reece believed, his own white father ran off. Afraid he wouldn't measure up. Now what about this muthafucker Gordon trying to steal Tish and the child? Reece didn't worry much about Tish. No matter how he treated her, she still had feelings for him, just like he did for her. *Aw, Tish*, he'd say. *Aw, Reece, nah, Reece*, with that love-light in her eyes, and the girl could flat-out ball, no lie. But the child? He regretted never putting much into her, for he knew that kids sometimes learned to hate their fathers. That sweet way she was with Gordon? Pierced his heart. Blood of his blood! No amount of money or pretending to be her father could change that, no more than pretending to be Richard A. Gordon had transformed him, for reals, into that sorry-assed white boy.

Back when his Moms would still show him the one picture of who she said was his dad (until he got too shitty with her about him being white), he would sometimes imagine he was white himself. He would study that damn picture. Skinny white kid, eyes squinting out under a ball cap, dirty blond hair, twenty-year-old peach fuzz mustache, the same shaped face Reece had inherited: narrow forehead and chin, wider at the cheekbones. He used to fantasize, even after he knew how stupid it was, about his dad showing up. He'd look just like him because he sure didn't look like his Moms or her brothers, which was his way of understanding back when he was coming up how much lighter he was. In school he took *bow-coo* shit about who or what his Moms boned. This one big kid called him *Nonky*, what you got, he said, when you crossed a nigger and a honky, and kept it up till Reece got brave enough to bounce a rock off his noggin. Even in high school, though he never used Mason, his father's name, and had begun telling anyone who'd listen he never knew it, just some white dick his Moms had slipped in, the Honky in the Woodpile, Reece fantasized he'd look up someday walking home or after he'd drained an NBA three playing for Ruskin, and not just any game, nah, the city finals or sectionals, and there his dad would be. And the most fucked-up part? His dad still looked just like that old picture.

Reece hauled himself off the couch. Byron's place was small, but he kept it nice, and Reece promised himself he'd do the same someday. He'd always stayed with family, his Moms, until she got sick, then his Auntie and Grams back down in Ruskin Heights. Never do that again, not unless things turned even more dire. He walked through B's bedroom to the bathroom, B's bed made, B long gone. That little nigger worked hard.

Reece stepped out of his boxers, exposing skinny, athletic flanks, his butt hardly a butt in terms of roundness, more a conjunction of abdomen and legs. He spread a towel in front of the tub to step on when he got out and turned on the shower. Later he'd stop by to see the child and hear how the operation went. And Pleasant Street? Nah, but don't that water feel good?

Dressed in jeans and a red do-rag like T. Thomas died in, Reece walked toward City Market. A burning trash smell hung over the whole neighborhood. Store owners had been up since dawn nailing plywood over busted-out windows. The butchers and fish markets, Asian and Middle Eastern groceries, had all been broken into and looked now as if they belonged in the abandoned part of C. City, M.O., which started out east of Brooklyn and continued south. Jimmi's BBQ, the one black-owned business near the Market, was also being barricaded. Big Jimmi worked on a ladder, his butt wide as a sofa cushion under the grimy shorts he wore cause it *hot* near the smoker, Jimmi's arms big as Reece's thighs, Jimmi nailing down the last corner of plywood.

Watching the big man work, Reece felt bad and decided he needed coffee. Only the Korean on Ninth would have the stones to stay open; word was Choi kept a shorty under the counter. Out the corner of his eye Reece spied a *Star* news truck across the square and headed toward it. Who should it be but the former newscaster Mayor Malcolm Wilson surrounded by other Very Important People, city council members Reece recognized from Sunday night as well as three suit-wearing niggers who looked like undertakers but were probably ministers. Reporters and cameramen shouldering the tools of their profession trailed the mayor and his group, who acted as if they were inspecting a natural disaster except there was nothing natural about it.

The mayor halted in front of Heist Fish and Poultry, which Reece recognized only because he'd been goofing on the name for years: *Rip-off Fish and Poultry.* Four four-by-eight plywood sheets covered the smashed storefront, covered the name too, and Reece felt mottled by guilt. He'd been part of that last night.

The mayor adjusted his spectacles. "This is all just senseless, random vandalism." He extended his hand to a white lady, who stepped into the center of attention beside His Honor. "Are all the windows gone?"

"Oh, yeah." She grimaced. "They hit everything. But we're still going to be here. We've been here since 1880. This neighborhood is our family."

Reece heard a reporter say into her camera, "That was Barb Heist, co-owner of Heist Fish and Poultry."

Barb Rip-off.

The reporters thrust their microphones at one of the ministers.

"Pastor Piphus, would you care to comment?"

Piphus drew himself up like a wading bird. "The hardest thing to do is *think*." He looked straight at Reece. "The easiest thing to do is react."

Fuck you, old man.

The other ministers preened and clucked, clucked and preened. Reece set off to find that cup of coffee.

Lorraine has been up since Richie left. She hardly sleeps at home, and with all that's happening here, she is so stirred up even when she falls asleep her eyes pop open after an hour or two. Then she can't get back to sleep. She knows she's tired, but she's also totally geeked up, waiting for Richie to call and report on Jada.

"We should just go up there; we're not helpless." Pammie's sipping coffee and smoking in the kitchen, not even on the balcony like she said she would. "We know what hospital it is."

"We don't have a car," Lorr replies then wishes she hadn't, because five minutes later Pammie's called a cab. Baby Sis is a whirl of irritable efficiency, and Lorr wonders how this happened. She recalls the awkward girl who loved The Monkees and Sweet Baby James, but now she's all about her dueling cell phones, though it's her business phone that gets all the action. It's as if Pammie's also had a personality job. Or maybe she evolved, and this is Twenty-First-Century Pammie, with high heels, smaller breasts, a pager, and a Blackberry, while Lorr remains hopelessly stuck in 1970. Same ideas, same hairdo, though now streaked with gray, and she has found in Redwood Valley a place as much out of time as she is, where it's still plausible to believe in peace, love, and marijuana.

As if there's anything wrong with that.

They're tucked into a Rocket Cab, driven by a white guy about her age, his bald spot half-concealed by the pullback into a gray ponytail. He looks a bit like George Carlin and a lot like Billy, one of the guys she used to sleep with until she started sleeping with younger guys. Truth be told, he looks like a lot of the guys she used to sleep with. Grizzled, kinda funky, but still sexy and into sex. Gold stud, barbwire tat edging out of his shirtsleeve. And something in Lorr perks up.

Peering in the mirror, he asks, "Where to, ladies?"

Lorr answers, "Children's Mercy Hospital."

"You got any idea where that is?"

"Not really." She grins. "We're not from around here."

Pammie elbows Lorr in the ribs.

"Let's just say," the driver says, "it's not the best part of town."

"Are they rioting there?" Pammie asks.

"Close enough. If I were you, I wouldn't walk around."

Pammie says, "That's why we called a cab."

The driver grins at Baby Sis in the rearview. When they've been driving a few minutes, he asks, "Who you visiting at Children's?"

Pammie shoots back, "A child."

"One a yours?"

"Not hardly. My sister's son's girlfriend's."

The driver's eyes root around in the rearview. "You must be the younger sister."

Pammie grins. "Much younger."

Lorr's not sure what's more astonishing, being so clearly identified as the *older* sister or Pammie casually referring to Richie as her son.

"Nothing serious?"

"Eye surgery," Lorr answers and leaves it at that. Richie's been vague about what happened, so vague he must not want them to know. Whatever it was must show Tisha in a bad funky light. It's worrisome how desperate Richie seems not only for them to like her but to think well of her himself, as if he's never had another girlfriend. She wonders if Jada got hurt at one of the riots, if Tisha took her and that's what Richie doesn't want them to know. As if Lorr would condemn anyone after what a totally shitty mom she's been. But Richie doesn't know her well enough to understand that. Or maybe this is about Richie blaming Tisha for what happened. Then Tisha would have freaked out and announced she didn't want him around for the operation. Which explains why Richie's been acting so strange, not just this morning but last night when he drove home through the riots.

This makes so much sense she must be right, but apparently, puzzling it through didn't happen in a heartbeat. Pammie's pinching her arm, whispering, "Earth to Lorr."

"What?"

"The driver asked for my number. Should I give it to him?"

"He's a fast worker."

"Actually, we're at the hospital. You were in some kind of fugue state."

Lorr looks up and recognizes the hospital complex just as the driver signals a left turn. She connects with his cagey eyes in the rearview.

"Why not?" And louder, "He's kind of cute, in a funky way. Hey, Driver Man."

"Name's Ray."

"You got a card? In case Baby Sis and I need a ride again?"

He slips it through the protective glass. "Call my cell." Then he turns into the hospital driveway.

Richie and LaTisha were slowly losing their minds. Doctor Williams had estimated the operation would take an hour and a half, but three hours had crept agonizingly by, and they still hadn't been buzzed. Richie had read and reread every *Time*, *Newsweek*, and *Sports Illustrated* in the waiting room. He had read the *Star*'s sports section and coverage of the riots a half-dozen times and was starting again, when Tisha laid her hand on his. "Richard, will you ask at the front desk?"

"I was thinking the same thing."

The volunteer knew nothing.

"Isn't there someone you can call? It's an hour and a half longer than we'd been told."

The girl turned to her beagle-eyed supervisor, who ran her finger down a phone list, then dialed. "Uh-huh," she said, the phone to her ear. "Uh-huh. Uh-huh, thanks."

Wondering what all the *uh-huh*'s could possibly mean, Richie found himself uttering a silent prayer, *Let Jada be all right.*

The supervisor said, "The OR nurse said it's just taking longer than they thought. And they started late."

"Did she say *why* it's taking longer?"

"She said, 'Tell them not to worry.'"

"How are we supposed to do that?"

The girl and the supervisor displayed sympathetic but condescending smiles that propelled Richie back toward LaTisha. When he reached her, Lorraine and Pammie were seated beside her.

"So what's the news?" Pammie asked.

Tisha's face looked like an overfilled balloon.

"They said don't worry, it's just taking longer. And they started late."

"See?" Lorraine said. "It's probably nothing."

Lorraine scooted over, and Richie sat beside Tisha, who laid her head on his shoulder.

"If anything happens," she whispered.

"Nothing's going to happen."

"You don't know that."

Fifteen minutes passed. Thirty. This worry about a child, a situation in which he could do nothing except wait and hope, was like nothing he'd experienced before. How did parents do it? And those who lost a child, like Angela Leisure, or had to raise a really sick one, what must that be like? What would it be like to watch a child starve to death, like Biafra or the Holocaust? Oh my God. And what about a child you'd given up, a child whose life you didn't even know about? He glanced at Lorraine, the splash of gray in her long hair, and she smiled, just around the eyes, as if she were patting his hand.

"How'd you two get here?" he asked.

"Pammie called Rocket Cab, and this cute cabbie picked us up." Lorraine grinned. "Then Pammie picked up the cabbie."

"He was sexy," Pammie said. "Lorr thought so too."

Tisha raised her head off Richie's shoulder. "Go, Auntie Pammie."

Pammie looked pleased with herself. "It's not like anything happened."

"It's going to be your lucky day. Jada's too." Lorraine patted Tisha's knee. "I just know she's going to be okay. And unlike Richie, I *do* know things."

What Tisha thought about that—was Lorraine claiming she had psychic powers?—he had no idea, and they lapsed into silent waiting. They waited. They also serve who sit and wait. Other adults, parents of Johnnie, Tiffany, Mariposa, and Keyshawn, were paged to the supervisor's desk, but Richie, Tisha, Lorraine, and Pammie waited. Richie wanted to jump up and pace to maintain some illusion of control, at least over his own body, but Tisha's head rested on his shoulder, her lips moving silently. He exchanged glances with Lorraine then let his own eyes close. He'd been up since five, had had almost no sleep. But his eyes wouldn't stay closed.

At last, just past two o'clock, the PA summoned the parents of Jada Gordon. He took Tisha's hand, and they walked to the supervisor's desk.

"Jada Gordon," Tisha said, barely a whisper. "I'm her mother."

"Doctor Williams will meet you in consultation room three."

"Is everything okay?" Richie asked.

"The doctor will answer your questions."

They waited inside the small room. Two straight chairs on one side of a table, a larger chair on the other.

"If anything happens to her," Tisha said. "I will die."

"She's fine," Richie said, imagining Jada blind in one eye or some terrible mistake, no blood to her brain. "You heard Lorraine."

"What's that? She *knows* things?"

A small door opened on their left, and Doctor Williams entered wearing blue scrubs, blue paper booties over his shoes, blue paper hair cap wrapping his head, blue everywhere except his hands and face; black-rimmed glasses covered tired eyes.

"Everything went fine," Williams said. "She's doing great."

Omigod. "What took so long? We thought—"

Beside him Tisha began to tremble.

"We started late, and there was more to do than we expected. Some fragments—"

"But she's fine, she really is *fine*?" Tisha asked in a strong clear voice he felt proud of her for possessing now.

"Yes," the doctor said. "We used a silicone plate. We don't always do that." Williams must have read the concern in their faces; before they could ask why, he continued, "Really, it's fine. In a few days, when the swelling goes down, and it could take as many as four or five, and she can open her eye, there may still be some double vision. If so, it will be vertical in orientation."

"For how long?" Richie asked, pressing Tisha's hand.

"A few days. Sometimes"—Williams's head bobbed, as if he were weighing how much to say—"it's permanent. But that's extremely rare."

"When will we know?" Tisha asked, her voice not sounding quite as vibrant this time.

"Hard to say."

Doctor Williams raised his hand to shake Tisha's and then Richie's, who was struck again by how large and meaty the doctor's palm and fingers were. Maybe that wasn't racist. Maybe it was just the truth.

"But I believe she'll do fine. And now, if you'll excuse me, I have another surgery."

"Thank you, Doctor Williams," Richie said, "thank you so much."

Williams inclined his head like an actor acknowledging applause then exited.

"There's a million things I forgot to ask," Tisha said.

"She's okay," Richie said. "That's the main thing. She's okay."

205

EIGHTEEN

Washing down a crème-filled with coffee purchased from the Koreans, Reece headed for the alley where Tim Thomas died. People had been visiting since the murder, but Reece had feared to feel what he might feel, what T. Thomas must have felt. The end of hope. Remorse for deeds undone. Never to see his child again, his mother, his woman, his friends. Never to ball or get high. How bad did it hurt? Did he have time to be afraid, to shout, "No, man, don't shoot!" before Officer Bug blew away every possibility?

Fucking parking tickets. Hatred of the black man.

Reece entered the alley from the direction Officer Bug had run in from, saw the fence T. Thomas leapt, where it must have all gone down, the very spot where T. Thomas laid down his burdens and his soul departed. Reece felt a *pop*, his scalp tingling under his head rag. Someone had tagged the blackened brick wall, now part-shrine, part-mausoleum: R.I.P. TIM.

Bouquets, plastic and real, lay against the wall—tulips, daffodils. Half-full quarts of malt liquor and wine. A football. A Chiefs cap, the C the same red as R.I.P. TIM. To his right a young girl cried softly. A gray-haired auntie knelt to place roses still wrapped in green paper, while two faux gangstas in new jeans and wife-beaters raised bottles, swallowed deep, then added their offerings to the concrete altar of green and brown glass containers.

What a damn waste. Reece faced the wall again, drowned in thought. He'd buried his Moms, who died of cancer. Two cousins and a friend, gunfire. This kind of shit or something very much like it had been going down, maybe on this very street, since Calhoun, the muthafucka this city named for, who famously believed slavery wasn't just a necessary evil but a positive good, helped arrange for the Compromises, the *Compromises* that made slavery legal in the great racist state of Missouri. No wonder they still hated and feared the black man. Now it was 2001. Third century, same old shit. Reece clenched and unclenched his fists. Something's gotta change. Something's got to. He exited the alley of T. Thomas's beatification not knowing what that change might be and joined the crowd at the corner of Twelfth and Race, which appeared to be as large as the one yesterday when Jada got hurt. That's what gotta change, the kids. Someone shouted, "Let's go," and the crowd surged forward. Where to, Reece didn't know and didn't much care. He pushed to the front of the crowd, which was marching down the middle of Twelfth. Up ahead, just past the corner of Vine, a squad of white-helmeted cops beat batons against riot shields, and Reece wondered if this was it. Would the cops let them pass? Hell no. They'd just as soon beat batons against black heads as their damn shields. As the crowd approached the helmeted cops, from out of nowhere a line of middle-aged black men, including some he'd seen that morning with the mayor, surged between the marchers and the police and joined hands.

"Stop!" they shouted. "Hold up!"

The lead marchers, including Reece, pushed back on the crowd behind them, shouting, "Stop, watch out! Yo, stop!"

Ten feet away, just past the line of old black men in suits, the cops massed like a Roman legion. The crowd chanted, "No justice, no peace! No justice, no peace! Hey, hey, don't shoot me!"

One minister stepped forward to confer with the leader of the cops, a lieutenant or a captain, judging by the gold on his collar. Reece was close enough to see their mouths move and to lip-read some words. *Got to, Got to, Got to.* They talked a minute, maybe less, tendons standing out on both necks, black and white. The crowd chanted, "Hey, hey, don't shoot me!" The cops beat their shields. Then the police commander nodded; the minister shook his hand and returned to the crowd.

"Everyone, listen up!" Reece waved his arms. "Y'all, quiet down!"

The minister, who looked sixty, bald as an eight ball except for tufts that looped the back of his skull, mouthed, "Thank you!" then raised his arms.

"The *po*-lice," he intoned, "is gonna let us pass! They gonna let us pass!"

The white and black sea of cops parted, and the crowd passed through, chanting, "No justice, no peace! No justice, no peace!" They turned south onto Vine and marched to the New Prospect Baptist Church, which Reece declined to enter, having little use for Jesus and his earthly minions, though that minister surely saved the day. Instead, he continued along Vine to Sixth to catch a bus.

After surgery Jada had returned to the same room, the other half of which was now occupied by an eight-year-old bitten on the back and neck by his estranged dad's Rottweiler. The boy's mom, who'd pulled the dog off her son, had also been mauled, and since Richie, Tisha, Lorraine, and Pammie had returned, there'd been a stream of visitors to the other side, including a uniformed policeman taking a report with an eye toward filing charges against the dad, who had brought the dog over allegedly to attack his ex. What a fucking world, Richie thought.

He'd been out in the hall talking to Lorraine, who said she'd be happy to stay with Jada, although she doubted Tisha would be willing to leave her daughter. But when they walked back in, past the dog-bit family, to their half of the room, Tisha, whose chin kept falling onto her chest, admitted she'd love to go home and sleep a few. Jada would likely be discharged in the morning, and if she hadn't slept before then? Pammie said she would have stayed too, but she'd already arranged for Ray the cabbie to pick her up for dinner, and she wanted to get back to Richie's apartment to fix herself up.

"Do you need a ride?" Richie asked, thinking that if he had to drive Pammie after taking Tisha home, he'd never get back to work.

"No thanks. Ray's going to drop me then pick me up again later." Pammie was actually *blushing*. "That way he'll know where the apartment is."

Richie grinned at Tisha but didn't ask the obvious. *Didn't the cabbie already pick you up there?* Instead, he, Tisha, and Pammie rode the elevator to the ground floor and headed to the gift shop, where he purchased its largest stuffed animal, a St. Bernard with floppy brown ears. He hugged Pammie and whispered, "I hope it's your lucky day."

Pammie blushed a second time then headed to the elevator with the stuffed animal Richie had purchased, No How Dawg, tucked under her arm.

"She seems so excited," Tisha said. "It kinda cute."

"I don't think she's had a date in a long time."

"You white devils is strange."

Richie briefly tasted her lips, then they headed for the parking elevator, holding hands.

Lorr is chair-dozing beside the hospital bed in which Jada, connected both to an IV and a heart and lung monitor, slumbers with her unencumbered arm encircling No How Dawg. The curtain retracts, but instead of some medical person entering to check vitals or in some other way harass the sleeping child, a tall, good-looking black man crowned by a red do-rag enters, sees Lorr, and scowls. Before he has time to ask why she's there, she knows why he is. Not only *knows* but wonders why no one has mentioned him before.

"Where's Tish?"

His voice is deep and smooth as whiskey; his skin tone isn't much different from how she remembers Ricardo's. He's got to be some kind of mix, with large, oddly colored eyes: green just under a surface brown.

"Went home to sleep."

"So, who the hell are you?"

Something about his anger moves her. She doesn't know why, isn't sure she wants to. "Richie's mom." This seems both to anger him further and to pain him. "You're Jada's dad."

He circles the child's bed, avoiding the side on which Lorr sits. "She gonna be okay?"

"The surgeon says so." Lorr stands so he doesn't loom quite so menacingly over her. Across Jada's sleeping body she offers her hand. "I'm Lorraine, but people call me Lorr."

Either he's intent on Jada, which she wants to believe, or chooses to ignore her. Lorr lowers her hand. "What do they call you?"

He pushes stray hair from the undamaged side of Jada's face. When Jada stirs, he draws back, and Lorr realizes he hasn't had much to do with his daughter.

"She's lovely."

"What you know about it?" His eyes cloud again with that pain/anger cocktail. "What they tell you anyway?"

"Nothing."

"Then how you know I'm the child's father?"

"She looks like you." His unsettling eyes settle on hers. "And how you look at her."

"Reece Q. Woodson."

This time he shakes her hand. "What's the Q for?"

"Not for anything."

"Nice to meet you, Reece just a Q."

He drags a chair to the foot of the bed. Jada does not stir, and he makes no attempt to awaken her. She suspects Jada scares him and that he's just as happy she's asleep. There are quite a few questions she would like to ask and quite a bit she could tell him she believes it would be good for him to know. Why should she care? She'll probably never see him again but suspects he could play a very important role or non-role in Richie and Tisha's life. And oh, she doesn't understand it, but she feels something for him. For shit's sake, he's younger than Richie, which makes her more than old enough to be his mother, but she doesn't feel maternal. She feels *engaged*, in what way she can't yet say.

"You don't see her much, do you?"

His eyes darken, but instead of going off, which she can feel he badly wants to do, he says, "That's right."

There's something in how he says it, something, too, in his easily bruised eyes, that heightens what she's feeling, and without realizing what she's about to say and certainly with no conscious intent, she responds, "I didn't see Richie most of his life."

"Why not?"

"My parents raised him."

"Why you telling me?"

"I thought." She hesitates. "I'm not sure."

Footsteps approach, though it's too early for anyone in their group to return, and Lorr is relieved when whoever it is veers toward the other child's half of the room. Reece seems as intent on the footsteps as she is, and his expression mirrors what she suspects is her own. Pleasure at not being interrupted.

"Richie tell you how we met?"

She shakes her head.

"You should ask him."

"Why don't you tell me? I'm a good listener."

"Nah." He smiles. "I bet you are."

Jada moves her head but still does not wake. Her right eye is so swollen it looks as if it might pop out of its socket.

"Your son," Reece announces suddenly, "is trying to steal the child's affection."

"That's not possible." Lorr surprises herself by touching Reece on his bony right knee. "Assuming Jada has any for you."

"She could, but he's in the way."

"Richie only met her a few months ago. Who was in the way before that?"

"I had a legal situation. Still do."

"I know about getting in your own way."

He looks at her. She assumes he means jail and wonders how long and for what. Is he dangerous? A threat to Richie? She knows men who attacked their lover's new man. A few years back there was a murder/suicide in Redwood Valley, and the guy who did it boarded his dogs with her. And she's seen the anger in Reece's eyes.

"What did they arrest you for?"

"Receiving stolen goods."

"Did you?"

"The DA thinks so." He raises an eyebrow. "Wouldn't be the first time."

"So what are you going to do?"

"You ask a lot of questions."

"That's right. So what *are* you going do?"

"My Legal Aid lawyer thinks she can plead it out two to three years, maybe I do eighteen months, and they keep me at the County."

"That doesn't sound so bad."

He looks at her, she thinks, showboating.

"You ever been inside, Lorraine?"

Now it's her turn. "Visiting."

"Then you know. Not a place I want the child to see me. But if she don't, by the time I get out she might truly forget me. So maybe, I been thinking, I just might leave."

Now it's his turn to look surprised by how much he's revealed. He stands up. "Tell Tish I stopped by."

"I will."

This time, when he shakes her hand, he leans forward to hug her.

"Pleased to meet you, Lorraine. You pretty cool to be Richie's momma, considering how uncool he is."

She could let that go but feels she ought to defend Richie, who is more important than this bizarre little flirtation she's allowed herself.

"Tisha seems to think he's cool. So does Jada."

He aims his slender trigger finger at her. "Got me. Maybe I see you again when I visit the child."

"Maybe you will."

He saunters out, long legged, loose limbed, and she hears his sneakers slapping linoleum long after he disappears.

NINETEEN

Richie answered e-mail and worked through the stacked memoranda Jeannie had left him. He decided to talk to her about how early she was leaving then came upon a memo detailing perceived and real dangers to C&M employees during the crisis, so perhaps he didn't need to. Maybe Jeannie was acting prudently, though nothing he'd seen seemed dangerous or unusual, nothing, of course, except the scene on Vine last night. Every time he thought about driving Lorraine through the riot, he couldn't believe he had. It just wasn't like him, clearly the most ill-considered, insane thing he'd ever done. No planning at all, just impulse.

Folgrow news, at least, was encouraging. Although it was going to take another few days for the distribution snag to untangle, initial placements were still within estimates, in fact above his median projection. My God, he realized, today was the official shelf date, and he'd barely had time to think about it. Just then his cell phone rang. Dave Manning, confirming their weekly drink at Havana Martini. Before he could explain about Jada, Dave added, urgently, "I really need to see you. We can meet someplace else if it's better."

"Havana's fine." At least he could walk. "But I only have time for one."

When Richie entered, Dave was already holding down a corner table, working on what Richie assumed to be a dirty Grey Goose, very dry. A second stem, which Dave edged forward, welcomed him.

"Ah." Richie sipped. "That's good."

In just three days since the seder Dave seemed to have aged

an equal number of years. In addition to uncharacteristic shabbiness—he hadn't shaved, and his hair was uncombed—his eyes glistened, whether from illness, lack of sleep, or something else entirely, Richie couldn't say. But the change was remarkable.

"What's wrong?"

"Laura's leaving me."

"Bullshit."

"Actually, she's kicking me out." Dave gulped what remained in his glass then waggled the fingers of his right hand overhead to attract a waitress. "I can't believe it."

A brunette Richie hadn't met before, one whom Hank would have called *zoftik*, arrived beside their table.

"Two more," Dave said. The girl smiled and departed, and they watched her hips rumba under her black skirt. Dave's cheek, the one closer to Richie, expanded under the pressure of his tongue as if the girl's waggle were pressing on it. "You remember a few months ago, I asked Anne for her number, only you didn't want it?"

"Yeah?"

"So I called her. One thing led to another. And another."

"You idiot."

"Monday night Laura was either listening in or hacked my e-mail, but she announced she knew all about Anne and wanted me gone. She's changing the locks."

"But you're having a baby."

"That's what she kept saying. 'We're having a baby!'"

Faster than he would have thought possible, the waitress returned, set down fresh martinis, and collected the empties on her tray. Richie watched Dave watch her go.

"To be honest, I was also thinking, 'We're having a baby. This will be my last fling forever, before I become a dad.' I kind of told you, Laura wouldn't have anything to do with me the last couple of months, not that that's any excuse."

"Do you love Anne?"

Dave grimaced, like, *Are you kidding?* "I'm in love with Laura. And she knows it." He sipped his drink, set it down. "But I have to admit, the sex was incredible."

Richie nearly shouted, *I don't want to hear it.* The possibility that Dave and Laura would break up, that Dave could do this—God, he'd give anything to have a baby with Tisha—made him want to punch Dave. "The most important thing," he began, falling back on analysis, "is figuring out how much Laura knows and how much she only thinks she knows."

"She knows I made a lot of calls, she knows I've been out of the house, and she knows, she says, that 'I've been acting distant.'"

"Did you admit sleeping with Anne?"

"Are you kidding? I buried it then buried the shovel. But Laura's no fool."

They sat in unsteady silence.

"And there's some history." Dave ran a hand over his stubbly cheek. "A grad student ten years ago."

Sometime during his second martini Richie told Dave about the injury to Jada's eye. By the end of their third and final drink they'd agreed the most help Richie could provide was to tell Laura about Jada and suggest she visit, which might get her mind off what an asshole her husband had been. Of course, he'd have to pretend to know nothing about Anne. If Dave showed up at the same time, in the rush of maternal feeling, perhaps her heart would soften.

"You really are an idiot," Richie announced when they were out on the street, his head flying from all that Grey Goose. "How could you do this to Laura?"

"Not everyone's as pure as you, my friend. But that doesn't make me evil, just human."

Richie shook Dave's hand but concluded that while Dave might not be evil, his actions were. "I'll call her tonight."

"You're a pal."

They headed in opposite directions as darkness fell.

Richie mostly sobered up on the walk to his office, retrieved his CRV, and zoomed south to get Tisha. Fifteen minutes away and half an hour late, he called to apologize and woke her. When all she could manage were grunts, he asked, "You sure you want me to get you?"

"Uh-huh."

"Don't forget Stripes."

"Uh-huh."

Richie drove. He couldn't process Dave's news, not because he hadn't suspected Dave might like the ladies as much as they seemed to like him but because the consequences—he didn't believe Laura would relent, not if this wasn't the first time— were so dire he couldn't believe Dave would risk them. Blow up the marriage? Lose the right to be a full-time dad? And that didn't take Laura's feelings into account, how much this must hurt her.

It wasn't that Richie was pure, rather that he'd conducted years of unintentional market research into what unloved and unlovable felt like. With Dave's good looks and flirty eyes that every woman—well, every waitress—seemed drawn to, Dave could have no idea, but Richie did. Having found someone to love him, he'd cut off his own left nut, and Dave's too, before doing anything to mess it up.

A short time later, castrating blade still very much in mind, he turned onto Tisha's street and found his way to her door. She was waiting, Stripes in one hand, a small overnight bag in the other. She climbed up into the CRV.

"Hey, Richard."

He snatched her into his arms and kissed her with such urgency that after she'd pushed him away her eyes ran over his face. "What's wrong?"

"I really, really love you."

"I know."

"I'd never do anything to hurt you."

"Richard, tell me."

"Nothing." He'd promised Dave. "I just wanted you to know."

She cut her eyes to show she wasn't fooled. She still looked tired but tired-lite: freshly made up, and the fishhook curls once again glistened beside each ear.

"What you looking at?"

"You." He reversed in her driveway and set out, planning to follow Troost north to Hale, the side street he'd taken that afternoon from the hospital, but when they passed through the light at Forest, he spotted something up ahead.

"Looks like a fire," Tisha said.

Damn them. "Now what?"

"I don't know."

Talking to Dave, he'd almost forgotten C. City's troubles. He glanced at Tisha, who stared straight ahead, lips parted. Whatever else was operating on her, the protests seemed to thrill her; her excitement felt almost pornographic. Richie? Unlike last night, he was frightened. He didn't want to drive near the fire, but he also feared what might be waiting on a side street. *The heart of fucking darkness.* This much was clear, the demonstrations—no, call a spade a spade, *You fucking racist!*—the riots, had spilled over into other parts of the city.

The line of cars edged forward, grills to brake lights, as if they were elephants on parade. A block and a half away he could see a fire was burning in the southbound lane. A young and as far as he could tell entirely black crowd surrounded the flames, waving signs and chanting something over a discord of horns. Lining the right-hand sidewalk, across the fire from the demonstrators, squads of grim-faced cops stood in heavy gear. Patrol cars, bubblegum tops popping *red, red, red,* blocked access to side streets, while in the near distance firetrucks raced toward them, sirens rising and falling. Richie glanced again at Tisha.

"Look at the signs," she said.

"'No justice, no peace?'"

She pointed. "HONK IF YOU'RE BLACK."

This was meaningful protest? Tim Thomas dead in an alley, *Honk if you're black?* But he never doubted which side he was on and what he would do. He leaned on the horn, and the CRV bleated, bleated, while a voice inside Richie roared, *Fucking idiot, you're as stupid as they are.* They nosed into the intersection, passed the fire, the cops and whirling lights, the signs and shaken fists, the city's unforgiving and unforgivable history burning at Troost and Forty-fourth, and continued through, not looking at each other, not thinking any more than they had to, at least Richie wasn't, all nerves and white knuckles, until he found an unbarricaded side street and turned left, trying to find his way to Children's Mercy.

Lorr sits beside Jada, who is just conscious enough to hug No How Dawg. In repose she looks like a tiny boxer, right eye swollen shut and twice normal size. An hour ago, looking like Jake in *Raging Bull*, she awakened and glanced at Lorr. "Who are you?"

"Richie's mommy," Lorr answered. "Remember?"

"Where's Momma?"

"She went home to sleep. She'll be here soon."

Now, forty-five minutes before the end of visiting hours and more than an hour after he promised to return, there's no sign of Richie, no phone call either, and Lorr's worried. It's not that she can't imagine what could be keeping them; it's that she can. Then footsteps enter the shared room turning left toward eye damage rather than right toward dog attack, and Tisha draws the curtain. Behind her Richie looks upset.

"Richie, Momma," Jada cries, "you brought Stripes!"

Tisha bends and hugs her. "Oh, baby," she says. "I'm so glad to see you."

Lorr scoots her chair back to give them room.

"How's she been?" Richie asks.

"Mostly sleeping."

Tisha glances over her shoulder. "Thank you so much."

Lorr glances from Tisha, whom she notices knows her way around the makeup counter, to Richie, trying to intuit what's wrong. Jada pushes the polka-dotted snow leopard into the dog's floppy ears and snout.

"Stripes, this No How Dawg. *Mmm, mmm, mmm.*" The cat growls. "No, no, no, Stripes, Dawg won't hurt you." Stripes keeps growling. Jada puts her face to the cat's ear and whispers something Lorr can't quite make out but which might be "I love you best."

Stripes stops his noise, and Jada, who has all six adult eyes fixed firmly on her, says, "See, Momma? Now they friends."

"I was getting worried," Lorr says. To Richie she adds, "You didn't come when you said."

"I was late getting to Tisha, and driving here—" He pauses and *something,* Lorr isn't sure what, moves between him and Tisha. "We passed through demonstrations."

"Like last night?" Lorr sees the brick arcing toward them, the surreal ride through the riots.

"The first one was kind of a bonfire. The second one, and we were only there because streets were blocked off, a woman was pulled out—"

"I don't think"—Tisha glances meaningfully at Jada—"we should discuss this now."

A short time later a nurse stops by and asks everyone who's not spending the night to leave.

Richie asks, "Do you want me to stay?"

Tisha shakes her head. "No need."

"I'll be back by seven-thirty." Richie looks both concerned and on edge. "That's when Doctor Williams said he'd stop by."

"What about work?"

"What about school?"

Tisha's face, which Lorr believes has worn a *Don't Come Near*

Me smile except when talking to Jada, softens a bit. "If you can, that'd be nice."

Richie kisses Tisha then moves toward Jada, who's fallen asleep hugging both stuffed animals. There's something about her swollen face pressed so close to the plush animals that tears at Lorr's heart.

Tisha says, "Thank you. It was such a help."

"It was nothing." Lorr hugs the younger woman, *her son's lover*, for shit's sake, and wonders if there's still anything between her and Reece Q, who made such an impression. Her lips brush Tisha's cheek, and Tisha's touch hers. "Let me know if there's anything else I can do."

While they're waiting for the elevator, Richie says, "We drove through one demonstration where they were all waving signs, 'Honk if you're black.'"

The elevator door opens, revealing a large, gray-haired black man, a maintenance worker, Lorr surmises from his clothing, and she feels Richie respond to the loss of privacy. "Did you?"

He nods. "But it was stupid, and Tisha knew I thought so." He glances toward the stranger. "Then we hit this detour and ended up east of where we wanted to be at another intersection with a fire burning, only this time there weren't any cops. The next thing I know."

The door slides back at the lobby, and they exit, including the stranger. "What happened?" he asks.

Lorr eyes him. Blue work clothes. Round face, salt-and-pepper beard.

"Three or four cars ahead? We're all stopped for a light, when a bunch of kids pull this woman out of an SUV and start beating on her."

Oh shit, oh shit, Lorr thinks, and now her stomach is not only churning but upside down.

"A white woman?" the stranger asks.

"What do you think?"

Oh shit.

"I'm trying to figure what to do. Get out of the car and help, like my girlfriend's telling me?"

Lorr glances at the stranger, who must assume his girlfriend's white.

"Or is that only going to make things worse and get my ass beat? I'm halfway out the door, when two women and two men, who turn out to live on the block, come running and pull the kids off her."

"And the woman?" Lorr asks.

"By this point there's a whole bunch of us standing around."

The stranger asks, "You mean, you got out of the car?"

"You know what?" Richie answers. "Why don't you mind your own damn business?"

The black man squints, and his eyes half-disappear in his cheeks. "You're just mad 'cause a white woman was getting beat on."

"*Because* she was white."

"That ain't right." The stranger shakes his head. "But now you know how it feels."

Lorr watches him walk out the door. Beside her Richie takes a deep, shuddering breath. "It was all I could do not to say things to him I would never say out loud."

Lorr drops her hand on Richie's shoulder then moves it to his cheek.

TWENTY

Long past dark Reece strode toward Byron's, eating the second of two beef and bean burritos purchased at the Taco Bell on Martin Luther King. Short on cash but long on hungry, he'd decided to exchange a long walk for a second beef and bean. If shit got desperate, he could beg money from his Grams, but she had borrowed against her house for his bail, so he was disinclined. He could eat out of Little B's fridge, but he was weary of B's charity. Bad enough to be staying not helping with rent. So Reece was walking, half an hour or more, to save two dollars, but he liked to walk, had the long arms and legs for it and did his best thinking while his body moved in tandem with his mind. *Walk bite, think chew, walk bite, think*, his Airs slapping sidewalk as he strode downhill and crossed Brooklyn, still a few blocks east of Troost. He'd used up half his remaining cell phone minutes trying to find Marshall King. No one knew why, but it seemed Marsh had disappeared and *fast*, about the time Reece got pinched with all the TVs. Maybe the nigger afraid Reece going to flip him, or maybe he flipped Reece? But Marsh *gone*, which explained Richard A. Gordon's unpaid cable bill. Nothing to be done for it now.

Up ahead trash can fires burned, embers circling the cans like orange gnats. Reece had passed other fires on this walk. And fiery groups of the very young to whom he'd nodded, their greetings containing neither thought nor meaning. *Yo, whass happening?* Walking, Reece had indulged an out-of-body lassitude, reliving the conversation with Lorraine. He knew from the IDs he'd found just lying there on Fourth and Race, and wasn't it weird how random shit became your life, that Richard A. Gordon would turn thirty-one next month, which put Lorraine near fifty? Even if she'd gotten knocked up really really young, she'd be forty-five. He'd never had no taste for older bitches, nor was he interested in the white girls who frequented the clubs—*Once they taste black, they never go back*—but he had to admit Lorraine looked good no matter what her age or color. Sitting with her in the child's room, and he was *pissed* when he learned who she was, like even Richie's momma had more claim than he did, something zip-zapped between them. If it wasn't sexual (and up to this point most everything that had passed between Reece and women, and there had been quite a bit, was bodily fluids), he didn't know what to call it. But they had definitely clicked, and Reece left the child's room feeling better, and better about himself, than when he'd entered.

He fed the folded, mostly tortilla last half-inch into his mouth, wiped his fingers on his jeans, and tossed the greasy wrapper in the gutter. Up ahead a crowd had gathered on the corner of what appeared to be Troost, where he'd turn south toward B's. Cops, too, including some on horseback. Reece reached for his cell, to see if B knew what was going on, when he heard what sounded like gunshots. What fool be blasting around all these cops, or was it cops blasting at them? Then he heard it again, no mistake—he'd heard enough guns, even fired a few himself, though never in anger. The crowd screeched toward him, mouths wide open. Reece was still fumbling for his cell, hand in his pocket, when two cops rushed up, the white one big as two men, looking not just angry but dumb as a boulder. The black cop—both wore white riot helmets—was nowhere near as big but just as angry.

"Don't move, asshole!" He shoved a shorty shotgun against Reece's forehead. "Now take your hand out your pocket, and you better have nothing that makes my finger slip."

Both cops looked like they wanted to kick his face in. Reece displayed a gray flip phone on his palm. The white cop patted him down then shook his huge head. The black one lessened the pressure of the barrel but did not remove it.

"Someone shot a cop."

"Not me."

A small crowd, a very small crowd considering how many people had been milling around just a minute ago, circled them. Then more cops, one of them older and apparently in charge, pushed through.

"Let him go, the shooter was older."

The black cop lowered his shotgun.

"Sorry for your trouble, *Sir*," said the white giant.

"Maybe you oughta go home and change your panties." The black cop's gaze shifted from Reece's face to his jeans, and Reece suddenly felt the wetness sluicing down his leg. His fist closed around the phone.

"Easy, stud."

"Let's go," said the cop in charge.

Reece's face burned now with shame instead of fear. Without acknowledging or registering if anyone spoke to him, *It all right, bro, you right to be scared,* he started for Byron's thinking, If he killed someone, if he just laid some muthafucker out, who could blame him?

Richie sits opposite Lorr at Hannigan's. She picks at a Caesar salad, wondering how much to tell him, when her phone rings: Pammie, announcing she won't be home (not that Lorr thought she would be) or only really, really late, is there still some way she could get in? Lorr covers the mouthpiece and explains. Richie, who looks two parts weary, one part sick at heart, pulls himself together enough to say, "Tell her to ring the buzzer, I'll get up." Lorr relays this to Pammie then asks her, "You all right?"

"Hell, yes." Baby Sis hangs up.

Lorr sips her chardonnay, which tastes thin and nasty. Now that it's time, she fears she won't be able to do it. And Rich-

227

ie? He looks like he's going to pass out, face-first, in his garlic mashed potatoes.

"Don't hate me, but I never told your dad I was pregnant."

He eyes her, fork and knife suspended. Then he bends to the task at hand: slicing his steak. He forks a bloody hunk to his lips and chews. Just when she's wondering if she's going to have to repeat her shameful confession, he asks, "So, you know who he is?"

It takes a moment then she's raging. "You think at seventeen I was fucking so many guys I didn't know?"

His wounded eyes remind her of Ricardo's, though the truth is—and this summons tears to her own eyes, though she's been promising herself every time she imagined this that she wouldn't cry—she can't remember exactly what Ricardo looked like. A vague outline has morphed into the reality of Richie.

"If you knew, why didn't you tell him?"

The truth, which at one time seemed too complex to find, comes into view. "He didn't love me anymore. And Daddy." She sips the awful wine. "Hank."

"I know who you meant."

"Wanted a little boy so bad."

"Wouldn't he have wanted a grandson?"

She wants to shout, *Why are you making this so hard?* And then she knows. Because it is hard. "Ricardo—"

"That's his name?"

"—was Puerto Rican, and Daddy, he had lots of good qualities. But he hated, he *hated*, and if we pretended you were his and Mommy's—"

"So I'm half–Puerto Rican?"

"That's right. Ricardo Delgas." She makes the surname sound as Latin as she can.

"So." Richie sips his own blood-red wine. "Did you stop loving him too?"

"No."

"Did you hate him because he was Puerto Rican?"

"How could I, when I loved him?"

His tongue tugs at the corner of his mustache. For a moment she watches him chew on himself. Then he whispers, "There's a part of me, this *voice*, that's always saying the most fucked-up things about Tisha."

"Like what?"

"They're too terrible to say."

"Maybe that's why only you hear them."

"Do you?"

She hesitates, so as not to shame him. "No, but I was too chickenshit to stand up to Daddy, who not only heard those things but said them all the time." She drains her wine and waves at the waiter. "I let him ruin things for me and Ricardo. And for you."

"You were only eighteen."

"Seventeen when it ended." She sees herself, crying in her room. "Eighteen when you were born."

"When I was eighteen, all I was doing was school."

"So, you don't think I'm horrible?"

"For not being a single mom?"

"For being such a chickenshit."

"I don't think you're horrible."

He pats her hand, and she's fighting tears again. Just then the waiter starts toward their table. "Last time I checked," she says quickly, "Ricardo wrote for one of the New York papers, I think the *Post*, about the Puerto Rican community."

"How long ago was that?"

"A few years." The waiter arrives beside them. "Another chardonnay, you got anything better than this crap?"

The waiter shakes his head.

They walked home in the dark. Sleepwalking, it felt like, or maybe he was dreaming. He wasn't Hank and Marilyn's little boy, okay. In some deep and deeply repressed part of his mind he'd known Hank and Marilyn were older than everyone else's parents, so maybe in that same roped-off and hidden place he'd always known. Or at least suspected. There'd been times when strangers looked at them oddly. At the very least, a few months after learning it, he was no longer completely surprised. But that he wasn't all Jewish and not even all white? Did that mean Hank had hated him too but hid it? He couldn't stand that. His own father, fuck it, his own grandfather, hated him? Richie Allan Delgas? *Half-Spic?* He'd always believed Hank loved him. He *knew* Hank loved him, and there was no doubt, racist or not, that he had loved Hank, that he still loved him. Maybe, he thought, Hank's heart had changed. Maybe raising him had changed Hank, and that's why he didn't remember Hank being a hater. If every racist raised a kid who didn't look like him, would that solve the race problem? It's hard, after all, to hate a two-year-old close up, unless he's crying. Or shitting his pants. *You're an asshole,* Richie thought, unsure whom he was cursing. Himself? Hank? He glanced at Lorraine, wondering if he'd said *asshole* out loud? With Lorraine sometimes it didn't matter. But she seemed lost inside herself, dark hair cloaking her face. Then his cell chirped and startled Richie, fearful something had gone wrong with Jada.

Dave asked, "Have you called Laura yet?"

"Oh shit."

"Call the house." Dave's voice buzzed against his ear. "I know she's there."

"Where are you?"

"In a bar." He sounded glum. "The news says the rioting is getting worse."

"After I left you, I drove through it."

"You okay?"

Richie glanced at Lorraine. "Define *okay.*"

"On the news they said Wilson's considering calling in the National Guard."

"You're shitting me."

"I shit you not. Call Laura and tell her to come tomorrow."

"Okay." He closed his phone.

Lorr asked, "What was that?"

He told her about the news report but not about Dave and Laura's troubles. She said, "If things keep getting worse, maybe you should bring Jada here tomorrow instead of Tisha's apartment. Pammie and I could get a motel room. Or sleep on the couch."

He hadn't thought about where Jada would come home to. Or who would take care of her when Tisha went back to school. "Do I look like Ricardo? Because I don't look like anyone else in the family."

"I always said, 'You look like you.'"

She seemed poised to say something more but didn't. When he unlocked the lobby door and held it open for her, she surprised him by touching his hair.

"Except your hair. Ricardo's exactly." She kissed his cheek. "I always loved his hair. You would have loved him too."

As so often happened, he didn't know what to say.

At five-thirty his eyes sprung open. What could have gotten him up? Pammie ringing the buzzer? He padded to the front door and checked the keypad. No, no one had buzzed. Pammie must still be out screwing the cabbie. Well, good for her. Or should he worry? *Ray* something. And they knew which cab company he drove for. Pammie could take care of herself. Hadn't she taken care of him? Maybe he should worry about the cabbie.

Richie headed for the kitchen. Five hours sleep, three the night before. Sometime soon he was going to crash but apparently not yet. He ground French roast and turned on the coffeemaker. While water gurgled up to drip onto the fresh grounds, he tried to extract from his dream-self what had awakened him. What had he forgotten to do? It was gone. But the hiss of steam and the first gouts of coffee scent hitting the pot retrieved it. He hadn't called Laura. Dave was going to kill him.

Richie sipped his first cup in the dark. He'd just decided maybe he should stop in the office on his way to Children's Mercy when he heard the guest bedroom door open. A moment later Lorraine arrived in the kitchen.

"Don't you sleep?" he asked.

"Oh shit!" She jumped back and switched on the light. "Why are you sitting in the dark?"

"Sorry."

She poured a cup. "No, I don't sleep much. Daddy didn't either."

He was about to ask her what else ran in the family besides racism and insomnia. Then the caffeine kicked in, and a million things he must have been thinking about began to jump around inside his head. *Should he contact Ricardo Delgas? What would Lorraine think if he did? What would Ricardo Delgas think? What about Tisha when he told her he wasn't all white?* Two rooms away his cell phone rang. Not even six a.m., what the fuck?

"Richard," Tisha breathed. "Did I wake you?"

"Is everything okay?"

"You coming to see Doctor Williams?"

"Of course. How's Jada?"

"They keep coming in and waking her."

"Did you get any sleep?"

"Richard, I've been so hateful."

"No, you haven't."

"I have! I woke up a few minutes ago in the chair beside her bed."

Suddenly he could hear other voices. "Where are you calling from?"

"The nurses' station. And I thought, 'It's not his fault he's white.'"

Not as white as you think.

"And now he's not going to come."

"I'll be there."

"It's not even your fault you have messed-up attitudes. You do, you know."

"I know. I love you. I'll be there soon."

He hung up, closed his door, then hurried to his clothes closet, feeling, although it wasn't even six o'clock, that he was already late and it was going to be another fucked-up day.

TWENTY-ONE

Reece woke on B's couch with last night's shame pressing him down. Peed his damn trow and had to walk to B's like a pissy baby, pee running down his leg; then, to make everything bad as it could be, B was boning one of his girls in the bedroom. Normally, Reece would have went, but he was so beat down he couldn't make himself go nowhere else to let B finish his business in peace. Instead, Reece locked himself in the john, stripped, and stood under the shower, where he couldn't hear the bed jouncing and the bitch moaning. He would have stayed in there all night, maybe even drowned like the worthless muthafucker he was beginning to think he was, except sometime later B began to pound the door instead of the bitch.

"Reece, hey Reece, open up."

On the couch, still shamed, Reece ran his hands over his face. It was dark, morning hours away. His cranium throbbed; his lips tasted chapped; he badly needed to pee. Damn that black bitch of a cop. After B's lady friend, Roxy, headed home to be with her kids—she needed to wash up, that's what had brought B to the door—Reece and him saluted an entire bottle of Captain Morgan. Reece tried but couldn't make himself tell B what happened, said only some cop, damn his black ass, got all up in my face, and it was bad, man, real bad. Put the barrel of a shorty right here. Walking to the bathroom, where his washed and still-wet jeans and boxers hung from the shower rod, Reece rubbed the spot on his temple then directed his stream into the bowl. Damn, why'd he have to do that?

"Fucked-up," B had agreed.

"Thought I was one dead nigger."

235

"A cop," B said, "ain't no color at all, not even a person."

"I'll kill his ass I see him again," Reece said. "Kill his ass."

"Nah," B answered. "You gotta be smart."

Reece returned to the couch. What had being smart ever got him? He was way smarter than B, and look who was sleeping on whose couch. Who had a job and who was going back to jail. Reece slipped into a pair of dirty jeans and selected the T-shirt that smelled least funky, though there wasn't much to choose from. Eau de Serious Funk. He'd lied last night, told B his Grams had gifted him, so here's a twenty, bro—in reality, one of Reece's last two—for the bottle of Captain. Reece slipped out of the apartment and down the stairwell, entering the dark street, where overhead morning stars still shone. He was hungry; he was angry. He started down Twelfth toward Race wondering what he'd do if that cop was still there. He wondered too, his stride lengthening, how long it would take to walk back up the hill to see the child, if Lorraine was still standing guard or if he'd grab some sweet time alone with Tish.

He couldn't remember the last time he'd been awake this early except when he'd been up all night. Walking through the empty, rubble-dusted streets was freaky. No cops, no kids, nothing and no one, just trash and boarded windows, the feeling *Nothing's going to change no matter what we do* clouding up the air like smoke. He could slip away and start over, maybe out west, but be who? Richard A. Gordon's cards no good anymore. Do your time? Get your head straight, maybe start correspondence courses and get a degree like Caroline Something-Something said? Use this brain he'd been given Lord knows why, make his Grams and the child, maybe even Tish, proud? Yeah, I knew that nigger once.

When he crossed MLK, Reece thought of the great man it was named for, how the times he'd endured were so much worse than these, how they'd threatened to and then really did murder him. It was early enough, Reece felt like Batman patrolling the sleeping city; there were cars stopped at the light, and he wondered why the drivers were up so early and what they thought about him, walking in the dark this weekday morning. Did they think he was going to work? Some no-account gangsta? That he had an injured child he was walking to see?

When Reece entered the hospital lobby, the hands of the clock pointed straight up: six o'clock. He'd prepared a story in case anyone hassled him, but no one sat at the information desk downstairs nor the nurses' station upstairs, and he approached the child's room unchallenged. The lights on both sides of the room were turned down. He hesitated then drew the curtain on the child's side. Tisha, splay-legged on a chair that made halfway into a bed, raised her head toward him, recalling happier times: all those mornings he'd awakened beside her fusty, warm-bodied self. He thought about joining her on the chair bed, kissing her gently then harder, retrieving all he'd lost. Then Tish seemed to rise into herself, and the anticipatory light in her eyes dimmed so far down he knew it had been meant for someone else.

"Hey, Reece, what you doing here?"

"Can't I see my child?"

On a raised bed the child slumbered, her cheek and eye swollen ugly.

"'Course you can. But maybe come back when she awake?"

"I was here last night and met Richie Gordon's momma. She tell you?"

Tish looked surprised.

"Why didn't you ask me if you needed someone to watch the child?"

"You know you never wanted nothing to do with her."

"That was before."

"That was *years*."

He was going to say *I've changed*, maybe get on his knees, say, *Tish, I been wrong, but I'm gonna get straight with the law, and when I come back, everything gonna be different. Maybe you and me—*

237

Just then a nurse stepped in, checked the child, and wrote on her chart. When she left, Reece said, "I'm here *now*."

Tish seemed about to answer, and though Reece wasn't sure what that answer might be—the child asleep, first light breaking outside the big window—he decided not to wait. He kissed her gently then hard, felt her lips' familiar softness, her breath quickening, *felt it*, then Tish's mouth went both firm and limp so it was like kissing raw meat.

"Nah, Reece, too late for that. And even if it wasn't"—she smiled, that hard, bitchy smile he remembered—"you way too stanky."

"What, you only like faggoty white boy smell?"

"Not just your stank, your attitude. *Forget about no job, I'm way too cool for that*, when all the time you just some great big loser, when you coulda been—"

"Fuck you, bitch."

"No, fuck you, bitch."

He didn't remember drawing back, but he slapped her hard, openhanded, across the face. Tish's eyes swelled, and she slapped him back, chest and shoulders heaving. He drew back and didn't know if he was going to punch her this time or throw her down and fuck her, he was so confused, so worked up, everything messed up in his head. Then the child, still hooked to IVs and monitors, sat up, screaming, "Don't hit my momma, don't hit my momma!"

Reece's head and heart froze. "I'm sorry," he stammered, whether to Tish or the child he didn't know. "This ain't me." He thrust his hand in his pocket, drew out his last twenty, and pressed it into Tish's palm. "Buy her one of them stuffed animals from me."

Tish nodded, soul-eyed again, and with the monitors pinging, medical staff probably racing toward them, and for sure the child screaming, "Don't hit, don't hit my *mo—ah-ahmma!*" Reece hurtled down the hall toward the elevator, where he nearly collided with Richard A. Gordon, who stepped off just as Reece stepped in. And if looks could have killed, there would have been two dead men sprawled on the floor. Reece pressed *L* and, eyes fixed straight ahead, waited for the damn thing to move. Last thing he saw was that sorry muthafucker's mustache twitching, then the silver door slid shut.

When he found Tisha trying to calm Jada, who was screaming and shrinking away from a nurse trying to reinsert her IV as if the nurse were Beelzebub in white, Richie let go of his desire to know *Right now!* what the fuck was going on. When Jada calmed down enough—the vein hit, the butterfly retaped—to stop shrieking and declare, "He hit my momma!" Tisha met his eyes, *Yes, he did!* Was that Reece's hand faintly outlined on her cheek? Richie wanted to chase after him, and what? Another black man brutally murdered by a white one?

The nurse departed; the story unfolded. Reece slapped her. She slapped him back. Jada tried to protect her, jerking the IV out of her hand, but it was over now. The whole time, standing somewhere outside himself watching Richie Gordon, Rican Jew, Spic Yid, with Tisha and Jada, he kept thinking if he'd had a gun when he'd heard what Reece did and Reece was still there? *Bam.* Racial hatred? Sexual jealousy? Which was more powerful? Then *Bam* a second time. "Why," he asked, "did Reece hit you?"

Tisha glanced at Jada, who'd fallen back asleep clutching Stripes and No How Dawg.

"He tried to kiss me, and I made him stop."

He knew it! He fucking *knew* it! What kind of primordial swamp was he being sucked into? And while he sat beside Tisha waiting for Doctor Williams, a good part of him remained outside himself, wondering how. How could he get back at Reece? How could he keep Jada—and Tisha—safe?

Some time later Doctor Williams, natty in black spectacles and a white lab coat with his name stitched on the breast pocket, and trailed by silent residents, one male, one female, carrying clipboards, drew back the curtain. "How's my favorite patient?" Williams collected Jada's chart from the foot of the bed then moved to her side.

"Fine."

"Good girl." Williams patted her unblemished cheek—the other remained a purple and yellow still life—then turned to Tisha. "As I told you yesterday, the operation went perfectly, but we won't know for sure about double vision until the swelling goes down."

Richie and Tisha squeezed each other's hand.

"She can go home later this morning, but she'll need to remain in bed and be kept quiet for several days."

"Would it be better," Richie asked, "if she stayed here another day?"

"It might be easier to keep her quiet," Williams said, "but for insurance reasons I don't believe that's an option."

"What if I guaranteed payment?"

Williams turned to his residents, who stared back blank faced. "I suppose that's between you and the billing office. Are you listed as the financially responsible party?"

"No," Tisha said, "I am."

"I'd be willing to sign whatever," Richie said. "If you think it's a good idea."

"Wherever you think she'll be best taken care of." Williams paused then added gently, "Some people think it's best to care for a sick child at home."

"Can we let you know?" Richie asked. "After we discuss it?"

Williams nodded.

"If she does stay, is it possible to get someone who has no legal right to be here barred from the room? Whose presence is upsetting Jada and resulted in the IV being ripped out of her arm this morning?"

Tisha released his hand.

Williams stepped closer. "Are we talking about the young man I met the day she was admitted?"

Richie nodded.

"It was my understanding"—Williams glanced at Tisha then back to Richie—"he was the father."

"I am, Richard Gordon. You can check the birth certificate."

Williams's gaze moved again to Tisha. Her eyes were brown glass, her lips fixed in *that* smile. "I can only advise you on medical matters. The rest is between you, the other young man, and possibly the police, who seem to have their hands full right now. Perhaps"—Williams's knowing eyes moved to Tisha, Jada, then back to Richie—"the best would be for me to discharge her."

Tisha asked, "What time?"

"Between eleven and twelve."

"Thank you," said LaTisha.

"Yes, thank you," Richie added.

"We'll see her Monday in my office. They'll schedule an appointment as part of the discharge and give you instructions for taking care of her."

Williams left, followed by his residents.

Lorr drinks cup after cup of black coffee. When nine a.m. arrives and departs without word from Pammie or Richie, and then it's past ten, she freaks and tries Pammie's cell for the umpteenth time. It goes straight to voice-mail as it has all morning. She tries Richie's and gets the message advising her to call his office. She doesn't want to bother him, but for shit's sake! She dials the office number. His secretary, who comes off kind of snotty, asks, "Who is this?" When Lorr identifies herself, the secretary sweetens up and says he hasn't come in yet, but if Lorraine hears from him, would she have him call *right away*? Two of his bosses are looking for him.

Give her yapping dogs and puking cats any time. Even cleaning out shit-strewn runs is better than this. Lorr switches on the television. On every local affiliate Malcolm Wilson, the mayor who used to do TV news, is declaring a state of emergency to quell the rioting; he has asked the governor to send in the Missouri National Guard to help enforce an eight p.m. to six a.m. curfew. C. City busses won't run during those hours. Anyone on the street after eight p.m. will be arrested. Wilson, for whom Lorr has conceived a bizarre affection—you see his pudding face and want to eat him up—His Honor peers earnestly into the cameras as if preparing to sign off from a nightly news report. Flashbulbs *boing-boing-boing*-ing, he declares, wide-eyed, "I have lived in this city all of my life, and I love it to death. I never thought I would sign an emergency order because of civil unrest."

Lorr finds it hard to watch the Q&A: reporters shouting, Wilson answering, his eyes growing sadder and rounder. On another channel there's an announcement that Kweisi Mfume, president of the NAACP, is flying into C. City to help African American leaders shape a unified response to the unrest and to demand a complete and immediate investigation not only of this shooting but the record of racial profiling by the Calhoun City Police Department.

The image cuts to a perky blonde, Annie Bell, who reads a statement from recently elected President George W. Bush, assuring the public the Bush administration is monitoring the events in Calhoun City and is prepared to offer any and all requested assistance. Lorr hates to hear the word *Bush* preceded by the word *President*, almost as much as she dislikes seeing his dopey mug on the screen. She still can't believe he was elected in November; in fact, she doesn't believe he *was* elected, and she switches off the set. A few moments later the buzzer rings. She can't figure out how to open the downstairs door, and after a few hysterical minutes of hearing Pammie's voice and shouting for her to wait, *For shit's sake, just wait,* she rides the elevator to the lobby and comes upon Baby Sis kissing Ray the cabbie just outside the street door. She pushes the door open, and they break off the kiss. The cabbie, looking rumpled and even funkier than he'd looked the night before, grins at Lorr then descends the front steps toward his hack parked curbside. Pammie waves. The cabbie waves back, and gray ponytail swinging, he ducks into his cab. When he drives off, tooting his horn, Lorr leads Pammie into the wood-paneled lobby and then into the elevator and up to Richie's eighth-floor apartment. The whole time Pammie is kind of grinning and humming without words. As soon as the apartment door closes behind them, Baby Sis steps out of her heels and begins shedding garments, reaching the guest bathroom wearing a powder blue bra and matching panties.

"Let's just say." Pammie appears as content as Lorr has seen her in years. "Ray knows how to handle a stick shift." She laughs and starts drawing a tub. "If I can change my ticket, I'll leave with you on Sunday. Right now I need a bath and sleep. We didn't close our eyes all night."

"You slut."

Pammie grins.

"He seems like a nice guy."

"The nicest things about him—" Baby Sis grins wider. "—can't be seen with his clothes on."

But sleep is not in the cards. Pammie has barely finished her bath and dozed off in the guest bedroom when the front door bangs open and LaTisha enters, carrying Jada, trailed by Richie. LaTisha sets her daughter down just inside the door. The poor kid's eye remains swollen shut, but she's alert, and as soon as her feet touch down, she pivots toward Richie.

"Can I have Stripes and Dawg?"

"*May* I have Stripes and Dawg?"

"For Chrissakes, Richard, just let her have them."

"*May I?*" Jada asks.

Richie hands her the animals.

What's going on? Whatever it is, though Lorr stands no more than fifteen feet away in front of the couch, they either haven't seen her, or they're so caught up in their own drama, they don't care. It's damn uncomfortable, and Lorr approaches, asking, "Jada, how are you?"

"My eye hurts."

"I'm so sorry. But you look much better than last night when I stayed with you. Do you remember?"

Jada looks confused, like *What?* Then her battered face breaks into a smile. "That's right. Is Auntie Pammie here?"

"She is." Lorr glances toward Richie and Tisha. "But she's sleeping."

"*Sleeping?*" Richie asks.

Tisha glares at him. "I told you we shouldn't have brought her here."

Richie says, "Jada needs to stay in bed for the next few days."

"I'm sure," Lorr begins, "Pammie would be happy to give her the bed. Or maybe Jada can spend the day in your bed, Richie, and this afternoon, when Pammie wakes up—"

"I told you, 'Take her to my place, Auntie Bertie can watch her,' but no! She stay there her whole life, but no, it might be dangerous, there's too many black folk—"

"Tisha, please."

"Don't *please* me, whose child is she? You think because some damn lie on a birth certificate? Doctor Williams knew. We *all* knew. What I don't get is why you believe your own bullshit?"

"It's not bullshit. No one could love her more than I do."

"That's a lie. And even if it's not, she's *my* child. I decide what's best."

Jada begins to cry.

"Maybe"—Lorr moves to Jada, who allows herself to be lifted, though Lorr fears it's the wrong move and Tisha will turn on her too—"I could get Jada settled in the big bedroom and let you two work this out."

Richie and Tisha nod. Jada settles her cheek against Lorr's

244

collarbone. Maybe she wouldn't have been such a terrible mother after all, though for thirty years, because little Richie preferred Pammie, she's believed small children disliked her. Halfway to the bedroom, with Jada in her arms, Lorr turns back as if toward Gomorrah. But it's Richie and Tisha who look like statues, salted in place several feet from each other.

"Your secretary said to call," Lorr says. "Someone needs to talk to you."

She continues on and closes the bedroom door, leaving the young people, and they suddenly seem very, very young, to face what's gone wrong between them.

TWENTY-TWO

Reece headed back toward B's place. With all the walking—miles and miles although the sun was barely cresting rooftops—his stomach growled like a grizzly's at the end of winter. Above its rumble he could hear his hand striking Tish's cheek and hers striking his, the child screaming, and the honey he had tasted on Tish's lips before it turned to acid. Girl could really ball, but that door forever closed though wide open for Richard A. Gordon. Just shows. Money talks, bullshit walks and walks and walks. Lord God, he wished he had that twenty back.

No, he wished he had more to give her. Liberated from his last Jackson, Reece not only felt hungry but free. From what? From every other day of his life. From whatever sense he might have once thought he had.

Reece continued downhill, the same route he'd followed last night before the black cop stuck the gun in his face and everything changed. He couldn't exactly say how or what but everything. This morning the streets were empty, cold, and bottle strewn. When he reached where it happened, prepared to get it right this time and stick the gun he didn't have into that black muthafucker's ear, watch him piss *his* pants, there was no one there except the increasingly loud echoes of what had happened before and before and before that. These streets haunted. Then this skinny wino, white and rheumy, reached out from the wall, shaking a cup. Reece dropped a quarter in, though he normally gave nothing to bums, white or black, and continued to Little B's, opened the door, which revealed B in the kitchen, wearing boxers and making coffee.

"Where you been?"

247

"Walking."

"You hungry?"

"Nah, already ate."

When B left for work, Reece lay down on the couch for an hour or so then turned on the TV and learned about the curfew. They murder black men, and now they setting curfews? Where were they, South Africa? Mississippi? Next they be using dogs. What would it mean for B, who worked after dark? For Tish, who went to school? Would they enforce the curfew everywhere or only east of Troost, making damn sure, like Boss Prendergast used to, that the niggers stayed on their side of town.

Reece headed to the kitchen. He'd decided not to eat any more of B's food, but if there was coffee in the pot, that would be all right. Least his head wouldn't come off from no caffeine. But his belly? Not hungry. He sipped coffee and dialed Caroline Something-Something. Wouldn't mind, no, not one bit. "Plead me out," he told her when she picked up then grabbed his last dollars and his stanky, pissy clothes, heading for the Fluff and Fold around the corner.

Although he was already terrified about what he'd find at work, Richie offered to drive Tisha to UMCC. Five minutes into the ride he wished he hadn't. She understood, *blah, blah*, he was only doing what he thought, *blah, blah, blah*, but she should never have let him convince her to bring Jada to his place; she couldn't even get there easy on a bus today. She accepted cab fare, but still. Jada her child, not his. She'd been caring for Jada her whole life and doing just fine, thank you.

All right.

All right, what?

All right, give it a rest.

She didn't speak again until he pulled over across from the main entrance to the university. This was the moment to tell her he wasn't all white.

"Richard," she said, before he could say anything. "I know you love Jada, I really do. More than you love me."

"That's not true."

"True for me. This isn't working right now."

"*This?*"

"You and me." Staring straight ahead, she continued, "I'm not saying I don't have feelings or that I haven't *grown* being with you. Like, what wine to order. Or that a man should be *proud* of me trying to better myself, or fuck him." She turned toward Richie, pursing lips she'd coated in purple gloss. "But it too hard right now. I'll take Jada home in the morning. You hang with your momma and your aunt."

"That's it?"

"And then we'll see."

"Are you going back to Reece?"

"You know what? Fuck you."

She jumped out of the CRV before he could tell her what he'd meant to. *You don't have to hate me, I'm not white.* Without looking back, Tisha crossed the street in her hip-hugging red coat, which reflected light, like blood.

As soon as he got to work, Haddy Horstmeyer, vice president of NBD, summoned him three floors up to ream him out not only for the problems in Ohio and Kentucky he hadn't taken care of yet but for missing two days of meetings. Then Horstmeyer, who was in his early forties and developing the sort of male pattern baldness Folgrow promised to correct, paused long enough to allow Richie to mention Jada's emergency surgery.

From behind his desk Horstmeyer said, "I didn't know you had kids."

"She's my girlfriend's daughter. My *live-in* girlfriend."

Live-in seemed to provide traction. Horstmeyer asked, "Why haven't I met her? Does she work in the building?"

Richie shook his head.

"I'd still like to meet her." Horstmeyer nodded, as if in agreement with his own opinion. "Look, fix the crap in Ohio. By the way how'd the little girl hurt her eye?"

Richie considered telling Horstmeyer the truth then said she'd gotten hurt at school.

Haddy grinned. "Sounds like a lawsuit."

Richie tried to look as if he agreed without actually saying so, a stratagem he found useful with superiors in general but especially with Horstmeyer. After reminding him not to forget about the curfew, Horstmeyer let him go, and Richie spent the rest of the afternoon in his office, much of it on the phone. He was going to have to fly to Cincinnati early next week, piggy-backing that stop on a previously scheduled trip to Chicago. He also had meetings at the Leawood research park, two reports to finish, and a quarterly model to build, but as soon as he got off the phone and tried to start working, that is *thinking*, his mind snapped back to Tisha telling him *this* wasn't working and the smile that wasn't a smile at all before she stepped away from his CRV. He looked in his wallet for the original picture of Jada, wondering if he'd have to give it back and if he'd ever get to tell Tisha about Ricardo Delgas. He pictured Jada reaching up to be carried, snuggling Stripes. Reece, that bastard, pushing past him onto the elevator, and he couldn't think, couldn't focus, might as well be home, but Horstmeyer would have his ass, so he remained in his office with his door closed pretending to work while outside C. City simmered, and Richie stared at his computer, unable to perform what had long been his passion and salvation. Then his cell phone rang, and he nearly knocked himself unconscious getting it out of his pocket. What if it were LaTisha calling to make up? Instead, the screen ID'd Dave Manning.

"Oh shit, I forgot to call Laura. I'll call right now."

"She's home," Dave said. "I'm hiding outside my own house like a fucking private detective."

"Jada's been released, she's at my place. But with this curfew starting—"

"For Chrissakes, you think they're going to hassle *white* people in your neighborhood?"

"You're right. I'll invite Laura over at six."

"You're the best. I'll be there six-fifteen."

Richie hung up and called Laura.

Lorr has spent the afternoon reading storybooks to Jada. Each time she thinks the child is falling into the nap she so badly needs, her good eye blinks open and she begs for another and another, and after she's heard them all, to hear them all again. This is the sort of intimacy she never shared with Richie: a small trusting body pressed against her own. As she opens *Frog and Toad's Wild Ride* for the third time, her mind travels to what might have been if she'd made it to the station with Richie in the stroller instead of abandoning him with Mom and Daddy. Who knows, who really knows? And who knows what's happening with Richie and Tisha? For shit's sake, she hadn't realized being in Richie's life would mean problems not only not of her own making but maybe not of his. A black girlfriend in a racially divided city, it didn't take an Einstein . . . She hears her own breathy voice describing Toad and the runaway wagon. If only there was something she could do to keep these kids safe, kids broadly defined as everyone younger than herself, even Pammie. Some way to reenter the moment when she said, *Yes, yes, you can keep him*, to scream, *No, no! He's mine.*

When Jada's undamaged eye finally closes, Lorr tucks the comforter under her chin and slips out, leaving the door ajar as they used to in the Sheepshead Bay bedroom that was hers before it became Richie's. She wonders who lives in that house now. She also wonders about Reece. What an intense, beautiful moment they shared last night. She considers venturing out for a late lunch then remembers she can't leave the apartment. She heats a Lean Cuisine then passes out on the couch. When she wakes, she can't recall the time or day, where she is or what she's meant to be doing, then identifies Richie's front door closing and his shape coming toward her.

"How's Jada?"

"Sleeping."

He walks toward his bedroom door, peeks in, and returns. "Any sign of Pammie?"

Lorr shakes her head. "I'm surprised you're home so early."

"So am I. You heard about the curfew?"

Lorr nods.

"I should tell you that Laura, the pregnant—"

"I remember her from the seder."

"—is coming over to see Jada." He starts toward the kitchen. "You want a drink?"

"It's kinda early."

"Not today it isn't." He returns with a stubby glass filled to the brim with what looks like scotch. "Dave and Laura are going through"—he hesitates—"some problems, and Dave is planning to show up to try to talk to her."

She doesn't know how she knows, but she does. "Who'd he sleep with?"

"How'd you know?"

She considers Richie's unhappy face. "I think I will have that drink. Any red wine left?"

Richie returns from the kitchen with a fresh bottle of Israeli Cabernet, left over from the seder, and a wine glass for her. When she's had her first sip, Lorr asks, "How well do you know Reece?"

"Who told you about Reece?"

"He stopped by the hospital last night."

"He's an asshole. He tell you how we met?"

"He said to ask you."

Richie slugs his Scotch. "For years, until he got arrested last fall, I don't even know for what—"

"Receiving stolen goods."

Richie looks at her. "He told you?"

She nods.

"He was using my IDs. When the police picked him up, they called me." He takes another, more moderate nip of Scotch. "Mixed in with my IDs was a picture of Jada and Tisha's number, in case of emergency. That's how I met her."

Then suddenly, inexplicably, he bursts into tears. She would like to comfort him, but she doesn't know how or for what.

"The scumbag never came around, but now that I'm there, he's like, 'Wait, I'm the dad.'"

"Just because someone's not around doesn't mean he stops being a parent."

He glares at her. "Bullshit."

"You're upset because Reece, who's going back to jail and has *nothing* in his life, wants to say, 'I have some rights here too?'"

"No. Because I've been so freaked-out and jealous, Tisha's breaking up with me."

Oh shit. Then, despite realizing she's mostly on Reece's side, she scoots over to provide her son with what little comfort she can.

Wearing clean clothes for the first time in what felt like weeks but was only days, Reece set out from B's carrying everything he owned. He figured it would take him an hour to walk, but he had way more time than money, and he wanted to say a proper good-bye to the child, never mind Tish herself. He didn't want the last time she saw him to be the slap and slap-back, the child screaming, "No, no, nooooooo!" though it was possible Tish wouldn't talk to him, possible, too, she would be neither at her place nor Children's Mercy but at the crib of Richard A. Gordon, muthafucker. He wished he'd done more with the IDs, wished Marshall had too, because if anyone was stealing anyone's identity it was Gordon stealing his. Stole Tish and the child, then just like the lying muthafucker he was, claimed he'd been the one done wrong.

Reece crossed Martin Luther King. It was past five, and he hadn't eaten since last night. Normally, he'd be aghast with hunger. With his hyped-up metabolism he had to eat every two hours. But today wasn't nobody's normal. Even carrying everything he owned—clothes, CDs, three pairs of shoes, a six-inch filleting knife, his prepaid cell with six minutes left—he felt unburdened by demands of the body. If Tish wasn't home, that old lady would know how to find her, maybe even know where Richard A. Gordon lived. And then? And then he'd be so gone.

It took him an hour and fifteen minutes, then Tish didn't answer the bell. Reece was trying to decide what to do when the other front door opened and Auntie Bertie hauled her big ass onto the porch.

"I'm looking for Tish."

"I know what you looking for."

"How you know that?"

"Yo kind always hunting the same thing. End of days."

"No, Auntie. I'm going *away*. I come to say good-bye to my child."

"Well, I ain't seen her."

"I bet you got a number for her boyfriend, though."

"Maybe I do, maybe I don't."

He thought of all the aunties he'd known, including his own Grams. "Please, Auntie Bertie, I'm trying to do the right thing, the *Christian* thing, by my child."

Shrewd eyes narrowed in the old woman's face. "If you lying, you going straight to hell, nigger. And let me tell you, it's real."

"I ain't lying."

Bertie stepped back inside her door and fastened the chain behind her, mistrustful old bitch that she was. But she was wrong about him. Reece was still waiting respectfully when she reappeared and passed him out a sheet of lined paper torn from a spiral notebook, on which she'd block-printed a phone number.

"I ain't seen nor heard from her in three days during these here riots, and I'm worry sick. If you find her, say, 'Call Bertie.'"

"I will."

The old woman closed the door and Reece heard locks click: one, two, and three, the last one being a chain sliding shut.

TWENTY-THREE

Wearing a red maternity blouse over green stretch slacks, Laura, who looked even larger than she had at Sunday's seder and in her outfit resembled nothing so much as a Christmas ornament, turned sideways to step through the door as if she feared getting stuck coming through. Eyes bright above flushed round cheeks, she asked, "How's Jada?"

"The surgeon says she's going to be fine." Richie brushed lips with his friend's wife. "But we won't know until the swelling goes down."

Laura followed him to the living room, where Lorraine, who'd answered the phone just as Laura arrived at the door, excused herself and headed toward the kitchen.

Laura asked, "How's Tisha holding up?"

While he fumbled for a commonplace, Laura answered her own question. "I'm sure she's a wreck, I know I'd be."

How could Dave do it to her? "She's at school. She hasn't been all week."

Laura raised a shiny silver gift bag. "I wanted to drop this off. I hope Jada likes to color."

"Please stay."

"Are you sure?"

He nodded.

"Just for a few. Do you have sparkling water?"

He found a Perrier for Laura, a fresh scotch for himself, then labored to find something to talk about that didn't bring in Tisha or Dave but soon gave up. "How's your hubby?"

"I don't know. And I don't care."

Now what? Laura clearly expected him to follow up. But their friendship, and yes, he could say his love for her, was mediated by his friendship with Dave. In fact, he'd never been alone with Laura. But just as he was about to ask, Pammie popped out of the guest bedroom, bare legged below a long blue T-shirt emblazoned with yellow script: ROCKET CAB across the chest, TAKES YOU THERE on the back.

"Whoops."

"You remember Laura."

Pammie raised her hand like a traffic cop toward Laura, who was struggling to rise from the couch. "Don't get up, I gotta pee like crazy."

She hurried toward the guest bathroom as Laura, grunting, heaved herself upright and stood supporting her belly with both hands. "I should really go."

"Please, I was just about to wake Jada."

"Are you sure you should?"

"Oh, yes." But he couldn't think of a single good reason why. "The present will mean more if you give it to her." Laura looked doubtful. "And I'm supposed to feed her dinner."

"I never heard of waking a sick child."

But she followed him to his bedroom, where Jada lay just as he'd left her, Stripes on one side, No How Dawg on the other. In the front room he heard the lobby buzzer sound.

"Doesn't she look sweet!" Laura said then sobbed.

"What's wrong?"

"Don't mind me, I cry all the time. Dogs, small children. My asshole husband."

Then she was hard at it, and Richie stepped forward to hug her.

"You know, don't you?" She pinned him with hot eyes. "He tells you everything. That fucking waitress. It's so humiliating." Laura wiped tears from both cheeks. "Be honest, everyone knew but me."

The doorbell rang, once then a second time. He heard footsteps, probably Lorraine's, head toward it. "He didn't tell me anything." He gazed into Laura's bleary eyes and thought, *What the fuck.* "Until after you found out."

"Richie," Lorraine called from outside the bedroom. "There's someone here to see you."

"Whoever it is," he answered, thinking, *Dave, at last!* "send him in." He bent and kissed Jada's cheek. "Jadakins, wake up."

Her good eye rolled open, and for a moment he believed the right one would too. But after a fluttery movement under the lid, it remained shut.

"Auntie Laura brought you a present."

He stepped back to allow Laura to move to Jada's side. Then he slipped from the room, thinking he'd let the mom-to-be have a moment with the child before bringing Dave in. Or maybe he should bring Laura out to Dave? But instead of finding Dave, he found Reece.

"I've come to see my child."

Richie's heart began to race. "Did Tisha bring you?"

"*Man.*" Reece's lips pulled back from his teeth in what may or may not have been a grin. "You don't know shit about Tish."

"What I do know is you're not welcome here."

"Now why you got to be like that?"

The top of Richie's head was about to come off. "If Tisha didn't bring you, how the hell did you get here?"

Reece drew himself up to his considerable height. "I walked."

"I don't care if you hopped like a bunny."

"First to Tisha's place. Bertie gave me your number, and then I walked here."

"Bertie doesn't know where I live."

"That's the only thing you right about." Grinning, Reece's long face looked even more wolfish than usual. "But your momma does, and she told me."

If there had been anything left of the top of Richie's head, it would have blown off and splattered Lorraine, who stood a few feet from Reece. "You had no fucking right!"

Lorraine flipped her hair back from her face. "Even if I know what it costs *everyone* when a parent disappears?"

"It's *because* you left you have no fucking right."

"Don't curse at your momma." Reece's outraged eyes met his own.

"Fuck you. She stopped being my *momma* when she left. Like you stopped being Jada's father when you put my name on her birth certificate."

"You bullshit, man."

The bell rang.

"No," Richie shouted, "*you* bullshit. You never cared one little shit about Jada."

"You got no idea what I care about, punk muthafucker."

The bell rang again. Footsteps hurried toward it, Pammie this time.

"How come you never came around? Or gave Tisha any money? Or is that how you"—he ignored the voice in his head urging him to say *You people*—"show you love someone? By being totally irresponsible? Like Jada was just some jism for Baby Momma to clean up?"

"If I didn't care about my child," Reese answered, so soft and low Richie had to lean in to hear him, "you'd be spitting teeth right now."

"Threaten me in my own house?" Richie shoved Reece in the chest with both hands and watched the taller man react. "You gonna bitch-slap me like you did Tisha?"

"Touch me again—"

"Richie," Lorraine shouted. "Reece!"

"—find out, y'little bitch."

Aiming for Reece's mouth, Richie swung as hard as he could, and if he'd hit what he'd aimed at, he might have done some damage. But Reece dodged right, and the punch spun past. Then he straightened and caught Richie with an uppercut that thudded against his cheek and knocked him down. Reece leapt onto his chest and landed a right above Richie's eye before Dave, who'd been ringing the bell that Pammie answered, raced in and yanked Reece off him. Finding himself outnumbered, Reece pulled the blade that must have been hidden in his waistband and slashed the air in front of Dave's astonished face and at Richie too, who was struggling to rise from the floor. And he might have cut more than air if Lorraine hadn't pushed between them.

"Reece," she said, her back to Dave and Richie, who was panting and still trying to get up. "If you want to hurt someone, hurt me."

"Did I come here to hurt someone?"

"I know," Lorraine said. "I know."

"I came to say good-bye to my child. And now these two white muthafuckers—"

From the corner of his eye Richie saw Dave, freshly shaved and with his hair slicked back, looking for a way around Lorraine, who stood like a dancer on point, knees bent, arms extended, while Reece backed up slowly toward the couch and his duffel bag, the thin, nasty-looking blade extended in front of him.

"—are trying to punk me."

"No, they're not, isn't that right, Richie?"

On his knees, cheek throbbing, his ears ringing from being punched, Richie gazed past Lorraine at Reece's reddish crown of hair, his eyes flitting back and forth in the light skin that wasn't and never would be white.

"Not that it makes any difference," Lorraine said, "but it's not two *white* muthafuckers because Richie's dad sure wasn't. Now put that knife—"

The bedroom door opened. Jada screamed, "Richie!" and Reece turned toward the child coming toward him holding Laura's hand. And maybe Dave thought Reece was threatening Laura and wanted to protect her. Or maybe he wanted to play the hero to win her back. But when Reece turned his head toward Jada, Dave pushed past Lorraine and launched himself at Reece who raised his knife hand, protecting the side of his face. The blade caught Dave high on his wrist or forearm then again on his shoulder or face. Dave screamed and fell backward.

"Muthafucker," Reece said. "Now look what you done."

"For shit's sake," Lorr screamed, "get away from him."

And before Richie moved forward to see how bad it all was, his gaze found Jada, her good eye stretched wide, her mouth forming a second, perfect circle. "Oh, no, oh no, oh no!"

Dave, Lorr decides, isn't going to die. He isn't going to lose an eye or even an ear, but he is bleeding from a substantial gash on his forearm and a smaller one on his cheek, and though Lorr is no expert on knife wounds, she has seen the aftermath of more than a few bar fights and suspects Dave should really have stitches to close the larger cut. But there's neither time nor much psychic space to think about Dave. She orders Pammie to the kitchen for a clean dish towel to apply pressure to the wound, directs Richie to find whatever first aid supplies he has, and after she demands and receives from Reece a six-inch filleting knife, which has a nasty pointed blade, she makes him swear to sit there and wait and above all try not to get into it again with Richie.

Lorr's doctored enough dogs to know the greatest danger is infection. Once she has Dave in the master bathroom, she upends the brown bottle of hydrogen peroxide on the larger gash then the smaller one and coats both with disinfectant. Both cuts are clean, and though the first is deep and won't stop bleeding, she's not worried. Dave is shaking a little, and she wonders if he's going into shock but decides he seems too coherent, moaning and cursing, insisting he's going to fuck Reece up but good. And after he fucked Reece up, he was going to press charges, someone should get out in the living room, make sure he doesn't get away.

But Laura, who somehow maneuvers her extremely large self into the crowded bathroom, announces, "The hell you are. Nothing would have happened if you hadn't leapt on him like an asshole."

"He had a knife!"

"Press this," Lorr says, placing gauze pads over the arm wound, "and raise your arm."

"I thought." Dave makes goo-goo eyes at his wife. "He was going to hurt you."

"Bullshit. *You're* the one who hurt me, and everyone knows it."

That silences Dave, and Lorr finishes bandaging his arm.

"To be honest," Laura continues, "I'm glad he stabbed you. Now you know how it feels."

Looking from Dave to Laura, whose eyes glisten, Lorr gets the hell out of the bathroom, leaving the wronged wife to administer to her husband's wounds. In the living room Richie and Reece sit opposite each other, Reece on the couch, Richie on the chair. They barely acknowledge her, and for a moment they strike her not so much as grown men looking for each other's weaknesses but as little boys, or even brothers, placed in time-out for fighting. They both have long rather than round faces, not a whit of excess flesh on either, their skins olive and off-white, really not so very different. Richie's hair is thicker, black, and curly. Reece's is kinked, reddish, and cropped short. They look, she thinks, as if they could have had the same mother but different fathers, and since she is mother, but not really Mom to one, and not mother, but maternal in her intentions to the other, she would love more than anything to make them feel as if they were brothers under the skin. Or at least not enemies, she would settle for that.

"Reece," she says, entering the dead space between them. "Richie, I want to talk to both of you." Their eyes edge toward her. "For Jada's sake you need to work some things out."

"How's Dave?" Richie asks.

"He's going to be fine."

"Stupid muthafucker," Reece mutters.

"Who you calling muthafucker?"

"Your boy, Dave."

"I think we can agree on three things," Lorr says. "One, let's tone down the fucking language." Reece rewards her with a grin. "Two, there's enough blame to go around. Invited or not, Reece came with good intentions, to say good-bye to Jada, and Richie, because he loves Jada, should have let him."

"I wouldn't say that," Richie says.

"I would," Lorr says, "and I'm right. And Reece, even if he thought he was going to be outnumbered, shouldn't have pulled that knife."

"My bad," Reece admits.

She glances from Reece to Richie to gauge his reaction then back to Reece trying to decide if he meant it. "Third, Dave's real problem aren't those cuts, even though he might need stitches for the one on his arm—"

"If he goes to an emergency room, they're gonna ask questions, and that's trouble for me."

"You should have thought about that," Richie says, "before you cut him."

"He jumped me."

"Will you boys shut up?" After a moment they nod. "As I was saying, Dave's problem isn't a little blood but how's he going to make things right with Laura"—Richie meets her eyes and shakes his head, but she's long past wanting to protect anyone's scummy secrets, not even her own—"for sleeping around on her when she was carrying his baby. Just like your real problem is the little girl in the next room, who was not only wounded by the world in all its ugliness but has seen the two men she loves—"

"She doesn't love him," Richie says.

"Of course, she does."

"Whose side are you on?"

"Jada's, and how do you think it makes her feel to see you two fighting?" Lorr glances from one to the other, and of the two Reece's eyes come more readily and warmly to hers.

"What do you want?" he asks.

"For the two of you, together, to tell her you love her and that it's okay for her to love both of you. And when Reece comes back." She looks at him, and he nods. Then she turns to see if Richie knows what she's talking about and sees that he does. "Whenever that may be, you're going to find some way you can both be part of her life. And that you're sorry for fighting and scaring her and that despite being the unevolved *men* you are"—Richie grins, and she grins back at him—"you're going to find some way to be friends because you love her and want her to be happy."

Reece asks, "You don't want much, do you?"

"Just the world."

After a moment Richie says, "The only problem, assuming Reece and I agree, is Tisha's breaking up with me. So I won't be around."

Lorr looks from her son to Reece and back again. "You don't know much about women, do you?"

"He sure don't know shit about Tish."

The master bedroom opens, and Dave emerges trailed by Laura. Dave's forearm is heavily taped. Band-Aids crisscross the center of his cheek.

"We're going." Laura takes Dave's undamaged left hand in her right. "We want to get home before curfew starts."

"What about the emergency room?" Lorr asks.

"He'll live," Laura answers.

Dave grins. What an asshole. Lorr doesn't envy Laura, but the woman's nine months pregnant, what is she going to do? Then Dave and Laura are out the door. Richie says, "I can do it if he can." He turns toward Reece. "Let's talk to Jada."

265

Lorr says, "You go in first. I want a minute with Reece."

Richie eyes her mistrustfully, but he's just going to have to suck it up. He hesitates then heads toward the guest bedroom.

"Come with me." Reece follows her to the kitchen, where she digs her wallet from her purse. "Have you called that lawyer yet?"

He nods.

"Good. Do your time then come out and make a life for yourself."

"Can I ask you something?"

She nods.

"What do you care?"

"I just do." She offers the contents of her wallet to him. "Take it, it's two hundred dollars."

"You buying me off?"

"I'm buying you in. I figure where you're going a little money's gonna come in handy."

"I don't get it."

"Just maybe," she says, wondering, and suddenly she knows it's true, "a long time ago, someone gave me two hundred dollars to go away. I'm giving you two hundred dollars to come back."

Reece slips the money into his pocket then asks her to give Richie a message. *Pleasant Street wasn't him, but it was his fault, and he's taken care of it.* Lorr decides not to ask any questions and says she'll tell Richie but isn't sure she will. Then Reece reaches down and wraps his long arms around her. "Thank you," he murmurs. "I won't forget this."

Lorr lets herself be hugged. Then feeling as if she's finally done something right, she follows Reece from the kitchen to join Jada, Richie, and Baby Sis.

TWENTY-FOUR

Tisha, who arrived just before curfew, slept in his bed, Jada between them, but she still wasn't talking to him. There'd been no mention of shifting Jada to her apartment in the morning perhaps because, as he overheard her tell Lorraine and Pammie, the Good Sam training supervisor had put her on probation, while her manager at work had warned, *Miss one more shift and you're gone.* Spending the night with him, therefore, hardly felt like a reaffirmation of affection, more like a practical solution, and Tisha, especially when it came to Jada, was nothing but practical. So, while he was glad she'd stayed—with the curfew, she didn't have much choice—he didn't feel she'd changed her opinion about how *This* was working for her. He lay awake, his mind sorely troubled, and thought back to when they'd met, how exciting and life changing it had all seemed. A black woman, a sexy black woman, willing to go out with him? She'd tongued the whipped cream from her fork at Kaldi's, like some über-fantasy of black sexuality, and he ate it up, he ate it up, IT ATE HIM UP. And then he fell in love with the woman, not the fantasy. And Jada too, he loved them both, though maybe he didn't deserve them. Not like Dave didn't deserve Laura, for something he'd done, but for the way he thought, the way he *was* inside, and there was nothing he could do about that, who he was, his innermost thoughts, the voices he heard in the cesspool of his mind. Though who he was, Yid Spic, Rican Jew, wasn't who he'd thought, and he wondered if he'd get the chance to tell her. Or if he should. Or why it should matter anyway.

Long after Jada and Tisha had fallen asleep, Richie lay awake wondering if it were true for him, if he'd wanted her for the wrong reasons—can you really want someone for the wrong reasons? does desire distinguish right and wrong?—then maybe it was true for her in November too, when he'd worried Tisha had only taken up with him for his money. Richard Gordon the good bet, the white paycheck, and she hadn't loved him then. What if that had never stopped being true?

Did he now want to earn points for *not* being white, when at first he'd maybe gotten them for being white? How sick was that? This was different than worrying she had feelings for Reece. This wasn't about Reece, he realized, and never had been, but whether she could see him as something more than a rich white guy. And even if he wasn't *really* a white guy, would that change, when he told her? Would it change her heart? And what kind of a heart would that mean she had if it did? Maybe he *shouldn't* tell her. Maybe he shouldn't tell anyone? Was it important to her or to him, that she love him thinking he was all white. Important, how? For the sake of her soul? For the sake of his? For the sake of his career? For a chance of happiness in this little life they were leading? Why would it be different if she loved him thinking he was Latino? Was race always, always there? Shit. These weren't soothing bedtime thoughts, and he lay awake in the dark for a long time.

Early Friday, the adults gathered in the kitchen for coffee. Friday's *Star*, open in front of Richie, reported 153 arrests for curfew violation but almost no violence. There was a picture of NAACP president Mfume talking in one of the black churches near Tisha's apartment just before curfew. The article below the photo discussed Mfume's anger at the death of another young black man and the community's distress at the canceling of Good Friday services because of the second night of curfew. Another article provided details of Timothy Thomas's funeral scheduled for Saturday. Both the news and editorial writers agreed that the response of the police and the African American community to the funeral was the city's next big test. "Would the Peace Hold?" asked the headline. No one seemed to know.

Richie glanced at Lorraine, who sat hunched over, cradling a coffee mug in both hands, her dark hair a curtain obscuring her face. He was still angry at her for taking Reece's side.

Tisha said, "I really want to thank you for watching Jada again. You sure it's okay?"

"I'm glad to, and it won't just be me. Pammie changed her flight."

"Still." Tisha patted the fishhook curls beside her ears. "It means a lot."

Richie glanced between the women. He felt a million miles from both of them.

"I can watch her tomorrow too," Lorraine added, "if you and Richie want to go to that funeral."

Goddamn! Would you ask me first? But one look at Tisha, tears welling in her eyes, revealed how wrong he was.

"That would mean so much!" Tisha reached across the table, pressing her cheek to Lorraine's. Across Tisha's glistening helmet of processed hair, Lorraine's eyes found his. *Thank you,* his said, at least he knew they should. *I know,* hers answered. *I really do.*

Tisha sat down. "I've been wanting to go, but of course"— she cast a cold eye at Richie—"I couldn't take Jada out into no crowd again. I don't know how to thank you."

"By cutting Richie some slack. He's really smart about some things, kinda dim about others."

"Like anything," Tisha said, "involving women. Or black people."

"But he's good with kids."

"That's right. And he's loyal." She slipped her hand onto his, the first time she'd touched him since their fight in the car. "Not like that playa friend a his."

269

"What an asshole, right?" Lorr grinned. "And he sure does love you."

"Yeah," Tisha admitted. "I guess he does."

He dropped her at school then put in his first full day at work since the trouble started. That night, with Pammie out again with Ray the cabbie, Richie brought in takeout Chinese, wonton soup with extra wontons for Jada, three or four more dishes than were needed for everyone else, and the four of them, Richie and the three females, mother, lover, and child, ate together in the dining room. When they finished, Jada, whose eye was still swollen shut but whose bruises were fading—they were still sickening shades of purple and yellow, just not as intense—demanded ice cream, and though it was twenty minutes to curfew, Richie ran out to the convenience store around the corner. Heading home just before eight with pints of cookies and cream and chocolate, he passed two different bars, Longworth's and the C. City Bar and Grill, which were still full of customers, every one of them white. Obviously, these bars weren't planning to close at eight. How fucked-up was that, he thought, but didn't think much more about it until he was reading about it the next morning in the *Star*.

Jada was watching cartoons. To no one's surprise Pammie hadn't returned last night, so Lorraine had had the guest room to herself and was finally getting some sleep. Tisha was showering; in an hour they would leave for the funeral. He sat beside Jada on the couch then lifted her with Stripes and No How Dawg onto his lap, enjoying her familiar weight and little girl smell until it was time to go.

They had to park way on the other side of Washington Park, not far from Kaldi's, where they'd met that first morning for brunch. It was sunny and warm for April, with the promise of an early summer as they walked west toward Elm on streets skirted with broken glass and boarded windows. It was exactly one week and eight or nine hours since Timothy Thomas died, and Richie couldn't help thinking a lot had changed but a lot hadn't, not only since the shooting but since he met Tisha. He was still nervous, scared if he were honest, to take her hand in public. Down here it wasn't what white people would think, as it was that first night at the movies, but what the other blacks would think on these charged and nervous streets. And even if he wasn't all white, he looked and he guessed he felt white and probably always would.

Tisha said, "It means a lot, you coming with me."

Should he say she was welcome? Or thank her for bringing him?

"I know in your heart, Richard, you scared of black people, and something like this, it's pretty scary."

"No," he began.

"It's all right." She pulled him to the side of the pavement closer to Washington Park, beside a big tree just starting to leaf out, to permit a group of ten or twelve teenagers to push past. "If we gonna have any chance, we gotta be honest. I know black folks scare you." Her eyes sought his. "And I know you kinda racist. You been telling me about that voice, so you must know it too."

"I've been hoping that voice wasn't really me."

"It's part of you."

More teenagers ran past, half of them wearing red do-rags.

"Then how can you love me? Sometimes I don't think you do."

"I don't love that part." She sucked her lips between her teeth and looked hard at him, not quite *that* look because it admitted too much pain. "There's not a whole lot I love about any white people right now, except maybe Lorraine. No black person could. But—" And now her smile, the one he'd first been taken with, broke from the hard, almost masculine lines of her

271

face. "I do love your sorry pale ass. Maybe at first because of how nice you treated Jada, but that's not all it is now, and you know it. I really hope we can make this work."

Later, he thought, he'd tell her about Ricardo Delgas, or maybe he wouldn't. Tell her he wasn't all white nor his ass as pale as she thought, though the fact that she'd learned to love it when she thought it was, was probably a good thing. Unless it wasn't. And if that's not love, he thought, it's close enough. A moment later they rejoined the crowd hurrying toward New Prospect Baptist Church. He was one of the only white people, and in his dark suit, white shirt and tie, he was obviously overdressed. All around them, both walking and on line outside the church to view the body, teenagers wore T-shirts silk-screened with Timothy Thomas's picture, the smiling one of him in a tuxedo that had been running every day in the *Star*. Lots of them, both male and female, wore red bandanas like the one T. Thomas had been wearing when he was shot.

"I'm really glad you're with me," Tisha said, when they'd been standing on the slow-moving line for almost an hour.

"It means a lot to me too." He laced their fingers together. "I should really thank Lorraine."

"Your momma, she's cool."

A little while later they entered the flower-filled church. Up front there was a gleaming silver casket—who paid for it? he wondered—and an honor guard of young men wearing New Black Panther Party berets. Risers were arranged for what was clearly going to be an extra-large choir. A large section of pews had been roped off for VIPs. There was a crowd of working press, including a dozen or so cameramen and maybe twenty radio and television reporters. If it hadn't been clear while they were on line outside, he could now see that there were hundreds and possibly a thousand more mourners than would fit inside the church.

Up front a sad-eyed woman in black who may or may not

have been Timothy Thomas's mother, Angela Leisure, was being helped to her seat. Beside the silver coffin there was a two-by three-foot enlargement of the photograph on the teenagers' shirts. A young woman, a girl really, stood nearby, holding a baby that must have been Tim Thomas's three-month-old son, Tywon. When Richie reached the coffin, he could see the bouquet of red roses tucked under the lid. "To Souljah Tim," read the card, and Richie felt as if he finally got it. *He's just a kid, he's somebody's kid*, and he left the church weeping, feeling for the first time just how terrible this was. The forces that had ended this boy's life, that woman's son, the life of that baby's father, must themselves be ended, though Richie doubted they ever would be, and that's what made his tears so bitter.

Surrounded by a thousand or maybe fifteen hundred other mourners, Richie and LaTisha listened to the service and eulogies delivered inside the church on loudspeakers in Washington Park. News helicopters whirred overhead, and once, when a police siren screamed somewhere close before fading, the huge crowd held its collective breath as if they were joined along a single raw nerve. When the voice of Kweisi Mfume, president of the NAACP, boomed and crackled over the loudspeaker, "God still uses ordinary people. And although ordinary in his life, Timothy Thomas is extraordinary in his death. Because he got us talking to each other and looking at each other," Richie looked at LaTisha, and she looked at him. *Maybe*, he thought, *we* will *be all right*.

After Martin Luther King III spoke, Mayor Malcolm Wilson declared, in a quavering voice, "I express my condolences to all of you and pledge to you all the city will be better. I don't know how or when, but I pray for peace, and I pray for justice."

Then Reverend Doctor Osborne Richards, pastor of New Life Outreach Church, where Timothy Thomas's mother sang in the choir, began the official eulogy, speaking with the sort of incantatory black preacher rhythm Richie had never heard in person. Reverend Doctor Richards spoke for a long time. Richie imagined him to be older, gray-haired, and balding but didn't really know because he couldn't see him. The sun beat down. Inside his dark suit, with bodies pressed close on every side, Richie could feel himself sweating. He squeezed Tisha's moist palm, and she squeezed his as Reverend Doctor Richards's voice ratcheted higher then higher again.

"Let tomorrow, the day Christians celebrate Jesus's resurrection, be the start of the resurrection—in Timothy Thomas's name—of Calhoun City. Whether you are white or black, he made you the way he wanted you to be in order to fit into this life. Because God, God has a plan! Everyone, white and black, black and white, has to work together to keep Tim Thomas's death from being in vain. So everyone turn to each other and say to your neighbor, 'Everything's gonna be all right!'"

Richie said it to Tisha, and she said it to him, "Everything's gonna be all right."

If only, he thought, it was that easy.

Then the crowd in and outside of the church shouted, "Amen," and a few moments later the church doors swung open. Pallbearers started down the steps carrying their silver burden. No one spoke or moved in the enormous crowd, which lined both sides of Elm Street. The only sounds were the clanking chains of the swing set behind them in Washington Park. The pallbearers lifted the coffin into the back of the hearse and closed the doors. Family members, VIPs black and white, and reporters descended the church steps, disappearing into waiting limousines and vans. No one spoke, not one word, until the procession started up Elm. Then the crowd moved into the street, feeling shriven, maybe even a little bit sanctified, and began to walk north. Richie and LaTisha followed, caught up in what seemed innocent motion.

"I've got something to tell you," Tisha said. "I didn't want to tell you before."

Maybe she's pregnant, Richie thought. One life ends, another begins, wouldn't that be something. But when she faced him full on, he saw that wasn't it at all, though he still hoped someday it would be.

"Remember the other night, when we were driving to the hospital and saw that white girl pulled out of her car, getting beat up?"

"I'll never forget it."

She squeezed his hand again, which she'd been holding for what seemed forever, since they got on line to enter the church.

"I learned yesterday from one of the nurses she wasn't white."

"She looked white."

"She's an albino black girl who goes to UMCC."

Richie looked into Tisha's face. Large eyes, high cheeks, straightened black hair ending in those fishhook curls. "Why are you telling me this now?"

"They was beating on her cause they thought she was white, only she wasn't. It's so fucked-up, Richard, all this hating, and I been hating too. I wanted you to know."

"I love you, Tisha." He would be a better man. He would make her love him as much as he loved her, and it would make him better. She nodded, signifying exactly what he did not know but hoped it meant she understood and felt it too.

He looked around. The large crowd was moving slowly, but it was moving, and again they were caught up in its motion. They approached Liberty, which was a main street, with traffic lights on every corner, two lanes in each direction. For some reason there were quite a few white people near them now, more than in most of the crowd, including a group of women carrying a hand-painted banner on a white sheet: KANSANS AGAINST POLICE ABUSE. Almost everywhere else the crowd was black and of every age: young mothers with strollers; eight- and ten-year-olds; teenagers wearing red bandanas and the smiling face of

Timothy Thomas on their chests. Near the front, maybe twenty feet away, there were several ministers, including the one he'd seen on television leading the demonstration at City Hall. The black-suited ministers stopped at the corner, turned around, and started to sing "We Shall Overcome."

After a few bars the crowd joined in. "We shall overcome some day-ay-ay-ay-ay-ay."

Richie could hear Tisha's honeyed voice, "Oh, oh, deep—"

And he started to sing too. ". . . in my heart, I do believe . . ."

As they were finishing the first verse, four police cars, bubble lights flashing, pulled up in front of them and blocked the intersection of Liberty and Elm. Eight cops piled out, and without a word two of them raised shotguns.

What the fuck?

"Get down," Tisha shouted.

The cops fired. A few feet away one of the white women from Kansas grabbed her neck and started to scream.

"Tisha," he asked. "You all right?"

She nodded, and he could see she wasn't hurt, just frightened. Richie stood up, shouting, "What's wrong with you?" Everyone shouted. It was crazy. The cops were stone-cold assholes. They'd said nothing, given no warning. The white woman who'd been hit kept screaming. The cops armed with beanbag shotguns retreated toward their cruisers. The minister Richie had seen on television raised a bullhorn. "Everyone sit down. Sit down right here! We gonna block the intersection till Stryker comes!"

The crowd, including Richie and Tisha, sat in the middle of the intersection, chanting, "We want Stryker! We want Wilson! We want Stryker! We want Wilson!"

Sitting beside her, chanting and not worrying, well, not worrying very much that he was ruining the pants of his six hundred—dollar suit or that someone from C&M would see him on TV and he'd be coached out in his next review, Richie kept thinking, *Those racist motherfuckers. Those muthafuckers!*

276

"We didn't do anything," he shouted to Tisha, above the chanting: *We want Stryker! We want Wilson!* "We weren't doing anything."

"We were here," she said. "We were guilty of being *here*."

Even after Chief Stryker arrived and the crowd shouted questions and he shouted answers, and Richie held Tisha's hand while Stryker joined his with the black ministers' and prayed for Calhoun City. And even though the white woman, who'd been hit in the neck not the eye, would no doubt be okay. And even though the sun shone and the day went on, he couldn't stop thinking, as if it were a revelation, though he knew it shouldn't have been. *We didn't do anything wrong. We weren't doing anything at all.* As if that made any difference at all.

And then they went home.

IN THE FLYOVER FICTION SERIES

To order or obtain more information on
these or other University of Nebraska Press
titles, visit www.nebraskapress.unl.edu.